**The Children's Golden Library**

**19**

**Grimm's Fairy Tales**
The Brothers Grimm

First published 1823



ISBN : 84-9789-021-3
Dep. Legal B-37921-2003

Printed and bound in Spain
by Printer Industria Gráfica, Barcelona



**www.mediasatgroup.com**

# THE BROTHERS GRIMM

# Grimm's Fairy Tales

THE CHILDREN'S GOLDEN LIBRARY

# *Hans In Luck*

Some men are born to good luck: all they do or try to do comes right — all that falls to them is so much gain — all their geese are swans — all their cards are trumps — toss them which way you will, they will always, like poor puss, alight upon their legs, and only move on so much the faster. The world may very likely not always think of them as they think of themselves, but what care they for the world? What can it know about the matter?

One of these lucky beings was neighbour Hans. Seven long years he had worked hard for his master. At last he said, 'Master, my time is up; I must go home and see my poor mother once more: so pray pay me my wages and let me go.' And the master said, 'You have been a faithful and good servant, Hans, so your pay shall be handsome.' Then he gave him a lump of silver as big as his head.

Hans took out his pocket-handkerchief, put the piece of silver into it, threw it over his shoulder, and jogged off on his road homewards. As he went lazily on, dragging one foot after another, a man came in sight, trotting gaily along on a capital horse. 'Ah!' said

Hans aloud, 'what a fine thing it is to ride on horseback! There he sits as easy and happy as if he was at home, in the chair by his fireside; he trips against no stones, saves shoe-leather, and gets on he hardly knows how.' Hans did not speak so softly but the horseman heard it all, and said, 'Well, friend, why do you go on foot then?' 'Ah!' said he, 'I have this load to carry: to be sure it is silver, but it is so heavy that I can't hold up my head, and you must know it hurts my shoulder sadly.' 'What do you say of making an exchange?' said the horseman. 'I will give you my horse, and you shall give me the silver; which will save you a great deal of trouble in carrying such a heavy load about with you.' 'With all my heart,' said Hans: 'but as you are so kind to me, I must tell you one thing — you will have a weary task to draw that silver about with you.' However, the horseman got off, took the silver, helped Hans up, gave him the bridle into one hand and the whip into the other, and said, 'When you want to go very fast, smack your lips loudly together, and cry "Jip!"'

Hans was delighted as he sat on the horse, drew himself up, squared his elbows, turned out his toes, cracked his whip, and rode merrily off, one minute whistling a merry tune, and another singing,

'No care and no sorrow,
A fig for the morrow!
We'll laugh and be merry,
Sing neigh down derry!'

After a time he thought he should like to go a little faster, so he smacked his lips and cried 'Jip!' Away went the horse full gallop; and before Hans knew what he was about, he was thrown off, and lay on his back by the road-side. His horse would have ran off, if a shepherd who was coming by, driving a cow, had not stopped it. Hans soon came to himself, and got upon his legs again, sadly vexed, and said to the shepherd, 'This riding is no joke, when a man has the luck to get upon a beast like this that stumbles and flings him off as if it would break his neck. However, I'm off now once for all: I like your cow now a great deal better than this smart beast that played me this trick, and has spoiled my best coat, you see, in this puddle; which, by the by, smells not very like a nosegay. One can walk along at one's leisure behind that cow — keep good company, and have milk, butter, and cheese, every day, into the bargain. What would I give to have such a prize!' 'Well,' said the shepherd, 'if you are so fond of her, I will change my cow for your horse; I like to do good to my neighbours, even though I lose by it myself.' 'Done!' said Hans, merrily. 'What a noble heart that good man has!' thought he. Then the shepherd jumped upon the horse, wished Hans and the cow good morning, and away he rode.

Hans brushed his coat, wiped his face and hands, rested a while, and then drove off his cow quietly, and thought his bargain a very lucky one. 'If I have only a piece of bread (and I certainly shall always be able to get that), I can, whenever I like, eat my butter and cheese with it; and when I am thirsty I can milk my cow and drink the milk: and what can I wish for more?' When he came to an inn, he halted, ate up all his bread, and gave away his last penny for a glass of beer. When he had rested himself he set off again, driving his cow towards his mother's village. But the heat grew greater as soon as noon came on, till at last, as he found himself on a wide heath that would take him more than an hour to cross, he began to be so hot and parched that his tongue clave to the roof of his mouth. 'I can find a cure for this,' thought he; 'now I will milk my cow and quench my thirst': so he tied her to the stump of a tree, and held his leathern cap to milk into; but not a drop was to be had. Who would have thought that this cow, which was to bring him milk and butter and cheese, was all that time utterly dry? Hans had not thought of looking to that.

While he was trying his luck in milking, and managing the matter very clumsily, the uneasy beast began to think him very troublesome; and at last gave him such a kick on the head as knocked him down; and there he lay a long while senseless. Luckily a butcher soon came by, driving a pig in a wheelbarrow. 'What is the matter with you, my man?' said the butcher, as he helped him up. Hans told him what had happened, how he was dry, and wanted to milk his cow, but found the cow was dry too. Then the butcher gave him a flask of ale, saying, 'There, drink and refresh yourself; your cow will give you no milk: don't you see she is an old beast, good for nothing but the slaughter-house?' 'Alas, alas!' said Hans, 'who would have thought it? What a shame to take my horse, and give me only a dry cow! If

I kill her, what will she be good for? I hate cow-beef; it is not tender enough for me. If it were a pig now — like that fat gentleman you are driving along at his ease — one could do something with it; it would at any rate make sausages.' 'Well,' said the butcher, 'I don't like to say no, when one is asked to do a kind, neighbourly thing. To please you I will change, and give you my fine fat pig for the cow.' 'Heaven reward you for your kindness and self-denial!' said Hans, as he gave the butcher the cow; and taking the pig off the wheel-barrow, drove it away, holding it by the string that was tied to its leg.

So on he jogged, and all seemed now to go right with him: he had met with some misfortunes, to be sure; but he was now well repaid for all. How could it be otherwise with such a travelling companion as he had at last got?

The next man he met was a countryman carrying a fine white goose. The countryman stopped to ask what was o'clock; this led to further chat; and Hans told him all his luck, how he had so many good bargains, and how all the world went gay and smiling with him. The countryman than began to tell his tale, and said he was going to take the goose to a christening. 'Feel,' said he, 'how heavy it is, and yet it is only eight weeks old. Whoever roasts and eats it will find plenty of fat upon it, it has lived so well!' 'You're right,' said Hans, as he weighed it in his hand; 'but if you talk of fat, my pig is no trifle.' Meantime the countryman began to look grave, and shook his head. 'Hark ye!' said he, 'my worthy friend, you seem a good sort of fellow, so I can't help doing you a kind turn. Your pig may get you into a scrape. In the village I just came from, the squire has had a pig stolen out of his sty. I was dreadfully afraid when I saw you that you had got the squire's pig. If you have, and they catch you, it will be a bad job for you. The least they will do will be to throw you into the horse-pond. Can you swim?'

Poor Hans was sadly frightened. 'Good man,' cried he, 'pray get me out of this scrape. I know nothing of where the pig was either bred or born; but he may have been the squire's for aught I can tell: you know this country better than I do, take my pig and give me the goose.' 'I ought to have something into the bargain,' said the countryman; 'give a fat goose for a pig, indeed! 'Tis not everyone would do so much for you as that. However, I will not be hard upon you, as you are in trouble.' Then he took the string in his hand, and drove off the pig by a side path; while Hans went on the way homewards free from care. 'After all,' thought he, 'that chap is pretty well taken in. I don't care whose pig it is, but wherever it came from it has been a very good friend to me. I have much the best of the bargain. First there will be a capital roast; then the fat will find me in goose-grease for six months; and then there are all the beautiful white feathers. I will put them into my pillow, and then I am sure I shall sleep soundly without rocking. How happy my mother will be! Talk of a pig, indeed! Give me a fine fat goose.'

As he came to the next village, he saw a scissor-grinder with his wheel, working and singing,

'O'er hill and o'er dale
So happy I roam,
Work light and live well,
All the world is my home;
Then who so blythe, so merry as I?'

Hans stood looking on for a while, and at last said, 'You must be well off, master grinder! You seem so happy at your work.' 'Yes,' said the other, 'mine is a golden trade; a good grinder never puts his hand into his pocket without finding money in it — but where did you get that beautiful goose?' 'I did not buy it, I gave a pig for it.' 'And where did you get the pig?' 'I gave a cow for it.' 'And the cow?' 'I gave a horse for it.' 'And the horse?' 'I gave a lump of silver as big as my head for it.' 'And the silver?' 'Oh! I worked hard for that seven long years.' 'You have thriven well in the world hitherto,' said the grinder, 'now if you could find money in your pocket whenever you put your hand in it, your fortune would be made.' 'Very true: but how is that to be managed?' 'How? Why, you must turn grinder like myself,' said the other; 'you only want a grindstone; the rest will come of itself. Here is one that is but little the worse for wear: I would not ask more than the value of your goose for it — will you buy?' 'How can you ask?' said Hans; 'I should be the happiest man in the world, if I could have money whenever I put my hand in my pocket: what could I want more? There's the goose.' 'Now,' said the grinder, as he gave him a common rough stone that lay by his side, 'this is a most capital stone; do but work it well enough, and you can make an old nail cut with it.'

Hans took the stone, and went his way with a light heart: his eyes sparkled for joy, and he said to himself, 'Surely I must have been born in a lucky hour; everything I could want or wish for comes of itself. People are so kind; they seem really to think I do them a favour in letting them make me rich, and giving me good bargains.'

Meantime he began to be tired, and hungry too, for he had given away his last penny in his joy at getting the cow.

At last he could go no farther, for the stone tired him sadly: and he dragged himself to the side of a river, that he might take a drink of water, and rest a while. So he laid the stone carefully by his side on the bank: but, as he stooped down to drink, he forgot it, pushed it a little, and down it rolled, plump into the stream.

For a while he watched it sinking in the deep clear water; then sprang up and danced for joy, and again fell upon his knees and thanked Heaven, with tears in his eyes, for its kindness in taking away his only plague, the ugly heavy stone.

'How happy am I!' cried he; 'nobody was ever so lucky as I.' Then up he got with a light heart, free from all his troubles, and walked on till he reached his mother's house, and told her how very easy the road to good luck was.

# *Little Red-Cap*
## *(Little Red Riding Hood)*

Once upon a time there was a dear little girl who was loved by everyone who looked at her, but most of all by her grandmother, and there was nothing that she would not have given to the child. Once she gave her a little cap of red velvet, which suited her so well that she would never wear anything else; so she was always called 'Little Red-Cap.'

One day her mother said to her: 'Come, Little Red-Cap, here is a piece of cake and a bottle of wine; take them to your grandmother, she is ill and weak, and they will do her good. Set out before it gets hot, and when you are going, walk nicely and quietly and do not run off the path, or you may fall and break the bottle, and then your grandmother will get nothing; and when you go into her room, don't forget to say, "Good morning", and don't peep into every corner before you do it.'

'I will take great care,' said Little Red-Cap to her mother, and gave her hand on it.

The grandmother lived out in the wood, half a league from the village, and just as Little Red-Cap entered the wood, a wolf met her. Red-Cap did not know what a wicked creature he was, and was not at all afraid of him.

'Good day, Little Red-Cap,' said he.

'Thank you kindly, wolf.'

'Whither away so early, Little Red-Cap?'

'To my grandmother's.'

'What have you got in your apron?'

'Cake and wine; yesterday was baking-day, so poor sick grandmother is to have something good, to make her stronger.'

'Where does your grandmother live, Little Red-Cap?'

'A good quarter of a league farther on in the wood; her house stands under the three large oak-trees, the nut-trees are just below; you surely must know it,' replied Little Red-Cap.

The wolf thought to himself: 'What a tender young creature! what a nice plump mouthful — she will be better to eat than the old woman. I must act craftily, so as to catch both.' So he walked for a short time by the side of Little Red-Cap, and then he said: 'See, Little Red-Cap, how pretty the flowers are about here — why do you not look round? I believe, too, that you do not hear how sweetly the little birds are singing; you walk gravely along as if you were going to school, while everything else out here in the wood is merry.'

Little Red-Cap raised her eyes, and when she saw the sunbeams dancing here and there through the trees, and pretty flowers growing everywhere, she thought: 'Suppose I take grandmother a fresh nosegay;

that would please her too. It is so early in the day that I shall still get there in good time'; and so she ran from the path into the wood to look for flowers. And whenever she had picked one, she fancied that she saw a still prettier one farther on, and ran after it, and so got deeper and deeper into the wood.

Meanwhile the wolf ran straight to the grandmother's house and knocked at the door.

'Who is there?'

'Little Red-Cap,' replied the wolf. 'She is bringing cake and wine; open the door.'

'Lift the latch,' called out the grandmother, 'I am too weak, and cannot get up.'

The wolf lifted the latch, the door sprang open, and without saying a word he went straight to the grandmother's bed, and devoured her. Then he put on her clothes, dressed himself in her cap, laid himself in bed, and drew the curtains.

Little Red-Cap, however, had been running about picking flowers, and when she had gathered so many that she could carry no more, she remembered her grandmother, and set out on the way to her.

She was surprised to find the cottage-door standing open, and when she went into the room, she had such a strange feeling that she said to herself: 'Oh dear! how uneasy I feel today, and at other times I like being with grandmother so much.' She called out: 'Good morning,' but received no answer; so she went to the bed and drew back the curtains. There lay her grandmother with her cap pulled far over her face, and looking very strange.

'Oh! grandmother,' she said, 'what big ears you have!'

'The better to hear you with, my child,' was the reply.

'But, grandmother, what big eyes you have!' she said.

'The better to see you with, my dear.'

'But, grandmother, what large hands you have!'

'The better to hug you with.'

'Oh! but, grandmother, what a terrible big mouth you have!'

'The better to eat you with!'

And scarcely had the wolf said this, than with one bound he was out of bed and swallowed up Red-Cap.

When the wolf had appeased his appetite, he lay down again in the bed, fell asleep and began to snore very loud. The huntsman was just passing the house, and thought to himself: 'How the old woman is snoring! I must just see if she wants anything.' So he went into the room, and when he came to the bed, he saw that the wolf was lying in it. 'Do I find you here, you old sinner!' said he. 'I have long sought you!' Then just as he was going to fire at him, it occurred to him that the wolf might have devoured the grandmother, and that she might still be saved, so he did not fire, but took a pair of scissors, and began to cut open the stomach of the sleeping wolf. When he had made two snips, he saw the little Red-Cap shining, and then he made two snips more, and the little girl sprang out, crying: 'Ah, how frightened I have been! How dark it was inside the wolf'; and after that the aged grandmother came out alive also, but scarcely able to breathe. Red-Cap, however, quickly fetched great stones with which they filled the wolf's belly, and when he awoke, he wanted to run away, but the stones were so heavy that he collapsed at once, and fell dead.

Then all three were delighted. The huntsman drew off the wolf's skin and went home with it; the grandmother ate the cake and drank the wine which Red-Cap had brought, and revived, but Red-Cap thought to herself: 'As long as I live, I will never by myself leave the path, to run into the wood, when my mother has forbidden me to do so.'

It also related that once when Red-Cap was again taking cakes to the old grandmother, another wolf spoke to her, and tried to entice her from the path. Red-Cap, however, was on her guard, and went straight forward on her way, and told her grandmother that she had met the wolf, and that he had said 'good morning' to her, but with such a wicked look in his eyes, that if they had not been on the public road she was certain he would have eaten her up. 'Well,' said the grandmother, 'we will shut the door, that he may not come in.' Soon afterwards the wolf knocked, and cried: 'Open the door, grandmother, I am Little Red-Cap, and am bringing you some cakes.' But they did not speak, or open the door, so the grey-beard stole twice or thrice round the house, and at last jumped on the roof, intending to wait until Red-Cap went home in the evening, and then to steal after her and devour her in the darkness. But the grandmother saw what was in his thoughts. In front of the house was a great stone trough, so she said to the child: 'Take the pail, Red-Cap; I made some sausages yesterday, so carry the water in which I boiled them to the trough.' Red-Cap carried until the great trough was quite full. Then the smell of the sausages reached the wolf, and he sniffed and peeped down, and at last stretched out his neck so far that he could no longer keep his footing and began to slip, and slipped down from the roof straight into the great trough, and was drowned. But Red-Cap went joyously home, and no one ever did anything to harm her again.

# *The Travelling Musicians*

An honest farmer had once an ass that had been a faithful servant to him a great many years, but was now growing old and every day more and more unfit for work. His master therefore was tired of keeping him and began to think of putting an end to him; but the ass, who saw that some mischief was in the wind, took himself slyly off, and began his journey towards the great city, 'For there,' thought he, 'I may turn musician.'

After he had travelled a little way, he spied a dog lying by the roadside and panting as if he were tired. 'What makes you pant so, my friend?' said the ass. 'Alas!' said the dog, 'my master was going to knock me on the head, because I am old and weak, and can no longer make myself useful to him in hunting; so I ran away; but what can I do to earn my livelihood?' 'Hark ye!' said the ass, 'I am going to the great city to turn musician: suppose you go with me, and try what you can do in the same way?' The dog said he was willing, and they jogged on together.

They had not gone far before they saw a cat sitting in the middle of the road and making a most rueful face. 'Pray, my good lady,' said the ass, 'what's the matter with you? You look quite out of spirits!' 'Ah, me!' said the cat, 'how can one be in good spirits when one's life is in danger? Because I am beginning to grow old, and had rather lie at my ease by the fire than run about the house after the mice, my mistress laid hold of me, and was going to drown me; and though I have been lucky enough to get away from her, I do not know what I am to live upon.' 'Oh,' said the ass, 'by all means go with us to the great city; you are a good night singer, and may make your fortune as a musician.' The cat was pleased with the thought, and joined the party.

Soon afterwards, as they were passing by a farmyard, they saw a cock perched upon a gate, and screaming out with all his might and main. 'Bravo!' said the ass; 'upon my word, you make a famous noise; pray what is all this about?' 'Why,' said the cock, 'I was just now saying that we should have fine weather for our washing-day, and yet my mistress and the cook don't thank me for my pains, but threaten to cut off my head tomorrow, and make broth of me for the guests that are coming on Sunday!' 'Heaven forbid!' said the ass, 'come with us Master Chanticleer; it will be better, at any rate, than staying here to have your head cut off! Besides, who knows? If we care to sing in tune, we may get up some kind of a concert; so come along with us.' 'With all my heart,' said the cock: so they all four went on jollily together.

They could not, however, reach the great city the first day; so when night came on, they went into a wood to sleep. The ass and the dog laid themselves down under a great tree, and the cat climbed up into the branches; while the cock, thinking that the higher he sat the safer he should be, flew up to the very top of the tree, and then, according to his custom, before he went to sleep, looked out on all sides of him to see that everything was well. In doing this, he saw afar off something bright and shining and calling to his companions said, 'There must be a house no great way off, for I see a light.' 'If that be the case,' said the ass, 'we had better change our quarters, for our lodging is not the best in the world!' 'Besides,' added the dog, 'I should not be the worse for a bone or two, or a bit of meat.' So they walked off together towards the spot where Chanticleer had seen the light, and as they drew near it became larger and brighter, till they at last came close to a house in which a gang of robbers lived.

The ass, being the tallest of the company, marched up to the window and peeped in. 'Well, Donkey,' said Chanticleer, 'what do you see?' 'What do I see?' replied the ass. 'Why, I see a table spread with all kinds of good things, and robbers sitting round it making merry.' 'That would be a noble lodging for us,' said the cock. 'Yes,' said the ass, 'if we could only get in'; so they consulted together how they should contrive to get the robbers out; and at last they hit upon a plan. The ass placed himself upright on his hind legs, with his forefeet resting against the window; the dog got upon his back; the cat scrambled up to the dog's shoulders, and the cock flew up and sat upon the cat's head. When all was ready a signal was given, and they began their music. The ass brayed, the dog barked, the cat mewed, and the cock screamed; and then they all broke through the window at once, and came tumbling into the room, amongst the broken glass, with a most hideous clatter! The robbers, who had been not a little frightened by the opening concert, had now no doubt that some frightful hobgoblin had broken in upon them, and scampered away as fast as they could.

The coast once clear, our travellers soon sat down and dispatched what the robbers had left, with as much eagerness as if they had not expected to eat again for a month. As soon as they had satisfied themselves, they put out the lights, and each once more sought out a resting-place to his own liking. The donkey laid himself down upon a heap of straw in the yard, the dog stretched himself upon a mat behind the door, the cat rolled herself up on the hearth before the warm ashes, and the cock perched upon a beam on the top of the house; and, as they were all rather tired with their journey, they soon fell asleep.

But about midnight, when the robbers saw from afar that the lights were out and that all seemed quiet, they began to think that they had been in too great a hurry to run away; and one of them, who was bolder than the rest, went to see what was going on. Finding everything still, he marched into the kitchen, and groped about till he found a match in order to light a candle; and then, espying the glittering fiery eyes of the cat, he mistook them for live coals, and held the match to them to light it. But the cat, not understanding this joke, sprang at his face, and spat, and scratched at him. This frightened him dreadfully, and away he ran to the back door; but there the dog jumped up and bit him in the leg; and as he was crossing over the yard the ass kicked him; and the cock, who had been awakened by the noise, crowed with all his might. At this the robber ran back as fast as he could to his comrades, and told the captain how a horrid witch had got into the house, and had spat at him and scratched his face with her long bony fingers; how a man with a knife in his hand had hidden himself behind the door, and stabbed him in the leg; how a black monster stood in the yard and struck him with a club, and how the devil had sat upon the top of the house and cried out, 'Throw the rascal up here!' After this the robbers never dared to go back to the house; but the musicians were so pleased with their quarters that they took up their abode there; and there they are, I dare say, at this very day.

## *Hansel And Gretel*

Hard by a great forest dwelt a poor wood-cutter with his wife and his two children. The boy was called Hansel and the girl Gretel. He had little to bite and to break, and once when great dearth fell on the land, he could no longer procure even daily bread. Now when he thought over this by night in his bed, and tossed about in his anxiety, he groaned and said to his wife: 'What is to become of us? How are we to feed our poor children, when we no longer have anything even for ourselves?' 'I'll tell you what, husband,' answered the woman, 'early tomorrow morning we will take the children out into the forest to where it is the thickest; there we will light a fire for them, and give each of them one more piece of bread, and then we will go to our work and leave them alone. They will not find the way home again, and we shall be rid of them.' 'No, wife,' said the man, 'I will not do that; how can I bear to leave my children alone in the forest? — the wild animals would soon come and tear them to pieces.' 'O, you fool!' said she, 'then we must all four die of hunger, you may as well plane the planks for our coffins,' and she left him no peace until he consented. 'But I feel very sorry for the poor children, all the same,' said the man.

The two children had also not been able to sleep for hunger, and had heard what their stepmother had said to their father. Gretel wept bitter tears, and said to Hansel: 'Now all is over with us.' 'Be quiet, Gretel,' said Hansel, 'do not distress yourself, I will soon find a way to help us.' And when the old folks had fallen asleep, he got up, put on his little coat, opened the door below, and crept outside. The moon shone brightly, and the white pebbles which lay in front of the house glittered like real silver pennies. Hansel stooped and stuffed the little pocket of his coat with as many as he could get in. Then he went back and said to Gretel: 'Be comforted, dear little sister, and sleep in peace, God will not forsake us,' and he lay down again in his bed. When day dawned, but before the sun had risen, the woman came and awoke the two children, saying: 'Get up, you sluggards! we are going into the forest to fetch wood.' She gave each a little piece of bread, and said: 'There is something for your dinner, but do not eat it up before then, for you will get nothing else.' Gretel took the bread under her apron, as Hansel had the pebbles in his pocket. Then they all set out together on the way to the forest. When they had walked a short time, Hansel stood still and peeped back at the house, and did so again and again. His father said: 'Hansel, what are you looking at there and staying behind for? Pay attention, and do not forget how to use your legs.' 'Ah, father,' said Hansel, 'I am looking at my little white cat, which is sitting up on the roof, and wants to say goodbye to me.' The wife said: 'Fool, that is not your little cat, that is the morning sun which is shining on the chimneys.' Hansel, however, had not been looking back at the cat, but had been constantly throwing one of the white pebble-stones out of his pocket on the road.

When they had reached the middle of the forest, the father said: 'Now, children, pile up some wood, and I will light a fire that you may not be cold.' Hansel and Gretel gathered brushwood together, as high as a little hill. The brushwood was lighted, and when the flames were burning very high, the woman said: 'Now, children, lay yourselves down by the fire and rest, we will go into the forest and cut some wood. When we have done, we will come back and fetch you away.'

Hansel and Gretel sat by the fire, and when noon came, each ate a little piece of bread, and as they heard the strokes of the wood-axe they believed that their father was near. It was not the axe, however, but a branch which he had fastened to a withered tree which the wind was blowing backwards and forwards. And as they had been sitting such a long time, their eyes closed with fatigue, and they fell fast asleep. When at last they awoke, it was already dark night. Gretel began to cry and said: 'How are we to get out of the forest now?' But Hansel comforted her and said: 'Just wait a little, until the moon has risen, and then we will soon find the way.' And when the full moon had risen, Hansel took his little sister by the hand, and followed the pebbles which shone like newly-coined silver pieces, and showed them the way.

They walked the whole night long, and by break of day came once more to their father's house. They knocked at the door, and when the woman opened it and saw that it was Hansel and Gretel, she said: 'You naughty children, why have you slept so long in the forest? — we thought you were never coming back at all!' The father, however, rejoiced, for it had cut him to the heart to leave them behind alone.

Not long afterwards, there was once more great dearth throughout the land, and the children heard their mother saying at night to their father: 'Everything is eaten again, we have one half loaf left, and that is the end. The children must go, we will take them farther into the wood, so that they will not find their way out again; there is no other means of saving ourselves!' The man's heart was heavy, and he thought: 'It would be better for you to share the last mouthful with your children.' The woman, however, would listen to nothing that he had to say, but scolded and reproached him. He who says A must say B, likewise, and as he had yielded the first time, he had to do so a second time also.

The children, however, were still awake and had heard the conversation. When the old folks were asleep, Hansel again got up, and wanted to go out and pick up pebbles as he had done before, but the woman had locked the door, and Hansel could not get out. Nevertheless he comforted his little sister, and said: 'Do not cry, Gretel, go to sleep quietly, the good God will help us.'

Early in the morning came the woman, and took the children out of their beds. Their piece of bread was given to them, but it was still smaller than the time before. On the way into the forest Hansel crumbled his in his pocket, and often stood still and threw a morsel on the ground. 'Hansel, why do you stop and look round?' said the father, 'go on.' 'I am looking back at my little pigeon which is sitting on the roof, and wants to say goodbye to me,' answered Hansel. 'Fool!' said the woman, 'that is not your little pigeon, that is the morning sun that is shining on the chimney.' Hansel, however, little by little, threw all the crumbs on the path.

The woman led the children still deeper into the forest, where they had never in their lives been before. Then a great fire was again made, and the mother said: 'Just sit there, you children, and when you are tired you may sleep a little; we are going into the forest to cut wood, and in the evening when we are done, we will come and fetch you away.' When it was noon, Gretel shared her piece of bread with Hansel, who had scattered his by the way. Then they fell asleep and evening passed, but no one came to the poor children. They did not awake until it was dark night, and Hansel comforted his little sister and said: 'Just wait, Gretel, until the moon rises, and then we shall see the crumbs of bread which I have strewn about, they will show us our way home again.' When the moon came they set out, but they found no crumbs, for the many thousands of birds which fly about in the woods and fields had picked them all up. Hansel said to Gretel:

'We shall soon find the way,' but they did not find it. They walked the whole night and all the next day too from morning till evening, but they did not get out of the forest, and were very hungry, for they had nothing to eat but two or three berries, which grew on the ground. And as they were so weary that their legs would carry them no longer, they lay down beneath a tree and fell asleep.

It was now three mornings since they had left their father's house. They began to walk again, but they always came deeper into the forest, and if help did not come soon, they must die of hunger and weariness. When it was mid-day, they saw a beautiful snow-white bird sitting on a bough, which sang so delightfully that they stood still and listened to it. And when its song was over, it spread its wings and flew away before them, and they followed it until they reached a little house, on the roof of which it alighted; and when they approached the little house they saw that it was built of bread and covered with cakes, but that the windows were of clear sugar. 'We will set to work on that,' said Hansel, 'and have a good meal. I will eat a bit of the roof, and you Gretel, can eat some of the window, it will taste sweet.' Hansel reached up above, and broke off a little of the roof to try how it tasted, and Gretel leant against the window and nibbled at the panes. Then a soft voice cried from the parlour:

'Nibble, nibble, gnaw,
Who is nibbling at my little house?'

The children answered:
'The wind, the wind,
The heaven-born wind,'

and went on eating without disturbing themselves. Hansel, who liked the taste of the roof, tore down a great piece of it, and Gretel pushed out the whole of one round window-pane, sat down, and enjoyed herself with it. Suddenly the door opened, and a woman as old as the hills, who supported herself on crutches, came creeping out. Hansel and Gretel were so terribly frightened that they let fall what they had in their hands. The old woman, however, nodded her head, and said: 'Oh, you dear children, who has brought you here? Do come in, and stay with me. No harm shall happen to you.' She took them both by the hand, and led them into her little house. Then good food was set before them, milk and pancakes, with sugar, apples, and nuts. Afterwards two pretty little beds were covered with clean white linen, and Hansel and Gretel lay down in them, and thought they were in heaven.

The old woman had only pretended to be so kind; she was in reality a wicked witch, who lay in wait for children, and had only built the little house of bread in order to entice them there. When a child fell into her power, she killed it, cooked and ate it, and that was a feast day with her. Witches have red eyes, and cannot see far, but they have a keen scent like the beasts, and are aware when human beings draw near. When Hansel and Gretel came into her neighbourhood, she laughed with malice, and said mockingly: 'I have them, they shall not escape me again!' Early in the morning before the children were awake, she was already up, and when she saw both of them sleeping and looking so pretty, with their plump and rosy cheeks she muttered to herself: 'That will be a dainty mouthful!' Then she seized Hansel with her shrivelled hand, carried him into a little stable, and locked him in behind a grated door. Scream as he might, it would not help him. Then she went to Gretel, shook her till she awoke, and cried: 'Get up, lazy thing, fetch some water, and cook something good for your brother, he is in the stable outside, and is to be made fat. When he is fat, I will eat him.' Gretel began to weep bitterly, but it was all in vain, for she was forced to do what the wicked witch commanded.

And now the best food was cooked for poor Hansel, but Gretel got nothing but crab-shells. Every morning the woman crept to the little stable, and cried: 'Hansel, stretch out your finger that I may feel if you will soon be fat.' Hansel, however, stretched out a little bone to her, and the old woman, who had dim eyes, could not see it, and thought it was Hansel's finger, and was astonished that there was no way of fattening him. When four weeks had gone by, and Hansel still remained thin, she was seized with impatience and would not wait any longer. 'Now, then, Gretel,' she cried to the girl, 'stir yourself, and bring some water. Let Hansel be fat or lean, tomorrow I will kill him, and cook him.' Ah, how the poor little sister did lament when she had to fetch the water, and how her tears did flow down her cheeks! 'Dear God, do help us,' she cried. 'If the wild beasts in the forest had but devoured us, we should at any rate have died together.' 'Just keep your noise to yourself,' said the old woman, 'it won't help you at all.'

Early in the morning, Gretel had to go out and hang up the cauldron with the water, and light the fire. 'We will bake first,' said the old woman, 'I have already heated the oven, and kneaded the dough.' She pushed poor Gretel out to the oven, from which flames of fire were already darting. 'Creep in,' said the witch, 'and see if it is properly heated, so that we can put the bread in.' And once Gretel was inside, she intended to shut the oven and let her bake in it, and then she would eat her, too. But Gretel saw what she had in mind, and said: 'I do not know how I am to do it; how do I get in?' 'Silly goose,' said the old woman. 'The door is big enough; just look, I can get in myself!' and she crept up and thrust her head into the oven. Then Gretel gave her a push that drove her far into it, and shut the iron door, and fastened the bolt. Oh! then she began to howl quite horribly, but Gretel ran away and the godless witch was miserably burnt to death.

Gretel, however, ran like lightning to Hansel, opened his little stable, and cried: 'Hansel, we are saved! The old witch is dead!' Then Hansel sprang like a bird from its cage when the door is opened. How they did rejoice and embrace each other, and dance about and kiss each other! And as they had no longer any need to fear her, they went into the witch's house, and in every corner there stood chests full of pearls and jewels. 'These are far better than pebbles!' said Hansel, and thrust into his pockets whatever could be got in, and Gretel said: 'I, too, will take something home with me,' and filled her pinafore full. 'But now we must be off,' said Hansel, 'that we may get out of the witch's forest.'

When they had walked for two hours, they came to a great stretch of water. 'We cannot cross,' said Hansel, 'I see no foot-plank, and no bridge.' 'And there is also no ferry,' answered Gretel, 'but a white duck is swimming there: if I ask her, she will help us over.' Then she cried:

'Little duck, little duck, dost thou see,
Hansel and Gretel are waiting for thee?
There's never a plank, or bridge in sight,
Take us across on thy back so white.'

The duck came to them, and Hansel seated himself on its back, and told his sister to sit by him. 'No,' replied Gretel, 'that will be too heavy for the little duck; she shall take us across, one after the other.' The good little duck did so, and when they were once safely across and had walked for a short time, the forest seemed to be more and more familiar to them, and at length they saw from afar their father's house. Then they began to run, rushed into the parlour, and threw themselves round their father's neck. The man had not known one happy hour since he had left the children in the forest; the woman, however, was dead.

Gretel emptied her pinafore until pearls and precious stones ran about the room, and Hansel threw one handful after another out of his pocket to add to them. Then all anxiety was at an end, and they lived together in perfect happiness. My tale is done, there runs a mouse; whosoever catches it, may make himself a big fur cap out of it.

# *Rumpelstiltskin*

By the side of a wood, in a country a long way off, ran a fine stream of water; and upon the stream there stood a mill. The miller's house was close by, and the miller, you must know, had a very beautiful daughter. She was, moreover, very shrewd and clever; and the miller was so proud of her, that he one day told the king of the land, who used to come and hunt in the wood, that his daughter could spin gold out of straw. Now this king was very fond of money; and when he heard the miller's boast his greediness was raised, and he sent for the girl to be brought before him. Then he led her to a chamber in his palace where there was a great heap of straw, and gave her a spinning-wheel, and said, 'All this must be spun into gold before morning, as you love your life.' It was in vain that the poor maiden said that it was only a silly boast of her father, for that she could do no such thing as spin straw into gold: the chamber door was locked, and she was left alone.

She sat down in one corner of the room, and began to bewail her hard fate; when on a sudden the door opened, and a droll-looking little man hobbled in, and said, 'Good morrow to you, my good lass; what are you weeping for?' 'Alas!' said she, 'I must spin this straw into gold, and I know not how.' 'What will you give me,' said the hobgoblin, 'to do it for you?' 'My necklace,' replied the maiden. He took her at her word, and sat himself down to the wheel, and whistled and sang:

'Round about, round about,
Lo and behold!
Reel away, reel away,
Straw into gold!'

And round about the wheel went merrily; the work was quickly done, and the straw was all spun into gold.

When the king came and saw this, he was greatly astonished and pleased; but his heart grew still more greedy of gain, and he shut up the poor miller's daughter again with a fresh task. Then she knew not what to do, and sat down once more to weep; but the dwarf soon opened the door, and said, 'What will you give me to do your task?' 'The ring on my finger,' said she. So her little friend took the ring, and began to work at the wheel again, and whistled and sang:

'Round about, round about,
Lo and behold!
Reel away, reel away,
Straw into gold!'

till, long before morning, all was done again.

The king was greatly delighted to see all this glittering treasure; but still he had not enough: so he took the miller's daughter to a yet larger heap, and said, 'All this must be spun tonight; and if it is, you shall be my queen.' As soon as she was alone that dwarf came in, and said, 'What will you give me to spin gold for you this third time?' 'I have nothing left,' said she. 'Then say you will give me,' said the little man, 'the first little child that you may have when you are queen.' 'That may never be,' thought the miller's daughter: and as she knew no other way to get her task done, she said she would do what he asked. Round went the wheel again to the old song, and the manikin once more spun the heap into gold. The king came in the morning, and, finding all he wanted, was forced to keep his word; so he married the miller's daughter, and she really became queen.

At the birth of her first little child she was very glad, and forgot the dwarf, and what she had said. But one day he came into her room, where she was sitting playing with her baby, and put her in mind of it. Then she grieved sorely at her misfortune, and said she would give him all the wealth of the kingdom if he would let her off, but in vain; till at last her tears softened him, and he said, 'I will give you three days' grace, and if during that time you tell me my name, you shall keep your child.'

Now the queen lay awake all night, thinking of all the odd names that she had ever heard; and she sent messengers all over the land to find out new ones. The next day the little man came, and she began with TIMOTHY, ICHABOD, BENJAMIN, JEREMIAH, and all the names she could remember; but to all and each of them he said, 'Madam, that is not my name.'

The second day she began with all the comical names she could hear of, BANDY-LEGS, HUNCHBACK, CROOK-SHANKS, and so on; but the little gentleman still said to every one of them, 'Madam, that is not my name.'

The third day one of the messengers came back, and said, 'I have travelled two days without hearing of any other names; but yesterday, as I was climbing a high hill, among the trees of the forest where the fox and the hare bid each other good night, I saw a little hut; and before the hut burnt a fire; and round about the fire a funny little dwarf was dancing upon one leg, and singing:

'"Merrily the feast I'll make.
Today I'll brew, tomorrow bake;
Merrily I'll dance and sing,
For next day will a stranger bring.
Little does my lady dream
Rumpelstiltskin is my name!"'

When the queen heard this she jumped for joy, and as soon as her little friend came she sat down upon her throne, and called all her court round to enjoy the fun; and the nurse stood by her side with the baby in her arms, as if it was quite ready to be given up. Then the little man began to chuckle at the thought of having the poor child, to take home with him to his hut in the woods; and he cried out, 'Now, lady, what is my name?' 'Is it JOHN?' asked she. 'No, madam!' 'Is it TOM?' 'No, madam!' 'Is it JEMMY?' 'It is not.' 'Can your name be RUMPLESTILTSKIN?' said the lady slyly.

'Some witch told you that! — some witch told you that!' cried the little man, and dashed his right foot in a rage so deep into the floor, that he was forced to lay hold of it with both hands to pull it out.

Then he made the best of his way off, while the nurse laughed and the baby crowed; and all the court jeered at him for having had so much trouble for nothing, and said, 'We wish you a very good morning, and a merry feast, MR RUMPLESTILTSKIN!'

# *The Dog And The Sparrow*

A shepherd's dog had a master who took no care of him, but often let him suffer the greatest hunger. At last he could bear it no longer; so he took to his heels, and off he ran in a very sad and sorrowful mood. On the road he met a sparrow that said to him, 'Why are you so sad, my friend?' 'Because,' said the dog, 'I am very very hungry, and have nothing to eat.' 'If that be all,' answered the sparrow, 'come with me into the next town, and I will soon find you plenty of food.' So on they went together into the town: and as they passed by a butcher's shop, the sparrow said to the dog, 'Stand there a little while till I peck you down a piece of meat.' So the sparrow perched upon the shelf: and having first looked carefully about her to see if anyone was watching her, she pecked and scratched at a steak that lay upon the edge of the shelf, till at last down it fell. Then the dog snapped it up, and scrambled away with it into a corner, where he soon ate it all up. 'Well,' said the sparrow, 'you shall have some more if you will; so come with me to the next shop, and I will peck you down another steak.' When the dog had eaten this too, the sparrow said to him, 'Well, my good friend, have you had enough now?' 'I have had plenty of meat,' answered he, 'but I should like to have a piece of bread to eat after it.' 'Come with me then,' said the sparrow, 'and you shall soon have that too.' So she took him to a baker's shop, and pecked at two rolls that lay in the window, till they fell down: and as the dog still wished for more, she took him to another shop and pecked down some more for him. When that was eaten, the sparrow asked him whether he had had enough now. 'Yes,' said he; 'and now let us take a walk a little way out of the town.' So they both went out upon the high road; but as the weather was warm, they had not gone far before the dog said, 'I am very much tired — I should like to take a nap.' 'Very well,' answered the sparrow, 'do so, and in the meantime I will perch upon that bush.' So the dog stretched himself out on the road, and fell fast asleep. Whilst he slept, there came by a carter with a cart drawn by three horses, and loaded with two casks of wine. The sparrow, seeing that the carter did not turn out of the way, but would go on in the track in which the dog lay, so as to drive over him, called out, 'Stop! stop! Mr Carter, or it shall be the worse for you.' But the carter, grumbling to himself, 'You make it the worse for me, indeed! What can you do?' cracked his whip, and drove his cart over the poor dog, so that the wheels crushed him to death. 'There,' cried the sparrow, 'thou cruel villain, thou hast killed my friend the dog. Now mind what I say. This deed of thine shall cost thee all thou art worth.' 'Do your worst, and welcome,' said the brute, 'what harm can you do me?' and passed on. But the sparrow crept under the tilt of the cart, and pecked at the bung of one of the casks till she loosened it; and than all the wine ran out, without the carter seeing it. At last he looked round, and saw that the cart was dripping, and the cask quite empty. 'What an unlucky wretch I am!' cried he. 'Not wretch enough yet!' said the sparrow, as she alighted upon the head of one of the horses, and pecked at him till he reared up and kicked. When the carter saw this, he drew out his hatchet and aimed a blow at the sparrow, meaning to kill her; but she flew away, and the blow fell upon the poor horse's head with such force, that he fell down dead. 'Unlucky wretch that I am!' cried he. 'Not wretch enough yet!' said the sparrow. And as the carter went on with the other two horses, she again crept under the tilt of the cart, and pecked out the bung of the second cask, so that all the wine ran out. When the carter saw this, he again cried out, 'Miserable wretch that I am!' But the sparrow answered, 'Not wretch enough yet!' and perched on the head of the second horse, and pecked at him too. The carter ran up and struck at her again with his hatchet; but away she flew, and the blow fell upon the second horse and killed him on the spot. 'Unlucky wretch that I am!' said he. 'Not wretch enough yet!' said the sparrow; and perching upon the third horse, she began to peck him too. The carter was mad with fury; and without looking about him, or caring what he was about, struck again at the sparrow; but killed his third horse as he done the other two. 'Alas! miserable wretch that I am!' cried he. 'Not wretch enough yet!' answered the sparrow as she flew away; 'now will

I plague and punish thee at thy own house.' The carter was forced at last to leave his cart behind him, and to go home overflowing with rage and vexation. 'Alas!' said he to his wife, 'what ill luck has befallen me! — my wine is all spilt, and my horses all three dead.' 'Alas! husband,' replied she, 'and a wicked bird has come into the house, and has brought with her all the birds in the world, I am sure, and they have fallen upon our corn in the loft, and are eating it up at such a rate!' Away ran the husband upstairs, and saw thousands of birds sitting upon the floor eating up his corn, with the sparrow in the midst of them. 'Unlucky wretch that I am!' cried the carter; for he saw that the corn was almost all gone. 'Not wretch enough yet!' said the sparrow; 'thy cruelty shall cost thee thy life yet!' and away she flew.

The carter seeing that he had thus lost all that he had, went down into his kitchen; and was still not sorry for what he had done, but sat himself angrily and sulkily in the chimney corner. But the sparrow sat on the outside of the window, and cried 'Carter! thy cruelty shall cost thee thy life!' With that he jumped up in a rage, seized his hatchet, and threw it at the sparrow; but it missed her, and only broke the window. The sparrow now hopped in, perched upon the window-seat, and cried, 'Carter! it shall cost thee thy life!' Then he became mad and blind with rage, and struck the window-seat with such force that he cleft it in two: and as the sparrow flew from place to place, the carter and his wife were so furious, that they broke all their furniture, glasses, chairs, benches, the table, and at last the walls, without touching the bird at all. In the end, however, they caught her: and the wife said, 'Shall I kill her at once?' 'No,' cried he, 'that is letting her off too easily: she shall die a much more cruel death; I will eat her.' But the sparrow began to flutter about, and stretch out her neck and cried, 'Carter! it shall cost thee thy life yet!' With that he could wait no longer: so he gave his wife the hatchet, and cried, 'Wife, strike at the bird and kill her in my hand.' And the wife struck; but she missed her aim, and hit her husband on the head so that he fell down dead, and the sparrow flew quietly home to her nest.

## *Ashputtel*

The wife of a rich man fell sick; and when she felt that her end drew nigh, she called her only daughter to her bed-side, and said, 'Always be a good girl, and I will look down from heaven and watch over you.' Soon afterwards she shut her eyes and died, and was buried in the garden; and the little girl went every day to her grave and wept, and was always good and kind to all about her. And the snow fell and spread a beautiful white covering over the grave; but by the time the spring came, and the sun had melted it away again, her father had married another wife. This new wife had two daughters of her own, that she brought home with her; they were fair in face but foul at heart, and it was now a sorry time for the poor little girl. 'What does the good-for-nothing want in the parlour?' said they; 'they who would eat bread should first earn it; away with the kitchen-maid!' Then they took away her fine clothes, and gave her an old grey frock to put on, and laughed at her, and turned her into the kitchen.

There she was forced to do hard work; to rise early before daylight, to bring the water, to make the fire, to cook and to wash. Besides that, the sisters plagued her in all sorts of ways, and laughed at her. In the evening when she was tired, she had no bed to lie down on, but was made to lie by the hearth among the ashes; and as this, of course, made her always dusty and dirty, they called her Ashputtel.

It happened once that the father was going to the fair, and asked his wife's daughters what he should bring them. 'Fine clothes,' said the first; 'Pearls and diamonds,' cried the second. 'Now, child,' said he to his own daughter, 'what will you have?' 'The first twig, dear father, that brushes against your hat when you turn your face to come homewards,' said she. Then he bought for the first two the fine clothes and pearls and diamonds they had asked for: and on his way home, as he rode through a green copse, a hazel twig brushed against him, and almost pushed off his hat: so he broke it off and brought it away; and when he got home he gave it to his daughter. Then she took it, and went to her mother's grave and planted it there; and cried so much that it was watered with her tears; and there it grew and became a fine tree. Three times every day she went to it and cried; and soon a little bird came and built its nest upon the tree, and talked with her, and watched over her, and brought her whatever she wished for.

Now it happened that the king of that land held a feast, which was to last three days; and out of those who came to it his son was to choose a bride for himself. Ashputtel's two sisters were asked to come; so they called her up, and said, 'Now, comb our hair, brush our shoes, and tie our sashes for us, for we are going to dance at the king's feast.' Then she did as she was told; but when all was done she could not help crying, for she thought to herself, she should so have liked to have gone with them to the ball; and at last she begged her mother very hard to let her go. 'You, Ashputtel!' said she; 'you who have nothing to wear, no clothes at all, and who cannot even dance — you want to go to the ball? And when she kept on begging, she said at last, to get rid of her, 'I will throw this dishful of peas into the ash-heap, and if in two hours' time you have picked them all out, you shall go to the feast too.'

Then she threw the peas down among the ashes, but the little maiden ran out at the back door into the garden, and cried out:

'Hither, hither, through the sky,
Turtle-doves and linnets, fly!
Blackbird, thrush, and chaffinch gay,
Hither, hither, haste away!
One and all come help me, quick!
Haste ye, haste ye! — pick, pick, pick!'

Then first came two white doves, flying in at the kitchen window; next came two turtle-doves; and after them came all the little birds under heaven, chirping and fluttering in: and they flew down into the ashes. And the little doves stooped their heads down and set to work, pick, pick, pick; and then the others began to pick, pick, pick: and among them all they soon picked out all the good grain, and put it into a dish but left the ashes. Long before the end of the hour the work was quite done, and all flew out again at the windows.

Then Ashputtel brought the dish to her mother, overjoyed at the thought that now she should go to the ball. But the mother said, 'No, no! you slut, you have no clothes, and cannot dance; you shall not go.' And when Ashputtel begged very hard to go, she said, 'If you can in one hour's time pick two of those dishes of peas out of the ashes, you shall go too.' And thus she thought she should at least get rid of her. So she shook two dishes of peas into the ashes.

But the little maiden went out into the garden at the back of the house, and cried out as before:

'Hither, hither, through the sky,
Turtle-doves and linnets, fly!
Blackbird, thrush, and chaffinch gay,
Hither, hither, haste away!
One and all come help me, quick!
Haste ye, haste ye! — pick, pick, pick!'

Then first came two white doves in at the kitchen window; next came two turtle-doves; and after them came all the little birds under heaven, chirping and hopping about. And they flew down into the ashes; and the little doves put their heads down and set to work, pick, pick, pick; and then the others began pick, pick, pick; and they put all the good grain into the dishes, and left all the ashes. Before half an hour's time all was done, and out they flew again. And then Ashputtel took the dishes to her mother, rejoicing to think that she should now go to the ball. But her mother said, 'It is all of no use, you cannot go; you have no clothes, and cannot dance, and you would only put us to shame': and off she went with her two daughters to the ball.

Now when all were gone, and nobody left at home, Ashputtel went sorrowfully and sat down under the hazel-tree, and cried out:

'Shake, shake, hazel-tree,
Gold and silver over me!'

Then her friend the bird flew out of the tree, and brought a gold and silver dress for her, and slippers of spangled silk; and she put them on, and followed her sisters to the feast. But they did not know her, and thought it must be some strange princess, she looked so fine and beautiful in her rich clothes; and they never once thought of Ashputtel, taking it for granted that she was safe at home in the dirt.

The king's son soon came up to her, and took her by the hand and danced with her, and no one else: and he never left her hand; but when anyone else came to ask her to dance, he said, 'This lady is dancing with me.'

Thus they danced till a late hour of the night; and then she wanted to go home: and the king's son said, 'I shall go and take care of you to your home'; for he wanted to see where the beautiful maiden lived. But she slipped away from him, unawares, and ran off towards home; and as the prince followed her, she jumped up into the pigeon-house and shut the door. Then he waited till her father came home, and told him that the unknown maiden, who had been at the feast, had hid herself in the pigeon-house. But when they had broken open the door they found no one within; and as they came back into the house, Ashputtel was lying, as she always did, in her dirty frock by the ashes, and her dim little lamp was burning in the chimney. For she had run as quickly as she could through the pigeon-house and on to the hazel-tree, and had there taken off her beautiful clothes, and put them beneath the tree, that the bird might carry them away, and had lain down again amid the ashes in her little grey frock.

The next day when the feast was again held, and her father, mother, and sisters were gone, Ashputtel went to the hazel-tree, and said:

'Shake, shake, hazel-tree,
Gold and silver over me!'

And the bird came and brought a still finer dress than the one she had worn the day before. And when she came in it to the ball, everyone wondered at her beauty: but the king's son, who was waiting for her, took her by the hand, and danced with her; and when anyone asked her to dance, he said as before, 'This lady is dancing with me.'

When night came she wanted to go home; and the king's son followed here as before, that he might see into what house she went: but she sprang away from him all at once into the garden behind her father's house. In this garden stood a fine large pear-tree full of ripe fruit; and Ashputtel, not knowing where to hide herself, jumped up into it without being seen. Then the king's son lost sight of her, and could not find out where she was gone, but waited till her father came home, and said to him, 'The unknown lady who danced with me has slipped away, and I think she must have sprung into the pear-tree.' The father thought to himself, 'Can it be Ashputtel?' So he had an axe brought; and they cut down the tree, but found no one upon it. And when they came back into the kitchen, there lay Ashputtel among the ashes; for she had slipped down on the other side of the tree, and carried her beautiful clothes back to the bird at the hazel-tree, and then put on her little grey frock.

The third day, when her father and mother and sisters were gone, she went again into the garden, and said:

'Shake, shake, hazel-tree,
Gold and silver over me!'

Then her kind friend the bird brought a dress still finer than the former one, and slippers which were all of gold: so that when she came to the feast no one knew what to say, for wonder at her beauty: and the king's son danced with nobody but her; and when anyone else asked her to dance, he said, 'This lady is my partner, sir.'

When night came she wanted to go home; and the king's son would go with her, and said to himself, 'I will not lose her this time'; but, however, she again slipped away from him, though in such a hurry that she dropped her left golden slipper upon the stairs.

The prince took the shoe, and went the next day to the king his father, and said, 'I will take for my wife the lady that this golden slipper fits.' Then both the sisters were overjoyed to hear it; for they had beautiful feet, and had no doubt that they could wear the golden slipper. The eldest went first into the room where the slipper was, and wanted to try it on, and the mother stood by. But her great toe could not go into it, and the shoe was altogether much too small for her. Then the mother gave her a knife, and said, 'Never mind, cut it off; when you are queen you will not care about toes; you will not want to walk.' So the silly girl cut off her great toe, and thus squeezed on the shoe, and went to the king's son. Then he took her for his bride, and set her beside him on his horse, and rode away with her homewards.

But on their way home they had to pass by the hazel-tree that Ashputtel had planted; and on the branch sat a little dove singing:

> 'Back again! back again! look to the shoe!
> The shoe is too small, and not made for you!
> Prince! prince! look again for thy bride,
> For she's not the true one that sits by thy side.'

Then the prince got down and looked at her foot; and he saw, by the blood that streamed from it, what a trick she had played him. So he turned his horse round, and brought the false bride back to her home, and said, 'This is not the right bride; let the other sister try and put on the slipper.' Then she went into the room and got her foot into the shoe, all but the heel, which was too large. But her mother squeezed it in till the blood came, and took her to the king's son: and he set her as his bride by his side on his horse, and rode away with her.

But when they came to the hazel-tree the little dove sat there still, and sang:

> 'Back again! back again! look to the shoe!
> The shoe is too small, and not made for you!
> Prince! prince! look again for thy bride,
> For she's not the true one that sits by thy side.'

Then he looked down, and saw that the blood streamed so much from the shoe, that her white stockings were quite red. So he turned his horse and brought her also back again. 'This is not the true bride,' said he to the father; 'have you no other daughters?' 'No,' said he; 'there is only a little dirty Ashputtel here, the child of my first wife; I am sure she cannot be the bride.' The prince told him to send her. But the mother said, 'No, no, she is much too dirty; she will not dare to show herself.' However, the prince would have her come; and she first washed her face and hands, and then went in and curtsied to him, and he reached her the golden slipper. Then she took her clumsy shoe off her left foot, and put on the golden slipper; and it fitted her as if it had been made for her. And when he drew near and looked at her face he knew her, and said, 'This is the right bride.' But the mother and both the sisters were frightened, and turned pale with anger as he took Ashputtel on his horse, and rode away with her. And when they came to the hazel-tree, the white dove sang:

'Home! home! look at the shoe!
Princess! the shoe was made for you!
Prince! prince! take home thy bride,

For she is the true one that sits by thy side!'

And when the dove had done its song, it came flying, and perched upon her right shoulder, and so went home with her.

## *Jorinda And Jorindel*

There was once an old castle, that stood in the middle of a deep gloomy wood, and in the castle lived an old fairy. Now this fairy could take any shape she pleased. All the day long she flew about in the form of an owl, or crept about the country like a cat; but at night she always became an old woman again. When any young man came within a hundred paces of her castle, he became quite fixed, and could not move a step till she came and set him free; which she would not do till he had given her his word never to come there again: but when any pretty maiden came within that space she was changed into a bird, and the fairy put her into a cage, and hung her up in a chamber in the castle. There were seven hundred of these cages hanging in the castle, and all with beautiful birds in them.

Now there was once a maiden whose name was Jorinda. She was prettier than all the pretty girls that ever were seen before, and a shepherd lad, whose name was Jorindel, was very fond of her, and they were soon to be married. One day they went to walk in the wood, that they might be alone; and Jorindel said, 'We must take care that we don't go too near to the fairy's castle.'

It was a beautiful evening; the last rays of the setting sun shone bright through the long stems of the trees upon the green underwood beneath, and the turtle-doves sang from the tall birches.

Jorinda sat down to gaze upon the sun; Jorindel sat by her side; and both felt sad, they knew not why; but it seemed as if they were to be parted from one another for ever. They had wandered a long way; and when they looked to see which way they should go home, they found themselves at a loss to know what path to take.

The sun was setting fast, and already half of its circle had sunk behind the hill: Jorindel on a sudden looked behind him, and saw through the bushes that they had, without knowing it, sat down close under the old walls of the castle. Then he shrank for fear, turned pale, and trembled. Jorinda was just singing,

> 'The ring-dove sang from the willow spray,
> Well-a-day! Well-a-day!
> He mourn'd for the fate of his darling mate,
> Well-a-day!'

when her song stopped suddenly. Jorindel turned to see the reason, and beheld his Jorinda changed into a nightingale, so that her song ended with a mournful jug, jug. An owl with fiery eyes flew three times round them, and three times screamed:

'Tu whu! Tu whu! Tu whu!'

Jorindel could not move; he stood fixed as a stone, and could neither weep, nor speak, nor stir hand or foot. And now the sun went quite down; the gloomy night came; the owl flew into a bush; and a moment after the old fairy came forth pale and meagre, with staring eyes, and a nose and chin that almost met one another.

She mumbled something to herself, seized the nightingale, and went away with it in her hand. Poor Jorindel saw the nightingale was gone — but what could he do? He could not speak, he could not move from the spot where he stood. At last the fairy came back and sang with a hoarse voice:

> 'Till the prisoner is fast,
> And her doom is cast,
> There stay! Oh, stay!
> When the charm is around her,
> And the spell has bound her,
> Hie away! away!'

On a sudden Jorindel found himself free. Then he fell on his knees before the fairy, and prayed her to give him back his dear Jorinda: but she laughed at him, and said he should never see her again; then she went her way.

He prayed, he wept, he sorrowed, but all in vain. 'Alas!' he said, 'what will become of me?' He could not go back to his own home, so he went to a strange village, and employed himself in keeping sheep. Many a time did he walk round and round as near to the hated castle as he dared go, but all in vain; he heard or saw nothing of Jorinda.

At last he dreamt one night that he found a beautiful purple flower, and that in the middle of it lay a costly pearl; and he dreamt that he plucked the flower, and went with it in his hand into the castle, and that everything he touched with it was disenchanted, and that there he found his Jorinda again.

In the morning when he awoke, he began to search over hill and dale for this pretty flower; and eight long days he sought for it in vain: but on the ninth day, early in the morning, he found the beautiful purple flower; and in the middle of it was a large dewdrop, as big as a costly pearl. Then he plucked the flower, and set out and travelled day and night, till he came again to the castle.

He walked nearer than a hundred paces to it, and yet he did not become fixed as before, but found that he could go quite close up to the door. Jorindel was very glad indeed to see this. Then he touched the door with the flower, and it sprang open; so that he went in through the court, and listened when he heard so many birds singing. At last he came to the chamber where the fairy sat, with the seven hundred birds singing in the seven hundred cages. When she saw Jorindel she was very angry, and screamed with rage; but she could not come within two yards of him, for the flower he held in his hand was his safeguard. He looked around at the birds, but alas! there were many, many nightingales, and how then should he find out which was his Jorinda? While he was thinking what to do, he saw the fairy had taken down one of the cages, and was making the best of her way off through the door. He ran or flew after her, touched the cage with the flower, and Jorinda stood before him, and threw her arms round his neck looking as beautiful as ever, as beautiful as when they walked together in the wood.

Then he touched all the other birds with the flower, so that they all took their old forms again; and he took Jorinda home, where they were married, and lived happily together many years: and so did a good many other lads, whose maidens had been forced to sing in the old fairy's cages by themselves, much longer than they liked.

## *The Frog-Prince*

One fine evening a young princess put on her bonnet and clogs, and went out to take a walk by herself in a wood; and when she came to a cool spring of water, that rose in the midst of it, she sat herself down to rest a while. Now she had a golden ball in her hand, which was her favourite plaything; and she was always tossing it up into the air, and catching it again as it fell. After a time she threw it up so high that she missed catching it as it fell; and the ball bounded away, and rolled along upon the ground, till at last it fell down into the spring. The princess looked into the spring after her ball, but it was very deep, so deep that she could not see the bottom of it. Then she began to bewail her loss, and said, 'Alas! if I could only get my ball again, I would give all my fine clothes and jewels, and everything that I have in the world.'

Whilst she was speaking, a frog put its head out of the water, and said, 'Princess, why do you weep so bitterly?' 'Alas!' said she, 'what can you do for me, you nasty frog? My golden ball has fallen into the spring.' The frog said, 'I want not your pearls, and jewels, and fine clothes; but if you will love me, and let me live with you and eat from off your golden plate, and sleep upon your bed, I will bring you your ball again.' 'What nonsense,' thought the princess, 'this silly frog is talking! He can never even get out of the spring to visit me, though he may be able to get my ball for me, and therefore I will tell him he shall have what he asks.' So she said to the frog, 'Well, if you will bring me my ball, I will do all you ask.' Then the frog put his head down, and dived deep under the water; and after a little while he came up again, with the ball in his mouth, and threw it on the edge of the spring. As soon as the young princess saw her ball, she ran to pick it up; and she was so overjoyed to have it in her hand again, that she never thought of the frog, but ran home with it as fast as she could. The frog called after her, 'Stay, princess, and take me with you as you said,' But she did not stop to hear a word.

The next day, just as the princess had sat down to dinner, she heard a strange noise — tap, tap — plash, plash — as if something was coming up the marble staircase: and soon afterwards there was a gentle knock at the door, and a little voice cried out and said:

'Open the door, my princess dear,
Open the door to thy true love here!
And mind the words that thou and I said
By the fountain cool, in the greenwood shade.'

Then the princess ran to the door and opened it, and there she saw the frog, whom she had quite forgotten. At this sight she was sadly frightened, and shutting the door as fast as she could came back to her seat.

The king, her father, seeing that something had frightened her, asked her what was the matter. 'There is a nasty frog,' said she, 'at the door, that lifted my ball for me out of the spring this morning: I told him that he should live with me here, thinking that he could never get out of the spring; but there he is at the door, and he wants to come in.'

While she was speaking the frog knocked again at the door, and said:

'Open the door, my princess dear,
Open the door to thy true love here!
And mind the words that thou and I said
By the fountain cool, in the greenwood shade.'

Then the king said to the young princess, 'As you have given your word you must keep it; so go and let him in.' She did so, and the frog hopped into the room, and then straight on — tap, tap — plash, plash — from the bottom of the room to the top, till he came up close to the table where the princess sat. 'Pray lift me upon chair,' said he to the princess, 'and let me sit next to you.' As soon as she had done this, the frog said, 'Put your plate nearer to me, that I may eat out of it.' This she did, and when he had eaten as much as he could, he said, 'Now I am tired; carry me upstairs, and put me into your bed.' And the princess, though very unwilling, took him up in her hand, and put him upon the pillow of her own bed, where he slept all night long. As soon as it was light he jumped up, hopped downstairs, and went out of the house. 'Now, then,' thought the princess, 'at last he is gone, and I shall be troubled with him no more.'

But she was mistaken; for when night came again she heard the same tapping at the door; and the frog came once more, and said:

> 'Open the door, my princess dear,
> Open the door to thy true love here!
> And mind the words that thou and I said
> By the fountain cool, in the greenwood shade.'

And when the princess opened the door the frog came in, and slept upon her pillow as before, till the morning broke. And the third night he did the same. But when the princess awoke on the following morning she was astonished to see, instead of the frog, a handsome prince, gazing on her with the most beautiful eyes she had ever seen, and standing at the head of her bed.

He told her that he had been enchanted by a spiteful fairy, who had changed him into a frog; and that he had been fated so to abide till some princess should take him out of the spring, and let him eat from her plate, and sleep upon her bed for three nights. 'You,' said the prince, 'have broken his cruel charm, and now I have nothing to wish for but that you should go with me into my father's kingdom, where I will marry you, and love you as long as you live.'

The young princess, you may be sure, was not long in saying 'Yes' to all this; and as they spoke a gay coach drove up, with eight beautiful horses, decked with plumes of feathers and a golden harness; and behind the coach rode the prince's servant, faithful Heinrich, who had bewailed the misfortunes of his dear master during his enchantment so long and so bitterly, that his heart had well-nigh burst.

They then took leave of the king, and got into the coach with eight horses, and all set out, full of joy and merriment, for the prince's kingdom, which they reached safely; and there they lived happily a great many years.

## *Frederick And Catherine*

There was once a man called Frederick: he had a wife whose name was Catherine, and they had not long been married. One day Frederick said. 'Kate! I am going to work in the fields; when I come back I shall be hungry so let me have something nice cooked, and a good draught of ale.' 'Very well,' said she, 'it shall all be ready.' When dinner-time drew nigh, Catherine took a nice steak, which was all the meat she had, and put it on the fire to fry. The steak soon began to look brown, and to crackle in the pan; and Catherine stood by with a fork and turned it: then she said to herself, 'The steak is almost ready, I may as well go to the cellar for the ale.' So she left the pan on the fire and took a large jug and went into the cellar and tapped the ale cask. The beer ran into the jug and Catherine stood looking on. At last it popped into her head, 'The dog is not shut up — he may be running away with the steak; that's well thought of.' So up she ran from the cellar; and sure enough the rascally cur had got the steak in his mouth, and was making off with it.

Away ran Catherine, and away ran the dog across the field: but he ran faster than she, and stuck close to the steak. 'It's all gone, and "what can't be cured must be endured",' said Catherine. So she turned round; and as she had run a good way and was tired, she walked home leisurely to cool herself.

Now all this time the ale was running too, for Catherine had not turned the cock; and when the jug was full the liquor ran upon the floor till the cask was empty. When she got to the cellar stairs she saw what had happened. 'My stars!' said she, 'what shall I do to keep Frederick from seeing all this slopping about?' So she thought a while; and at last remembered that there was a sack of fine meal bought at the last fair, and that if she sprinkled this over the floor it would suck up the ale nicely. 'What a lucky thing,' said she, 'that we kept that meal! We have now a good use for it.' So away she went for it: but she managed to set it down just upon the great jug full of beer, and upset it; and thus all the ale that had been saved was set swimming on the floor also. 'Ah! well,' said she, 'when one goes another may as well follow.' Then she strewed the meal all about the cellar, and was quite pleased with her cleverness, and said, 'How very neat and clean it looks!'

At noon Frederick came home. 'Now, wife,' cried he, 'what have you for dinner?' 'O Frederick!' answered she, 'I was cooking you a steak; but while I went down to draw the ale, the dog ran away with it; and while I ran after him, the ale ran out; and when I went to dry up the ale with the sack of meal that we got at the fair, I upset the jug: but the cellar is now quite dry, and looks so clean!' 'Kate, Kate,' said he, 'how could you do all this? Why did you leave the steak to fry, and the ale to run, and then spoil all the meal?' 'Why, Frederick,' said she, 'I did not know I was doing wrong; you should have told me before.'

The husband thought to himself, 'If my wife manages matters thus, I must look sharp myself.' Now he had a good deal of gold in the house: so he said to Catherine, 'What pretty yellow buttons these are! I shall put them into a box and bury them in the garden; but take care that you never go near or meddle with them.' 'No, Frederick,' said she, 'that I never will.' As soon as he was gone, there came by some pedlars with earthenware plates and dishes, and they asked her whether she would buy. 'Oh dear me, I should like to buy very much, but I have no money: if you had any use for yellow buttons, I might deal with you.' 'Yellow buttons!' said they: 'let us have a look at them.' 'Go into the garden and dig where I tell you, and you will find the yellow buttons: I dare not go myself.' So the rogues went: and when they found what these yellow buttons were, they took them all away, and left her plenty of plates and dishes. Then she set them all about the house for a show: and when Frederick came back, he cried out, 'Kate, what have you been doing?' 'See,' said she, 'I have bought all these with your yellow buttons: but I did not touch them myself; the pedlars went themselves and dug them up.' 'Wife, wife,' said Frederick, 'what a pretty piece of work you have made! Those yellow buttons were all my money: how came you to do such a thing?' 'Why,' answered she, 'I did not know there was any harm in it; you should have told me.'

Catherine stood musing for a while, and at last said to her husband, 'Hark ye, Frederick, we will soon get the gold back: let us run after the thieves.' 'Well, we will try,' answered he; 'but take some butter and cheese with you, that we may have something to eat by the way.' 'Very well,' said she; and they set out: and as Frederick walked the fastest, he left his wife some way behind. 'It does not matter,' thought she: 'when we turn back, I shall be so much nearer home than he.'

Presently she came to the top of a hill, down the side of which there was a road so narrow that the cart wheels always chafed the trees on each side as they passed. 'Ah, see now,' said she, 'how they have bruised and wounded those poor trees; they will never get well.' So she took pity on them, and made use of the butter to grease them all, so that the wheels might not hurt them so much. While she was doing this kind office one of her cheeses fell out of the basket, and rolled down the hill. Catherine looked, but could not see where it had gone; so she said, 'Well, I suppose the other will go the same way and find you; he has younger legs than I have.' Then she rolled the other cheese after it; and away it went, nobody knows where, down the hill. But she said she supposed that they knew the road, and would follow her, and she could not stay there all day waiting for them.

At last she overtook Frederick, who desired her to give him something to eat. Then she gave him the dry bread. 'Where are the butter and cheese?' said he. 'Oh!' answered she, 'I used the butter to grease those poor trees that the wheels chafed so: and one of the cheeses ran away so I sent the other after it to find it, and I suppose they are both on the road together somewhere.' 'What a goose you are to do such silly things!' said the husband. 'How can you say so?' said she; 'I am sure you never told me not.'

They ate the dry bread together; and Frederick said, 'Kate, I hope you locked the door safe when you came away.' 'No,' answered she, 'you did not tell me.' 'Then go home, and do it now before we go any farther,' said Frederick, 'and bring with you something to eat.'

Catherine did as he told her, and thought to herself by the way, 'Frederick wants something to eat; but I don't think he is very fond of butter and cheese: I'll bring him a bag of fine nuts, and the vinegar, for I have often seen him take some.'

When she reached home, she bolted the back door, but the front door she took off the hinges, and said, 'Frederick told me to lock the door, but surely it can nowhere be so safe if I take it with me.' So she took her time by the way; and when she overtook her husband she cried out, 'There, Frederick, there is the door itself, you may watch it as carefully as you please.' 'Alas! alas!' said he, 'what a clever wife I have! I sent you to make the house fast, and you take the door away, so that everybody may go in and out as they please — however, as you have brought the door, you shall carry it about with you for your pains.' 'Very well,' answered she, 'I'll carry the door; but I'll not carry the nuts and vinegar bottle also — that would be too much of a load; so if you please, I'll fasten them to the door.'

Frederick of course made no objection to that plan,

and they set off into the wood to look for the thieves; but they could not find them: and when it grew dark, they climbed up into a tree to spend the night there. Scarcely were they up, than who should come by but the very rogues they were looking for. They were in truth great rascals, and belonged to that class of people who find things before they are lost; they were tired; so they sat down and made a fire under the very tree where Frederick and Catherine were. Frederick slipped down on the other side, and picked up some stones. Then he climbed up again, and tried to hit the thieves on the head with them: but they only said, 'It must be near morning, for the wind shakes the fir-apples down.'

Catherine, who had the door on her shoulder, began to be very tired; but she thought it was the nuts upon it that were so heavy: so she said softly, 'Frederick, I must let the nuts go.' 'No,' answered he, 'not now, they will discover us.' 'I can't help that: they must go.' 'Well, then, make haste and throw them down, if you will.' Then away rattled the nuts down among the boughs and one of the thieves cried, 'Bless me, it is hailing.'

A little while after, Catherine thought the door was still very heavy: so she whispered to Frederick, 'I must throw the vinegar down.' 'Pray don't,' answered he, 'it will discover us.' 'I can't help that,' said she, 'go it must.' So she poured all the vinegar down; and the thieves said, 'What a heavy dew there is!'

At last it popped into Catherine's head that it was the door itself that was so heavy all the time: so she whispered, 'Frederick, I must throw the door down soon.' But he begged and prayed her not to do so, for he was sure it would betray them. 'Here goes, however,' said she: and down went the door with such a clatter upon the thieves, that they cried out 'Murder!' and not knowing what was coming, ran away as fast as they could, and left all the gold. So when Frederick and Catherine came down, there they found all their money safe and sound.

# *Old Sultan*

A shepherd had a faithful dog, called Sultan, who was grown very old, and had lost all his teeth. And one day when the shepherd and his wife were standing together before the house the shepherd said, 'I will shoot old Sultan tomorrow morning, for he is of no use now.' But his wife said, 'Pray let the poor faithful creature live; he has served us well a great many years, and we ought to give him a livelihood for the rest of his days.' 'But what can we do with him?' said the shepherd, 'he has not a tooth in his head, and the thieves don't care for him at all; to be sure he has served us, but then he did it to earn his livelihood; tomorrow shall be his last day, depend upon it.'

Poor Sultan, who was lying close by them, heard all that the shepherd and his wife said to one another, and was very much frightened to think tomorrow would be his last day; so in the evening he went to his good friend the wolf, who lived in the wood, and told him all his sorrows, and how his master meant to kill him in the morning. 'Make yourself easy,' said the wolf, 'I will give you some good advice. Your master, you know, goes out every morning very early with his wife into the field; and they take their little child with them, and lay it down behind the hedge in the shade while they are at work. Now do you lie down close by the child, and pretend to be watching it, and I will come out of the wood and run away with it; you must run after me as fast as you can, and I will let it drop; then you may carry it back, and they will think you have saved their child, and will be so thankful to you that they will take care of you as long as you live.' The dog liked this plan very well; and accordingly so it was managed. The wolf ran with the child a little way; the shepherd and his wife screamed out; but Sultan soon overtook him, and carried the poor little thing back to his master and mistress. Then the shepherd patted him on the head, and said, 'Old Sultan has saved our child from the wolf, and therefore he shall live and be well taken care of, and have plenty to eat. Wife, go home, and give him a good dinner, and let him have my old cushion to sleep on as long as he lives.' So from this time forward Sultan had all that he could wish for.

Soon afterwards the wolf came and wished him joy, and said, 'Now, my good fellow, you must tell no tales, but turn your head the other way when I want to taste one of the old shepherd's fine fat sheep.' 'No,' said the Sultan; 'I will be true to my master.' However, the wolf thought he was in joke, and came one night to get a dainty morsel. But Sultan had told his master what the wolf meant to do; so he laid wait for him behind the barn door, and when the wolf was busy looking out for a good fat sheep, he had a stout cudgel laid about his back, that combed his locks for him finely.

Then the wolf was very angry, and called Sultan 'an old rogue,' and swore he would have his revenge. So the next morning the wolf sent the boar to challenge Sultan to come into the wood to fight the matter. Now Sultan had nobody he could ask to be his second but the shepherd's old three-legged cat; so he took her with him, and as the poor thing limped along with some trouble, she stuck up her tail straight in the air.

The wolf and the wild boar were first on the ground; and when they espied their enemies coming, and saw the cat's long tail standing straight in the air, they thought she was carrying a sword for Sultan to fight with; and every time she limped, they thought she was picking up a stone to throw at them; so they said they should not like this way of fighting, and the boar lay down behind a bush, and the wolf jumped up into a tree. Sultan and the cat soon came up, and looked about and wondered that no one was there. The boar, however, had not quite hidden himself, for his ears stuck out of the bush; and when he shook one of them a little, the cat, seeing something move, and thinking it was a mouse, sprang upon it, and bit and scratched it, so that the boar jumped up and grunted, and ran away, roaring out, 'Look up in the tree, there sits the one who is to blame.' So they looked up, and espied the wolf sitting amongst the branches; and they called him a cowardly rascal, and would not suffer him to come down till he was heartily ashamed of himself, and had promised to be good friends again with old Sultan.

# *The Seven Ravens*

There was once a man who had seven sons, and last of all one daughter. Although the little girl was very pretty, she was so weak and small that they thought she could not live; but they said she should at once be christened.

So the father sent one of his sons in haste to the spring to get some water, but the other six ran with him. Each wanted to be first at drawing the water, and so they were in such a hurry that all let their pitchers fall into the well, and they stood very foolishly looking at one another, and did not know what to do, for none dared go home. In the meantime the father was uneasy, and could not tell what made the young men stay so long. 'Surely,' said he, 'the whole seven must have forgotten themselves over some game of play'; and when he had waited still longer and they yet did not come, he flew into a rage and wished them all turned into ravens. Scarcely had he spoken these words when he heard a croaking over his head, and looked up and saw seven ravens as black as coal flying round and round. Sorry as he was to see his wish so fulfilled, he did not know how what was done could be undone, and comforted himself as well as he could for the loss of his seven sons with his dear little daughter, who soon became stronger and every day more beautiful.

For a long time she did not know that she had ever had any brothers; for her father and mother took care not to speak of them before her: but one day by chance she heard the people about her speak of them. 'Yes,' said they, 'she is beautiful indeed, but still 'tis a pity that her brothers should have been lost for her sake.' Then she was much grieved, and went to her father and mother, and asked if she had any brothers, and what had become of them. So they dared no longer hide the truth from her, but said it was the will of Heaven, and that her birth was only the innocent cause of it; but the little girl mourned sadly about it every day, and thought herself bound to do all she could to bring her brothers back; and she had neither rest nor ease, till at length one day she stole away, and set out into the wide world to find her brothers, wherever they might be, and free them, whatever it might cost her.

She took nothing with her but a little ring which her father and mother had given her, a loaf of bread in case she should be hungry, a little pitcher of water in case she should be thirsty, and a little stool to rest upon when she should be weary. Thus she went on and on, and journeyed till she came to the world's end; then she came to the sun, but the sun looked much too hot and fiery; so she ran away quickly to the moon, but the moon was cold and chilly, and said, 'I smell flesh and blood this way!' so she took herself away in a hurry and came to the stars, and the stars were friendly and kind to her, and each star sat upon his own little stool; but the morning star rose up and gave her a little piece of wood, and said, 'If you have not this little piece of wood, you cannot unlock the castle that stands on the glass-mountain, and there your brothers live.' The little girl took the piece of wood, rolled it up in a little cloth, and went on again until she came to the glass-mountain, and found the door shut. Then she felt for the little piece of wood; but when she unwrapped the cloth it was not there, and she saw she had lost the gift of the good stars. What was to be done? She wanted to save her brothers, and had no key of the castle of the glass-mountain; so this faithful little sister took a knife out of her pocket and cut off her little finger, that was just the size of the piece of wood she had lost, and put it in the door and opened it.

As she went in, a little dwarf came up to her, and said, 'What are you seeking for?' 'I seek for my brothers, the seven ravens,' answered she. Then the dwarf said, 'My masters are not at home; but if you will wait till they come, pray step in.' Now the little dwarf was getting their dinner ready, and he brought their food upon seven little plates, and their drink in seven little glasses, and set them upon the table, and out of each little plate their sister ate a small piece, and out of each little glass she drank a small drop; but she let the ring that she had brought with her fall into the last glass.

On a sudden she heard a fluttering and croaking in the air, and the dwarf said, 'Here come my masters.' When they came in, they wanted to eat and drink, and looked for their little plates and glasses. Then said one after the other,

'Who has eaten from my little plate? And who has been drinking out of my little glass?'

'Caw! Caw! well I ween
Mortal lips have this way been.'

When the seventh came to the bottom of his glass, and found there the ring, he looked at it, and knew that it was his father's and mother's, and said, 'O that our little sister would but come! Then we should be free.' When the little girl heard this (for she stood behind the door all the time and listened), she ran forward, and in an instant all the ravens took their right form again; and all hugged and kissed each other, and went merrily home.

## *The Mouse, The Bird And The Sausage*

Once upon a time, a mouse, a bird, and a sausage, entered into partnership and set up house together. For a long time all went well; they lived in great comfort, and prospered so far as to be able to add considerably to their stores. The bird's duty was to fly daily into the wood and bring in fuel; the mouse fetched the water, and the sausage saw to the cooking.

When people are too well off they always begin to long for something new. And so it came to pass, that the bird, while out one day, met a fellow bird, to whom he boastfully expatiated on the excellence of his household arrangements. But the other bird sneered at him for being a poor simpleton, who did all the hard work, while the other two stayed at home and had a good time of it. For, when the mouse had made the fire and fetched in the water, she could retire into her little room and rest until it was time to set the table. The sausage had only to watch the pot to see that the food was properly cooked, and when it was near dinner-time, he just threw himself into the broth, or rolled in and out among the vegetables three or four times, and there they were, buttered, and salted, and ready to be served. Then, when the bird came home and had laid aside his burden, they sat down to table, and when they had finished their meal, they could sleep their fill till the following morning: and that was really a very delightful life.

Influenced by those remarks, the bird next morning refused to bring in the wood, telling the others that he had been their servant long enough, and had been a fool into the bargain, and that it was now time to make a change, and to try some other way of arranging the work. Beg and pray as the mouse and the sausage might, it was of no use; the bird remained master of the situation, and the venture had to be made. They therefore drew lots, and it fell to the sausage to bring in the wood, to the mouse to cook, and to the bird to fetch the water.

And now what happened? The sausage started in search of wood, the bird made the fire, and the mouse put on the pot, and then these two waited till the sausage returned with the fuel for the following day. But the sausage remained so long away, that they became uneasy, and the bird flew out to meet him. He had not flown far, however, when he came across a dog who, having met the sausage, had regarded him as his legitimate booty, and so seized and swallowed him. The bird complained to the dog of this bare-faced robbery, but nothing he said was of any avail, for the dog answered that he found false credentials on the sausage, and that was the reason his life had been forfeited.

He picked up the wood, and flew sadly home, and

told the mouse all he had seen and heard. They were both very unhappy, but agreed to make the best of things and to remain with one another.

So now the bird set the table, and the mouse looked after the food and, wishing to prepare it in the same way as the sausage, by rolling in and out among the vegetables to salt and butter them, she jumped into the pot; but she stopped short long before she reached the bottom, having already parted not only with her skin and hair, but also with life.

Presently the bird came in and wanted to serve up the dinner, but he could nowhere see the cook. In his alarm and flurry, he threw the wood here and there about the floor, called and searched, but no cook was to be found. Then some of the wood that had been carelessly thrown down, caught fire and began to blaze. The bird hastened to fetch some water, but his pail fell into the well, and he after it, and as he was unable to recover himself, he was drowned.

# *The Fisherman And His Wife*

There was once a fisherman who lived with his wife in a pigsty, close by the seaside. The fisherman used to go out all day long a-fishing; and one day, as he sat on the shore with his rod, looking at the sparkling waves and watching his line, all on a sudden his float was dragged away deep into the water: and in drawing it up he pulled out a great fish. But the fish said, 'Pray let me live! I am not a real fish; I am an enchanted prince: put me in the water again, and let me go!' 'Oh, ho!' said the man, 'you need not make so many words about the matter; I will have nothing to do with a fish that can talk: so swim away, sir, as soon as you please!' Then he put him back into the water, and the fish darted straight down to the bottom, and left a long streak of blood behind him on the wave.

When the fisherman went home to his wife in the pigsty, he told her how he had caught a great fish, and how it had told him it was an enchanted prince, and how, on hearing it speak, he had let it go again. 'Did not you ask it for anything?' said the wife, 'we live very wretchedly here, in this nasty dirty pigsty; do go back and tell the fish we want a snug little cottage.'

The fisherman did not much like the business: however, he went to the seashore; and when he came back there the water looked all yellow and green. And he stood at the water's edge, and said:

'O man of the sea!
Hearken to me!
My wife Ilsabill
Will have her own will,
And hath sent me to beg a boon of thee!'

Then the fish came swimming to him, and said, 'Well, what is her will? What does your wife want?' 'Ah!' said the fisherman, 'she says that when I had caught you, I ought to have asked you for something before I let you go; she does not like living any longer in the pigsty, and wants a snug little cottage.' 'Go home, then,' said the fish; 'she is in the cottage already!' So the man went home, and saw his wife standing at the door of a nice trim little cottage. 'Come in, come in!' said she; 'is not this much better than the filthy pigsty we had?' And there was a parlour, and a bed-chamber, and a kitchen; and behind the cottage there was a little garden, planted with all sorts of flowers and fruits; and there was a courtyard behind, full of ducks and chickens. 'Ah!' said the fisherman, 'how happily we shall live now!' 'We will try to do so, at least,' said his wife.

Everything went right for a week or two, and then Dame Ilsabill said, 'Husband, there is not near room enough for us in this cottage; the courtyard and the garden are a great deal too small; I should like to have a large stone castle to live in: go to the fish again and tell him to give us a castle.' 'Wife,' said the fisherman, 'I don't like to go to him again, for perhaps he will be angry; we ought to be easy with this pretty cottage to live in.' 'Nonsense!' said the wife; 'he will do it very willingly, I know; go along and try!'

The fisherman went, but his heart was very heavy: and when he came to the sea, it looked blue and gloomy, though it was very calm; and he went close to the edge of the waves, and said:

'O man of the sea!
Hearken to me!
My wife Ilsabill
Will have her own will,
And hath sent me to beg a boon of thee!'

'Well, what does she want now?' said the fish. 'Ah!' said the man, dolefully, 'my wife wants to live in a stone castle.' 'Go home, then,' said the fish; 'she is standing at the gate of it already.' So away went the fisherman, and found his wife standing before the gate of a great castle. 'See,' said she, 'is not this grand?' With that they went into the castle together, and found a great many servants there, and the rooms all richly furnished, and full of golden chairs and tables; and behind the castle was a garden, and around it was a park half a mile long, full of sheep, and goats, and hares, and deer; and in the courtyard were stables and cow-houses. 'Well,' said the man, 'now we will live cheerful and happy in this beautiful castle for the rest of our lives.' 'Perhaps we may,' said the wife; 'but let us sleep upon it, before we make up our minds to that.' So they went to bed.

The next morning when Dame Ilsabill awoke it was broad daylight, and she jogged the fisherman with her elbow, and said, 'Get up, husband, and bestir yourself, for we must be king of all the land.' 'Wife, wife,' said the man, 'why should we wish to be the king? I will not be king.' 'Then I will,' said she. 'But, wife,' said the fisherman, 'how can you be king — the fish cannot make you a king?' 'Husband,' said she, 'say no more about it, but go and try! I will be king.' So the man went away quite sorrowful to think that his wife should want to be king. This time the sea looked a dark grey colour, and was overspread with curling waves and the ridges of foam as he cried out:

'O man of the sea!
Hearken to me!
My wife Ilsabill
Will have her own will,
And hath sent me to beg a boon of thee!'

'Well, what would she have now?' said the fish. 'Alas!' said the poor man, 'my wife wants to be king.' 'Go home,' said the fish; 'she is king already.'

Then the fisherman went home; and as he came close to the palace he saw a troop of soldiers, and heard the sound of drums and trumpets. And when he went in he saw his wife sitting on a throne of gold and diamonds, with a golden crown upon her head; and on each side of her stood six fair maidens, each a head taller than the other. 'Well, wife,' said the fisherman, 'are you king?' 'Yes,' said she, 'I am king.' And when he had looked at her for a long time, he said, 'Ah, wife! what a fine thing it is to be king! Now we shall never have anything more to wish for as long as we live.' 'I don't know how that may be,' said she; 'never is a long time. I am king, it is true; but I begin to be tired of that, and I think I should like to be emperor.' 'Alas, wife! why should you wish to be emperor?' said the fisherman. 'Husband,' said she, 'go to the fish! I say I will be emperor.' 'Ah, wife!' replied the fisherman, 'the fish cannot make an emperor, I am sure, and I should not like to ask him for such a thing.' 'I am king,' said Ilsabill, 'and you are my slave; so go at once!'

So the fisherman was forced to go; and he muttered as he went along, 'This will come to no good, it is too much to ask; the fish will be tired at last, and then we shall be sorry for what we have done.' He soon came to the seashore; and the water was quite black and muddy, and a mighty whirlwind blew over the waves and rolled them about, but he went as near as he could to the water's brink, and said:

'O man of the sea!
Hearken to me!
My wife Ilsabill
Will have her own will,
And hath sent me to beg a boon of thee!'

'What would she have now?' said the fish. 'Ah!' said the fisherman, 'she wants to be emperor.' 'Go home,' said the fish; 'she is emperor already.'

So he went home again; and as he came near he saw his wife Ilsabill sitting on a very lofty throne made of solid gold, with a great crown on her head full two yards high; and on each side of her stood her guards and attendants in a row, each one smaller than the other, from the tallest giant down to a little dwarf no bigger than my finger. And before her stood princes, and dukes, and earls: and the fisherman went up to her and said, 'Wife, are you emperor?' 'Yes,' said she, 'I am emperor.' 'Ah!' said the man, as he gazed upon her, 'what a fine thing it is to be emperor!' 'Husband,' said she, 'why should we stop at being emperor? I will be pope next.' 'O wife, wife!' said he, 'how can you be pope? there is but one pope at a time in Christendom.' 'Husband,' said she, 'I will be pope this very day.' 'But,' replied the husband, 'the fish cannot make you pope.' 'What nonsense!' said she; 'if he can make an emperor, he can make a pope: go and try him.'

So the fisherman went. But when he came to the shore the wind was raging and the sea was tossed up and down in boiling waves, and the ships were in trouble, and rolled fearfully upon the tops of the billows. In the middle of the heavens there was a little piece of blue sky, but towards the south all was red, as if a dreadful storm was rising. At this sight the fisherman was dreadfully frightened, and he trembled so that his knees knocked together: but still he went down near to the shore, and said:

> 'O man of the sea!
> Hearken to me!
> My wife Ilsabill
> Will have her own will,
> And hath sent me to beg a boon of thee!'

'What does she want now?' said the fish. 'Ah!' said the fisherman, 'my wife wants to be pope.' 'Go home,' said the fish; 'she is pope already.'

Then the fisherman went home, and found Ilsabill sitting on a throne that was two miles high. And she had three great crowns on her head, and around her stood all the pomp and power of the Church. And on each side of her were two rows of burning lights, of all sizes, the greatest as large as the highest and biggest tower in the world, and the least no larger than a small rushlight. 'Wife,' said the fisherman, as he looked at all this greatness, 'are you pope?' 'Yes,' said she, 'I am pope.' 'Well, wife,' replied he, 'it is a grand thing to be pope; and now you must be easy, for you can be nothing greater.' 'I will think about that,' said the wife. Then they went to bed: but Dame Ilsabill could not sleep all night for thinking what she should be next. At last, as she was dropping asleep, morning broke, and the sun rose. 'Ha!' thought she, as she woke up and looked at it through the window, 'after all I cannot prevent the sun rising.' At this thought she was very angry, and wakened her husband, and said, 'Husband, go to the fish and tell him I must be lord of the sun and moon.' The fisherman was half asleep, but the thought frightened him so much that he started and fell out of bed. 'Alas, wife!' said he, 'cannot you be easy with being pope?' 'No,' said she, 'I am very uneasy as long as the sun and moon rise without my leave. Go to the fish at once!'

Then the man went shivering with fear; and as he was going down to the shore a dreadful storm arose, so that the trees and the very rocks shook. And all the heavens became black with stormy clouds, and the lightnings played, and the thunders rolled; and you might have seen in the sea great black waves, swelling up like mountains with crowns of white foam upon their heads. And the fisherman crept towards the sea, and cried out, as well as he could:

'O man of the sea!
Hearken to me!
My wife Ilsabill
Will have her own will,
And hath sent me to beg a boon of thee!'

'What does she want now?' said the fish. 'Ah!' said he, 'she wants to be lord of the sun and moon.' 'Go home,' said the fish, 'to your pigsty again.'

And there they live to this very day.

# *The Salad*

As a merry young huntsman was once going briskly along through a wood, there came up a little old woman, and said to him, 'Good day, good day; you seem merry enough, but I am hungry and thirsty; do pray give me something to eat.' The huntsman took pity on her, and put his hand in his pocket and gave her what he had. Then he wanted to go his way; but she took hold of him, and said, 'Listen, my friend, to what I am going to tell you; I will reward you for your kindness; go your way, and after a little time you will come to a tree where you will see nine birds sitting on a cloak. Shoot into the midst of them, and one will fall down dead: the cloak will fall too; take it, it is a wishing-cloak, and when you wear it you will find yourself at any place where you may wish to be. Cut open the dead bird, take out its heart and keep it, and you will find a piece of gold under your pillow every morning when you rise. It is the bird's heart that will bring you this good luck.'

The huntsman thanked her, and thought to himself, 'If all this does happen, it will be a fine thing for me.' When he had gone a hundred steps or so, he heard a screaming and chirping in the branches over him, and looked up and saw a flock of birds pulling a cloak with their bills and feet; screaming, fighting, and tugging at each other as if each wished to have it himself. 'Well,' said the huntsman, 'this is wonderful; this happens just as the old woman said'; then he shot into the midst of them so that their feathers flew all about. Off went the flock chattering away; but one fell down dead, and the cloak with it. Then the huntsman did as the old woman told him, cut open the bird, took out the heart, and carried the cloak home with him.

The next morning when he awoke he lifted up his pillow, and there lay the piece of gold glittering underneath; the same happened next day, and indeed every day when he arose. He heaped up a great deal of gold, and at last thought to himself, 'Of what use is this gold to me whilst I am at home? I will go out into the world and look about me.'

Then he took leave of his friends, and hung his bag and bow about his neck, and went his way. It so happened that his road one day led through a thick wood, at the end of which was a large castle in a green meadow, and at one of the windows stood an old woman with a very beautiful young lady by her side looking about them. Now the old woman was a witch, and said to the young lady, 'There is a young man coming out of the wood who carries a wonderful prize; we must get it away from him, my dear child, for it is more fit for us than for him. He has a bird's heart that brings a piece of gold under his pillow every morning.' Meantime the huntsman came nearer and looked at the lady, and said to himself, 'I have been travelling so long that I should like to go into this castle and rest myself, for I have money enough to pay for anything I want'; but the real reason was, that he wanted to see more of the beautiful lady. Then he went into the house, and was welcomed kindly; and it was not long before he was so much in love that he thought of nothing else but looking at the lady's eyes, and doing everything that she wished. Then the old woman said, 'Now is the time for getting the bird's heart.' So the lady stole it away, and he never found any more gold under his pillow, for it lay now under the young lady's, and the old woman took it away every morning; but he was so much in love that he never missed his prize.

'Well,' said the old witch, 'we have got the bird's heart, but not the wishing-cloak yet, and that we must also get.' 'Let us leave him that,' said the young lady; 'he has already lost his wealth.' Then the witch was very angry, and said, 'Such a cloak is a very rare and wonderful thing, and I must and will have it.' So she did as the old woman told her, and set herself at the window, and looked about the country and seemed very sorrowful; then the huntsman said, 'What makes you so sad?' 'Alas! dear sir,' said she, 'yonder lies the granite rock where all the costly diamonds grow, and I want so much to go there, that whenever I think of it I cannot help being sorrowful, for who can reach it? only the birds and the flies — man cannot.' 'If that's all your grief,' said the huntsman, 'I'll take there you with all my heart'; so he drew her under his cloak, and the moment he wished to be on the granite mountain they were both there. The diamonds glittered so on all sides that they were delighted with the sight and picked up the finest. But the old witch made a deep sleep come upon him, and he said to the young lady, 'Let us sit down and rest ourselves a little, I am so tired that I cannot stand any longer.' So they sat down, and he laid his head in her lap and fell asleep; and whilst he was sleeping on she took the cloak from his shoulders, hung it on her own, picked up the diamonds, and wished herself home again.

When he awoke and found that his lady had tricked him, and left him alone on the wild rock, he said, 'Alas! what roguery there is in the world!' and there he sat in great grief and fear, not knowing what to do. Now this rock belonged to fierce giants who lived upon it; and as he saw three of them striding about, he thought to himself, 'I can only save myself by feigning to be asleep'; so he laid himself down as if he were in a sound sleep. When the giants came up to him, the first pushed him with his foot, and said, 'What worm is this that lies here curled up?' 'Tread upon him and kill him,' said the second. 'It's not worth the trouble,' said the third; 'let him live, he'll go climbing higher up the mountain, and some cloud will come rolling and carry him away.' And they passed on. But the huntsman had heard all they said; and as soon as they were gone, he climbed to the top of the mountain, and when he had sat there a short time a cloud came rolling around him, and caught him in a whirlwind and bore him along for some time, till it settled in a garden, and he fell quite gently to the ground amongst the greens and cabbages.

Then he looked around him, and said, 'I wish I had something to eat, if not I shall be worse off than before; for here I see neither apples nor pears, nor any kind of fruits, nothing but vegetables.' At last he thought to himself, 'I can eat salad, it will refresh and strengthen me.' So he picked out a fine head and ate of it; but scarcely had he swallowed two bites when he felt himself quite changed, and saw with horror that he was turned into an ass. However, he still felt very hungry, and the salad tasted very nice; so he ate on till he came to another kind of salad, and scarcely had he tasted it when he felt another change come over him, and soon saw that he was lucky enough to have found his old shape again.

Then he laid himself down and slept off a little of his weariness; and when he awoke the next morning he broke off a head both of the good and the bad salad, and thought to himself, 'This will help me to my fortune again, and enable me to pay off some folks for their treachery.' So he went away to try and find the castle of his friends; and after wandering about a few days he luckily found it. Then he stained his face all over brown, so that even his mother would not have known him, and went into the castle and asked for a lodging; 'I am so tired,' said he, 'that I can go no farther.' 'Countryman,' said the witch, 'who are you? and what is your business?' 'I am,' said he, 'a messenger sent by the king to find the finest salad that grows under the sun. I have been lucky enough to find it, and have brought it with me; but the heat of the sun scorches so that it begins to wither, and I don't know that I can carry it farther.'

When the witch and the young lady heard of his beautiful salad, they longed to taste it, and said, 'Dear countryman, let us just taste it.' 'To be sure,' answered he; 'I have two heads of it with me, and will give you one'; so he opened his bag and gave them the bad. Then the witch herself took it into the kitchen to be dressed; and when it was ready she could not wait till it was carried up, but took a few leaves immediately and put them in her mouth, and scarcely were they swallowed when she lost her own form and ran braying down into the court in the form of an ass. Now the servant-maid came into the kitchen, and seeing the salad ready, was going to carry it up; but on the way she too felt a wish to taste it as the old woman had done, and ate some leaves; so she also was turned into an ass and ran after the other, letting the dish with the salad fall on the ground. The messenger sat all this time with the beautiful young lady, and as nobody came with the salad and she longed to taste it, she said, 'I don't know where the salad can be.' Then he thought something must have happened, and said, 'I will go into the kitchen and see.' And as he went he saw two asses in the court running about, and the salad lying on the ground. 'All right!' said he; 'those two have had their share.' Then he took up the rest of the leaves, laid them on the dish and brought them to the young lady, saying, 'I bring you the dish myself that you may not wait any longer.' So she ate of it, and like the others ran off into the court braying away.

Then the huntsman washed his face and went into the court that they might know him. 'Now you shall be paid for your roguery,' said he; and tied them all three to a rope and took them along with him till he came to a mill and knocked at the window. 'What's the matter?' said the miller. 'I have three tiresome beasts here,' said the other; 'if you will take them, give them food and room, and treat them as I tell you, I will pay you whatever you ask.' 'With all my heart,' said the miller; 'but how shall I treat them?' Then the huntsman said, 'Give the old one stripes three times a day and hay once; give the next (who was the servant-maid) stripes once a day and hay three times; and give the youngest (who was the beautiful lady) hay three times a day and no stripes': for he could not find it in his heart to have her beaten. After this he went back to the castle, where he found everything he wanted.

Some days after, the miller came to him and told him that the old ass was dead; 'The other two,' said he, 'are alive and eat, but are so sorrowful that they cannot last long.' Then the huntsman pitied them, and told the miller to drive them back to him, and when they came, he gave them some of the good salad to eat. And the beautiful young lady fell upon her knees before him, and said, 'O dearest huntsman! forgive me all the ill I have done you; my mother forced me to it, it was against my will, for I always loved you very much. Your wishing-cloak hangs up in the closet, and as for the bird's heart, I will give it you too.' But he said, 'Keep it, it will be just the same thing, for I mean to make you my wife.' So they were married, and lived together very happily till they died.

# *The Blue Light*

There was once upon a time a soldier who for many years had served the king faithfully, but when the war came to an end could serve no longer because of the many wounds which he had received. The king said to him: 'You may return to your home, I need you no longer, and you will not receive any more money, for he only receives wages who renders me service for them.' Then the soldier did not know how to earn a living, went away greatly troubled, and walked the whole day, until in the evening he entered a forest. When darkness came on, he saw a light, which he went up to, and came to a house wherein lived a witch. 'Do give me one night's lodging, and a little to eat and drink,' said he to her, 'or I shall starve.' 'Oho!' she answered, 'who gives anything to a run-away soldier? Yet will I be compassionate, and take you in, if you will do what I wish.' 'What do you wish?' said the soldier. 'That you should dig all round my garden for me, tomorrow.' The soldier consented, and next day laboured with all his strength, but could not finish it by the evening. 'I see well enough,' said the witch, 'that you can do no more today, but I will keep you yet another night, in payment for which you must tomorrow chop me a load of wood, and chop it small.' The soldier spent the whole day in doing it, and in the evening the witch proposed that he should stay one night more. 'Tomorrow, you shall only do me a very trifling piece of work. Behind my house, there is an old dry well, into which my light has fallen, it burns blue, and never goes out, and you shall bring it up again.' Next day the old woman took him to the well, and let him down in a basket. He found the blue light, and made her a signal to draw him up again. She did draw him up, but when he came near the edge, she stretched down her hand and wanted to take the blue light away from him. 'No,' said he, perceiving her evil intention, 'I will not give you the light until I am standing with both feet upon the ground.' The witch fell into a passion, let him fall again into the well, and went away.

The poor soldier fell without injury on the moist ground, and the blue light went on burning, but of what use was that to him? He saw very well that he could not escape death. He sat for a while very sorrowfully, then suddenly he felt in his pocket and found his tobacco pipe, which was still half full. 'This shall be my last pleasure,' thought he, pulled it out, lit it at the blue light and began to smoke. When the smoke had circled about the cavern, suddenly a little black dwarf stood before him, and said: 'Lord, what are your commands?' 'What my commands are?' replied the soldier, quite astonished. 'I must do everything you bid me,' said the little man. 'Good,' said the soldier; 'then in the first place help me out of this well.' The little man took him by the hand, and led him through an underground passage, but he did not forget to take the blue light with him. On the way the dwarf showed him the treasures which the witch had collected and hidden there, and the soldier took as much gold as he could carry. When he was above, he said to the little man: 'Now go and bind the old witch, and carry her before the judge.' In a short time she came by like the wind, riding on a wild tom-cat and screaming frightfully. Nor was it long before the little man reappeared. 'It is all done,' said he, 'and the witch is already hanging on the gallows. What further commands has my lord?' inquired the dwarf. 'At this moment, none,' answered the soldier; 'you can return home, only be at hand immediately, if I summon you.' 'Nothing more is needed than that you should light your pipe at the blue light, and I will appear before you at once.' Thereupon he vanished from his sight.

The soldier returned to the town from which he come. He went to the best inn, ordered himself handsome clothes, and then bade the landlord furnish him a room as handsome as possible. When it was ready and the soldier had taken possession of it, he summoned the little black manikin and said: 'I have served the king faithfully, but he has dismissed me, and left me to hunger, and now I want to take my revenge.' 'What am I to do?' asked the little man. 'Late at night, when the king's daughter is in bed, bring her here in her sleep, she shall do servant's work for me.' The manikin said: 'That is an easy thing for me to do, but a very dangerous thing for you, for if it is discovered, you will fare ill.' When twelve o'clock had struck, the door sprang open, and the manikin carried in the princess. 'Aha! are you there?' cried the soldier, 'get to your work at once! Fetch the broom and sweep the chamber.' When she had done this, he ordered her to come to his chair, and then he stretched out his feet and said: 'Pull off my boots,' and then he threw them in her face, and made her pick them up again, and clean and brighten them. She, however, did everything he bade her, without opposition, silently and with half-shut eyes. When the first cock crowed, the manikin carried her back to the royal palace, and laid her in her bed.

Next morning when the princess arose she went to her father, and told him that she had had a very strange dream. 'I was carried through the streets with the rapidity of lightning,' said she, 'and taken into a soldier's room, and I had to wait upon him like a servant, sweep his room, clean his boots, and do all kinds of menial work. It was only a dream, and yet I am just as tired as if I really had done everything.' 'The dream may have been true,' said the king. 'I will give you a piece of advice. Fill your pocket full of peas, and make a small hole in the pocket, and then if you are carried away again, they will fall out and leave a track in the streets.' But unseen by the king, the manikin was standing beside him when he said that, and heard all. At night when the sleeping princess was again carried through the streets, some peas certainly did fall out of her pocket, but they made no track, for the crafty manikin had just before scattered peas in every street there was. And again the princess was compelled to do servant's work until cock-crow.

Next morning the king sent his people out to seek the track, but it was all in vain, for in every street poor children were sitting, picking up peas, and saying: 'It must have rained peas, last night.' 'We must think of something else,' said the king; 'keep your shoes on when you go to bed, and before you come back from the place where you are taken, hide one of them there, I will soon contrive to find it.' The black manikin heard this plot, and at night when the soldier again ordered him to bring the princess, revealed it to him, and told him that he knew of no expedient to counteract this stratagem, and that if the shoe were found in the soldier's house it would go badly with him. 'Do what I bid you,' replied the soldier, and again this third night the princess was obliged to work like a servant, but before she went away, she hid her shoe under the bed.

Next morning the king had the entire town searched for his daughter's shoe. It was found at the soldier's, and the soldier himself, who at the entreaty of the dwarf had gone outside the gate, was soon brought back, and thrown into prison. In his flight he had forgotten the most valuable things he had, the blue light and the gold, and had only one ducat in his pocket. And now loaded with chains, he was standing at the window of his dungeon, when he chanced to see one of his comrades passing by. The soldier tapped at the pane of glass, and when this man came up, said to him: 'Be so kind as to fetch me the small bundle I have left lying in the inn, and I will give you a ducat for doing it.' His comrade ran thither and brought him what he wanted. As soon as the soldier was alone again, he lighted his pipe and summoned the black manikin. 'Have no fear,' said the latter to his master. 'Go wheresoever they take you, and let them do what they will, only take the blue light with you.' Next day the soldier was tried, and though he had done nothing wicked, the judge condemned him to death. When he was led forth to die, he begged a last favour of the king. 'What is it?' asked the king. 'That I may smoke one more pipe on my way.' 'You may smoke three,' answered the king, 'but do not imagine that I will spare your life.' Then the soldier pulled out his pipe and lighted it at the blue light, and as soon as a few wreaths of smoke had ascended, the manikin was there with a small cudgel in his hand, and said: 'What does my lord command?' 'Strike down to earth that false judge there, and his constable, and spare not the king who has treated me so ill.' Then the manikin fell on them like lightning, darting this way and that way, and whosoever was so much as touched by his cudgel fell to earth, and did not venture to stir again. The king was terrified; he threw himself on the soldier's mercy, and merely to be allowed to live at all, gave him his kingdom for his own, and his daughter to wife.

## *The King Of The Golden Mountain*

There was once a merchant who had only one child, a son, that was very young, and barely able to run alone. He had two richly laden ships then making a voyage upon the seas, in which he had embarked all his wealth, in the hope of making great gains, when the news came that both were lost. Thus from being a rich man he became all at once so very poor that nothing was left to him but one small plot of land; and there he often went in an evening to take his walk, and ease his mind of a little of his trouble.

One day, as he was roaming along in a brown study, thinking with no great comfort on what he had been and what he now was, and was like to be, all on a sudden there stood before him a little, rough-looking, black dwarf. 'Prithee, friend, why so sorrowful?' said he to the merchant; 'what is it you take so deeply to heart?' 'If you would do me any good I would willingly tell you,' said the merchant. 'Who knows but I may?' said the little man: 'tell me what ails you, and perhaps you will find I may be of some use.' Then the merchant told him how all his wealth was gone to the bottom of the sea, and how he had nothing left but that little plot of land. 'Oh, trouble not yourself about that,' said the dwarf; 'only undertake to bring me here, twelve years hence, whatever meets you first on your going home, and I will give you as much as you please.' The merchant thought this was no great thing to ask; that it would most likely be his dog or his cat, or something of that sort, but forgot his little boy Heinel; so he agreed to the bargain, and signed and sealed the bond to do what was asked of him.

But as he drew near home, his little boy was so glad to see him that he crept behind him, and laid fast hold of his legs, and looked up in his face and laughed. Then the father started, trembling with fear and horror, and saw what it was that he had bound himself to do; but as no gold was come, he made himself easy by thinking that it was only a joke that the dwarf was playing him, and that, at any rate, when the money came, he should see the bearer, and would not take it in.

About a month afterwards he went upstairs into a lumber-room to look for some old iron, that he might sell it and raise a little money; and there, instead of his iron, he saw a large pile of gold lying on the floor. At the sight of this he was overjoyed, and forgetting all about his son, went into trade again, and became a richer merchant than before.

Meantime little Heinel grew up, and as the end of the twelve years drew near the merchant began to call to mind his bond, and became very sad and thoughtful; so that care and sorrow were written upon his face. The boy one day asked what was the matter, but his father would not tell for some time; at last, however, he said that he had, without knowing it, sold him for gold to a little, ugly-looking, black dwarf, and that the twelve years were coming round when he must keep his word. Then Heinel said, 'Father, give yourself very little trouble about that; I shall be too much for the little man.'

When the time came, the father and son went out together to the place agreed upon: and the son drew a circle on the ground, and set himself and his father in the middle of it. The little black dwarf soon came, and walked round and round about the circle, but could not find any way to get into it, and he either could not, or dared not, jump over it. At last the boy said to him. 'Have you anything to say to us, my friend, or what do you want?' Now Heinel had found a friend in a good fairy, that was fond of him, and had told him what to do; for this fairy knew what good luck was in store for him. 'Have you brought me what you said you would?' said the dwarf to the merchant. The old man held his tongue, but Heinel said again, 'What do you want here?' The dwarf said, 'I come to talk with your father, not with you.' 'You have cheated and taken in my father,' said the son; 'pray give him up his bond at once.' 'Fair and softly,' said the little old man; 'right is right; I have paid my money, and your father has had it, and spent it; so be so good as to let me have what I paid it for.' 'You must have my consent to that first,' said Heinel, 'so please to step in here, and let us talk it over.' The old man grinned, and showed his teeth, as if he should have been very glad to get into the circle if he could. Then at last, after a long talk, they came to terms. Heinel agreed that his father must give him up, and that so far the dwarf should have his way: but, on the other hand, the fairy had told Heinel what fortune was in store for him, if he followed his own course; and he did not choose to be given up to his hump-backed friend, who seemed so anxious for his company.

So, to make a sort of drawn battle of the matter, it was settled that Heinel should be put into an open boat, that lay on the sea-shore hard by; that the father should push him off with his own hand, and that he should thus be set adrift, and left to the bad or good luck of wind and weather. Then he took leave of his father, and set himself in the boat, but before it got far off a wave struck it, and it fell with one side low in the water, so the merchant thought that poor Heinel was lost, and went home very sorrowful, while the dwarf went his way, thinking that at any rate he had had his revenge.

The boat, however, did not sink, for the good fairy took care of her friend, and soon raised the boat up again, and it went safely on. The young man sat safe within, till at length it ran ashore upon an unknown land. As he jumped upon the shore he saw before him a beautiful castle but empty and dreary within, for it was enchanted. 'Here,' said he to himself, 'must I find the prize the good fairy told me of.' So he once more searched the whole palace through, till at last he found a white snake, lying coiled up on a cushion in one of the chambers.

Now the white snake was an enchanted princess; and she was very glad to see him, and said, 'Are you at last come to set me free? Twelve long years have I waited here for the fairy to bring you hither as she promised, for you alone can save me. This night twelve men will come: their faces will be black, and they will be dressed in chain armour. They will ask what you do here, but give no answer; and let them do what they will — beat, whip, pinch, prick, or torment you — bear all; only speak not a word, and at twelve o'clock they must go away. The second night twelve others will come: and the third night twenty-four, who will even cut off your head; but at the twelfth hour of that night their power is gone, and I shall be free, and will come and bring you the Water of Life, and will wash you with it, and bring you back to life and health.' And all came to pass as she had said; Heinel bore all, and spoke not a word; and the third night the princess came, and fell on his neck and kissed him. Joy and gladness burst forth throughout the castle, the wedding was celebrated, and he was crowned king of the Golden Mountain.

They lived together very happily, and the queen had a son. And thus eight years had passed over their heads, when the king thought of his father; and he began to long to see him once again. But the queen was against his going, and said, 'I know well that misfortunes will come upon us if you go.' However, he gave her no rest till she agreed. At his going away she gave him a wishing-ring, and said, 'Take this ring, and put it on your finger; whatever you wish it will bring you; only promise never to make use of it to bring me hence to your father's house.' Then he said he would do what she asked, and put the ring on his finger, and wished himself near the town where his father lived.

Heinel found himself at the gates in a moment; but the guards would not let him go in, because he was so strangely clad. So he went up to a neighbouring hill, where a shepherd dwelt, and borrowed his old frock, and thus passed unknown into the town. When he came to his father's house, he said he was his son; but the merchant would not believe him, and said he had had but one son, his poor Heinel, who he knew was long since dead: and as he was only dressed like a poor shepherd, he would not even give him anything to eat. The king, however, still vowed that he was his son, and said, 'Is there no mark by which you would know me if I am really your son?' 'Yes,' said his mother, 'our Heinel had a mark like a raspberry on his right arm.' Then he showed them the mark, and they knew that what he had said was true.

He next told them how he was king of the Golden Mountain, and was married to a princess, and had a son seven years old. But the merchant said, 'that can never be true; he must be a fine king truly who travels about in a shepherd's frock!' At this the son was vexed; and forgetting his word, turned his ring, and wished for his queen and son. In an instant they stood before him; but the queen wept, and said he had broken his word, and bad luck would follow. He did all he could to soothe her, and she at last seemed to be appeased; but she was not so in truth, and was only thinking how she should punish him.

One day he took her to walk with him out of the town, and showed her the spot where the boat was set adrift upon the wide waters. Then he sat himself down, and said, 'I am very much tired; sit by me, I will rest my head in your lap, and sleep a while.' As soon as he had fallen asleep, however, she drew the ring from his finger, and crept softly away, and wished herself and her son at home in their kingdom. And when he awoke he found himself alone, and saw that the ring was gone from his finger. 'I can never go back to my father's house,' said he; 'they would say I am a sorcerer: I will journey forth into the world, till I come again to my kingdom.'

So saying he set out and travelled till he came to a hill, where three giants were sharing their father's goods; and as they saw him pass they cried out and said, 'Little men have sharp wits; he shall part the goods between us.' Now there was a sword that cut off an enemy's head whenever the wearer gave the words, 'Heads off!'; a cloak that made the owner invisible, or gave him any form he pleased; and a pair of boots that carried the wearer wherever he wished. Heinel said they must first let him try these wonderful things, then he might know how to set a value upon them. Then they gave him the cloak, and he wished himself a fly, and in a moment he was a fly.

'The cloak is very well,' said he: 'now give me the sword.' 'No,' said they; 'not unless you undertake not to say, "Heads off!" for if you do we are all dead men.' So they gave it him, charging him to try it on a tree. He next asked for the boots also; and the moment he had all three in his power, he wished himself at the Golden Mountain; and there he was at once. So the giants were left behind with no goods to share or quarrel about.

As Heinel came near his castle he heard the sound of merry music; and the people around told him that his queen was about to marry another husband. Then he threw his cloak around him, and passed through the castle hall, and placed himself by the side of the queen, where no one saw him. But when anything to eat was put upon her plate, he took it away and ate it himself; and when a glass of wine was handed to her, he took it and drank it; and thus, though they kept on giving her meat and drink, her plate and cup were always empty.

Upon this, fear and remorse came over her, and she went into her chamber alone, and sat there weeping; and he followed her there. 'Alas!' said she to herself, 'was I not once set free? Why then does this enchantment still seem to bind me?'

'False and fickle one!' said he. 'One indeed came who set thee free, and he is now near thee again; but how have you used him? Ought he to have had such treatment from thee?' Then he went out and sent away the company, and said the wedding was at an end, for that he was come back to the kingdom. But the princes, peers, and great men mocked at him. However, he would enter into no parley with them, but only asked them if they would go in peace or not. Then they turned upon him and tried to seize him; but he drew his sword. 'Heads Off!' cried he; and with the word the traitors' heads fell before him, and Heinel was once more king of the Golden Mountain.

# *The Goose-Girl*

The king of a great land died, and left his queen to take care of their only child. This child was a daughter, who was very beautiful; and her mother loved her dearly, and was very kind to her. And there was a good fairy too, who was fond of the princess, and helped her mother to watch over her. When she grew up, she was betrothed to a prince who lived a great way off; and as the time drew near for her to be married, she got ready to set off on her journey to his country. Then the queen her mother, packed up a great many costly things; jewels, and gold, and silver; trinkets, fine dresses, and in short everything that became a royal bride. And she gave her a waiting-maid to ride with her, and give her into the bridegroom's hands; and each had a horse for the journey. Now the princess's horse was the fairy's gift, and it was called Falada, and could speak.

When the time came for them to set out, the fairy went into her bed-chamber, and took a little knife, and cut off a lock of her hair, and gave it to the princess, and said, 'Take care of it, dear child; for it is a charm that may be of use to you on the road.' Then they all took a sorrowful leave of the princess; and she put the lock of hair into her bosom, got upon her horse, and set off on her journey to her bridegroom's kingdom.

One day, as they were riding along by a brook, the princess began to feel very thirsty: and she said to her maid, 'Pray get down, and fetch me some water in my golden cup out of yonder brook, for I want to drink.' 'Nay,' said the maid, 'if you are thirsty, get off yourself, and stoop down by the water and drink; I shall not be your waiting-maid any longer.' Then she was so thirsty that she got down, and knelt over the little brook, and drank; for she was frightened, and dared not bring out her golden cup; and she wept and said, 'Alas! what will become of me?' And the lock answered her, and said:

'Alas! alas! if thy mother knew it,
Sadly, sadly, would she rue it.'

But the princess was very gentle and meek, so she said nothing to her maid's ill behaviour, but got upon her horse again.

Then all rode farther on their journey, till the day grew so warm, and the sun so scorching, that the bride began to feel very thirsty again; and at last, when they came to a river, she forgot her maid's rude speech, and said, 'Pray get down, and fetch me some water to drink in my golden cup.' But the maid answered her, and even spoke more haughtily than before: 'Drink if you will, but I shall not be your waiting-maid.' Then the princess was so thirsty that she got off her horse, and lay down, and held her head over the running stream, and cried and said, 'What will become of me?' And the lock of hair answered her again:

> 'Alas! alas! if thy mother knew it,
> Sadly, sadly, would she rue it.'

And as she leaned down to drink, the lock of hair fell from her bosom, and floated away with the water. Now she was so frightened that she did not see it; but her maid saw it, and was very glad, for she knew the charm; and she saw that the poor bride would be in her power, now that she had lost the hair. So when the bride had done drinking, and would have got upon Falada again, the maid said, 'I shall ride upon Falada, and you may have my horse instead'; so she was forced to give up her horse, and soon afterwards to take off her royal clothes and put on her maid's shabby ones.

At last, as they drew near the end of their journey, this treacherous servant threatened to kill her mistress if she ever told anyone what had happened. But Falada saw it all, and marked it well.

Then the waiting-maid got upon Falada, and the real bride rode upon the other horse, and they went on in this way till at last they came to the royal court. There was great joy at their coming, and the prince flew to meet them, and lifted the maid from her horse, thinking she was the one who was to be his wife; and she was led upstairs to the royal chamber; but the true princess was told to stay in the court below.

Now the old king happened just then to have nothing else to do; so he amused himself by sitting at his kitchen window, looking at what was going on; and he saw her in the courtyard. As she looked very pretty, and too delicate for a waiting-maid, he went up into the royal chamber to ask the bride who it was she had brought with her, that was thus left standing in the court below. 'I brought her with me for the sake of her company on the road,' said she; 'pray give the girl some work to do, that she may not be idle.' The old king could not for some time think of any work for her to do; but at last he said, 'I have a lad who takes care of my geese; she may go and help him.' Now the name of this lad, that the real bride was to help in watching the king's geese, was Curdken.

But the false bride said to the prince, 'Dear husband, pray do me one piece of kindness.' 'That I will,' said the prince. 'Then tell one of your slaughterers to cut off the head of the horse I rode upon, for it was very unruly, and plagued me sadly on the road'; but the truth was, she was very much afraid lest Falada should some day or other speak, and tell all she had done to the princess. She carried her point, and the faithful Falada was killed; but when the true princess heard of it, she wept, and begged the man to nail up Falada's head against a large dark gate of the city, through which she had to pass every morning and evening, that there she might still see him sometimes. Then the slaughterer said he would do as she wished; and cut off the head, and nailed it up under the dark gate.

Early the next morning, as she and Curdken went out through the gate, she said sorrowfully:

'Falada, Falada, there thou hangest!'
and the head answered:
'Bride, bride, there thou gangest!
Alas! alas! if thy mother knew it,
Sadly, sadly, would she rue it.'

Then they went out of the city, and drove the geese on. And when she came to the meadow, she sat down upon a bank there, and let down her waving locks of hair, which were all of pure silver; and when Curdken saw it glitter in the sun, he ran up, and would have pulled some of the locks out, but she cried:

'Blow, breezes, blow!
Let Curdken's hat go!
Blow, breezes, blow!
Let him after it go!
O'er hills, dales, and rocks,
Away be it whirl'd
Till the silvery locks
Are all comb'd and curl'd!

Then there came a wind, so strong that it blew off Curdken's hat; and away it flew over the hills: and he was forced to turn and run after it; till, by the time he came back, she had done combing and curling her hair, and had put it up again safe. Then he was very angry and sulky, and would not speak to her at all; but they watched the geese until it grew dark in the evening, and then drove them homewards.

The next morning, as they were going through the dark gate, the poor girl looked up at Falada's head, and cried:

'Falada, Falada, there thou hangest!'
and the head answered:
'Bride, bride, there thou gangest!
Alas! alas! if they mother knew it,
Sadly, sadly, would she rue it.'

Then she drove on the geese, and sat down again in the meadow, and began to comb out her hair as before; and Curdken ran up to her, and wanted to take hold of it; but she cried out quickly:

'Blow, breezes, blow!
Let Curdken's hat go!
Blow, breezes, blow!
Let him after it go!
O'er hills, dales, and rocks,
Away be it whirl'd
Till the silvery locks
Are all comb'd and curl'd!

Then the wind came and blew away his hat; and off it flew a great way, over the hills and far away, so that he had to run after it; and when he came back she had bound up her hair again, and all was safe. So they watched the geese till it grew dark.

In the evening, after they came home, Curdken went to the old king, and said, 'I cannot have that strange girl to help me to keep the geese any longer.' 'Why?' said the king. 'Because, instead of doing any good, she does nothing but tease me all day long.' Then the king made him tell him what had happened. And Curdken said, 'When we go in the morning through the dark gate with our flock of geese, she cries and talks with the head of a horse that hangs upon the wall, and says:

'Falada, Falada, there thou hangest!'
and the head answers:
'Bride, bride, there thou gangest!
Alas! alas! if they mother knew it,
Sadly, sadly, would she rue it.'

And Curdken went on telling the king what had happened upon the meadow where the geese fed; how his hat was blown away; and how he was forced to run after it, and to leave his flock of geese to themselves. But the old king told the boy to go out again the next day: and when morning came, he placed himself behind the dark gate, and heard how she spoke to Falada, and how Falada answered. Then he went into the field, and hid himself in a bush by the meadow's side; and he soon saw with his own eyes how they drove the flock of geese; and how, after a little time, she let down her hair that glittered in the sun. And then he heard her say:

'Blow, breezes, blow!
Let Curdken's hat go!
Blow, breezes, blow!
Let him after it go!
O'er hills, dales, and rocks,
Away be it whirl'd
Till the silvery locks
Are all comb'd and curl'd!

And soon came a gale of wind, and carried away Curdken's hat, and away went Curdken after it, while the girl went on combing and curling her hair. All this the old king saw: so he went home without being seen; and when the little goose-girl came back in the evening he called her aside, and asked her why she did so: but she burst into tears, and said, 'That I must not tell you or any man, or I shall lose my life.'

But the old king begged so hard, that she had no peace till she had told him all the tale, from beginning to end, word for word. And it was very lucky for her that she did so, for when she had done the king ordered royal clothes to be put upon her, and gazed on her with wonder, she was so beautiful. Then he called his son and told him that he had only a false bride; for that she was merely a waiting-maid, while the true bride stood by. And the young king rejoiced when he saw her beauty, and heard how meek and patient she had been; and without saying anything to the false bride, the king ordered a great feast to be got ready for all his court. The bridegroom sat at the top, with the false princess on one side, and the true one on the other; but nobody knew her again, for her beauty was quite dazzling to their eyes; and she did not seem at all like the little goose-girl, now that she had her brilliant dress on.

When they had eaten and drank, and were very merry, the old king said he would tell them a tale. So he began, and told all the story of the princess, as if it was one that he had once heard; and he asked the true waiting-maid what she thought ought to be done to anyone who would behave thus. 'Nothing better,' said this false bride, 'than that she should be thrown into a cask stuck round with sharp nails, and that two white horses should be put to it, and should drag it from street to street till she was dead.' 'Thou art she!' said the old king; 'and as thou has judged thyself, so shall it be done to thee.' And the young king was then married to his true wife, and they reigned over the kingdom in peace and happiness all their lives; and the good fairy came to see them, and restored the faithful Falada to life again.

# *The Adventures Of Chanticleer And Partlet*

## *1. How They Went To The Mountains To Eat Nuts*

'The nuts are quite ripe now,' said Chanticleer to his wife Partlet, 'suppose we go together to the mountains, and eat as many as we can, before the squirrel takes them all away.' 'With all my heart,' said Partlet, 'let us go and make a holiday of it together.'

So they went to the mountains; and as it was a lovely day, they stayed there till the evening. Now, whether it was that they had eaten so many nuts that they could not walk, or whether they were lazy and would not, I do not know: however, they took it into their heads that it did not become them to go home on foot. So Chanticleer began to build a little carriage of nutshells: and when it was finished, Partlet jumped into it and sat down, and bid Chanticleer harness himself to it and draw her home. 'That's a good joke!' said Chanticleer; 'no, that will never do; I had rather by half walk home; I'll sit on the box and be coachman, if you like, but I'll not draw.' While this was passing, a duck came quacking up and cried out, 'You thieving vagabonds, what business have you in my grounds? I'll give it you well for your insolence!' and upon that she fell upon Chanticleer most lustily. But Chanticleer was no coward, and returned the duck's blows with his sharp spurs so fiercely that she soon began to cry out for mercy; which was only granted her upon condition that she would draw the carriage home for them. This she agreed to do; and Chanticleer got upon the box, and drove, crying, 'Now, duck, get on as fast as you can.' And away they went at a pretty good pace.

After they had travelled along a little way, they met a needle and a pin walking together along the road: and the needle cried out, 'Stop, stop!' and said it was so dark that they could hardly find their way, and such dirty walking they could not get on at all: he told them that he and his friend, the pin, had been at a public-house a few miles off, and had sat drinking till they had forgotten how late it was; he begged therefore that the travellers would be so kind as to give them a lift in their carriage. Chanticleer observing that they were but thin fellows, and not likely to take up much room, told them they might ride, but made them promise not to dirty the wheels of the carriage in getting in, nor to tread on Partlet's toes.

Late at night they arrived at an inn; and as it was bad travelling in the dark, and the duck seemed much tired, and waddled about a good deal from one side to the other, they made up their minds to fix their quarters there: but the landlord at first was unwilling, and said his house was full, thinking they might not be very respectable company: however, they spoke civilly to him, and gave him the egg which Partlet had laid by the way, and said they would give him the duck, who was in the habit of laying one every day: so at last he let them come in, and they bespoke a handsome supper, and spent the evening very jollily.

Early in the morning, before it was quite light, and when nobody was stirring in the inn, Chanticleer awakened his wife, and, fetching the egg, they pecked a hole in it, ate it up, and threw the shells into the fireplace: they then went to the pin and needle, who were fast asleep, and seizing them by the heads, stuck one into the landlord's easy chair and the other into his handkerchief; and, having done this, they crept away as softly as possible. However, the duck, who slept in the open air in the yard, heard them coming, and jumping into the brook which ran close by the inn, soon swam out of their reach.

An hour or two afterwards the landlord got up, and took his handkerchief to wipe his face, but the pin ran into him and pricked him: then he walked into the kitchen to light his pipe at the fire, but when he stirred it up the eggshells flew into his eyes, and almost blinded him. 'Bless me!' said he, 'all the world seems to have a design against my head this morning': and so saying, he threw himself sulkily into his easy chair; but, oh dear! the needle ran into him; and this time the pain was not in his head. He now flew into a very great passion, and, suspecting the company who had come in the night before, he went to look after them, but they were all off; so he swore that he never again would take in such a troop of vagabonds, who ate a great deal, paid no reckoning, and gave him nothing for his trouble but their apish tricks.

## *2. How Chanticleer And Partlet Went To Visit Mr Korbes*

Another day, Chanticleer and Partlet wished to ride out together; so Chanticleer built a handsome carriage with four red wheels, and harnessed six mice to it; and then he and Partlet got into the carriage, and away they drove. Soon afterwards a cat met them, and said, 'Where are you going?' And Chanticleer replied,

'All on our way
A visit to pay
To Mr Korbes, the fox, today.'

Then the cat said, 'Take me with you,' Chanticleer said, 'With all my heart: get up behind, and be sure you do not fall off.'

'Take care of this handsome coach of mine,
Nor dirty my pretty red wheels so fine!
Now, mice, be ready,
And, wheels, run steady!
For we are going a visit to pay
To Mr Korbes, the fox, today.'

Soon after came up a millstone, an egg, a duck, and a pin; and Chanticleer gave them all leave to get into the carriage and go with them.

When they arrived at Mr Korbes's house, he was not at home; so the mice drew the carriage into the coach-house, Chanticleer and Partlet flew upon a beam, the cat sat down in the fireplace, the duck got into the washing cistern, the pin stuck himself into the bed pillow, the millstone laid himself over the house door, and the egg rolled himself up in the towel.

When Mr Korbes came home, he went to the fireplace to make a fire; but the cat threw all the ashes in his eyes: so he ran to the kitchen to wash himself; but there the duck splashed all the water in his face; and when he tried to wipe himself, the egg broke to pieces in the towel all over his face and eyes. Then he was very angry, and went without his supper to bed; but when he laid his head on the pillow, the pin ran into his cheek: at this he became quite furious, and, jumping up, would have run out of the house; but when he came to the door, the millstone fell down on his head, and killed him on the spot.

### *3. How Partlet Died And Was Buried, And How Chanticleer Died Of Grief*

Another day Chanticleer and Partlet agreed to go again to the mountains to eat nuts; and it was settled that all the nuts which they found should be shared equally between them. Now Partlet found a very large nut; but she said nothing about it to Chanticleer, and kept it all to herself: however, it was so big that she could not swallow it, and it stuck in her throat. Then she was in a great fright, and cried out to Chanticleer, 'Pray run as fast as you can, and fetch me some water, or I shall be choked.' Chanticleer ran as fast as he could to the river, and said, 'River, give me some water, for Partlet lies in the mountain, and will be choked by a great nut.' The river said, 'Run first to the bride, and ask her for a silken cord to draw up the water.' Chanticleer ran to the bride, and said, 'Bride, you must give me a silken cord, for then the river will give me water, and the water I will carry to Partlet, who lies on the mountain, and will be choked by a great nut.' But the bride said, 'Run first, and bring me my garland that is hanging on a willow in the garden.' Then Chanticleer ran to the garden, and took the garland from the bough where it hung, and brought it to the bride; and then the bride gave him the silken cord, and he took the silken cord to the river, and the river gave him water, and he carried the water to Partlet; but in the meantime she was choked by the great nut, and lay quite dead, and never moved any more.

Then Chanticleer was very sorry, and cried bitterly; and all the beasts came and wept with him over poor Partlet. And six mice built a little hearse to carry her to her grave; and when it was ready they harnessed themselves before it, and Chanticleer drove them. On the way they met the fox. 'Where are you going, Chanticleer?' said he. 'To bury my Partlet,' said the other. 'May I go with you?' said the fox. 'Yes; but you must get up behind, or my horses will not be able to draw you.' Then the fox got up behind; and presently the wolf, the bear, the goat, and all the beasts of the wood, came and climbed upon the hearse.

So on they went till they came to a rapid stream.

'How shall we get over?' said Chanticleer. Then said a straw, 'I will lay myself across, and you may pass over upon me.' But as the mice were going over, the straw slipped away and fell into the water, and the six mice all fell in and were drowned. What was to be done? Then a large log of wood came and said, 'I am big enough; I will lay myself across the stream, and you shall pass over upon me.' So he laid himself down; but they managed so clumsily, that the log of wood fell in and was carried away by the stream. Then a stone, who saw what had happened, came up and kindly offered to help poor Chanticleer by laying himself across the stream; and this time he got safely to the other side with the hearse, and managed to get Partlet out of it; but the fox and the other mourners, who were sitting behind, were too heavy, and fell back into the water and were all carried away by the stream and drowned.

Thus Chanticleer was left alone with his dead Partlet; and having dug a grave for her, he laid her in it, and made a little hillock over her. Then he sat down by the grave, and wept and mourned, till at last he died too; and so all were dead.

## *The Fox And The Horse*

A farmer had a horse that had been an excellent faithful servant to him: but he was now grown too old to work; so the farmer would give him nothing more to eat, and said, 'I want you no longer, so take yourself off out of my stable; I shall not take you back again until you are stronger than a lion.' Then he opened the door and turned him adrift.

The poor horse was very melancholy, and wandered up and down in the wood, seeking some little shelter from the cold wind and rain. Presently a fox met him: 'What's the matter, my friend?' said he, 'why do you hang down your head and look so lonely and woebegone?' 'Ah!' replied the horse, 'justice and avarice never dwell in one house; my master has forgotten all that I have done for him so many years, and because I can no longer work he has turned me adrift, and says unless I become stronger than a lion he will not take me back again; what chance can I have of that? He knows I have none, or he would not talk so.'

However, the fox bid him be of good cheer, and said, 'I will help you; lie down there, stretch yourself out quite stiff, and pretend to be dead.' The horse did as he was told, and the fox went straight to the lion who lived in a cave close by, and said to him, 'A little way off lies a dead horse; come with me and you may make an excellent meal of his carcass.' The lion was greatly pleased, and set off immediately; and when they came to the horse, the fox said, 'You will not be able to eat him comfortably here; I'll tell you what — I will tie you fast to his tail, and then you can draw him to your den, and eat him at your leisure.'

This advice pleased the lion, so he laid himself down quietly for the fox to make him fast to the horse. But the fox managed to tie his legs together and bound all so hard and fast that with all his strength he could not set himself free. When the work was done, the fox clapped the horse on the shoulder, and said, 'Jip! Dobbin! Jip!' Then up he sprang, and moved off, dragging the lion behind him. The beast began to roar and bellow, till all the birds of the wood flew away for fright; but the horse let him sing on, and made his way quietly over the fields to his master's house.

'Here he is, master,' said he, 'I have got the better of him': and when the farmer saw his old servant, his heart relented, and he said. 'Thou shalt stay in thy stable and be well taken care of.' And so the poor old horse had plenty to eat, and lived — till he died.

# *The Juniper-Tree*

Long, long ago, some two thousand years or so, there lived a rich man with a good and beautiful wife. They loved each other dearly, but sorrowed much that they had no children. So greatly did they desire to have one, that the wife prayed for it day and night, but still they remained childless.

In front of the house there was a court, in which grew a juniper-tree. One winter's day the wife stood under the tree to peel some apples, and as she was peeling them, she cut her finger, and the blood fell on the snow. 'Ah,' sighed the woman heavily, 'if I had but a child, as red as blood and as white as snow,' and as she spoke the words, her heart grew light within her, and it seemed to her that her wish was granted, and she returned to the house feeling glad and comforted. A month passed, and the snow had all disappeared; then another month went by, and all the earth was green. So the months followed one another, and first the trees budded in the woods, and soon the green branches grew thickly intertwined, and then the blossoms began to fall. Once again the wife stood under the juniper-tree, and it was so full of sweet scent that her heart leaped for joy, and she was so overcome with her happiness, that she fell on her knees. Presently the fruit became round and firm, and she was glad and at peace; but when they were fully ripe she picked the berries and ate eagerly of them, and then she grew sad and ill. A little while later she called her husband, and said to him, weeping. 'If I die, bury me under the juniper-tree.' Then she felt comforted and happy again, and before another month had passed she had a little child, and when she saw that it was as white as snow and as red as blood, her joy was so great that she died.

Her husband buried her under the juniper-tree, and wept bitterly for her. By degrees, however, his sorrow grew less, and although at times he still grieved over his loss, he was able to go about as usual, and later on he married again.

He now had a little daughter born to him; the child of his first wife was a boy, who was as red as blood and as white as snow. The mother loved her daughter very much, and when she looked at her and then looked at the boy, it pierced her heart to think that he would always stand in the way of her own child, and she was continually thinking how she could get the whole of the property for her. This evil thought took possession of her more and more, and made her behave very unkindly to the boy. She drove him from place to place with cuffings and buffetings, so that the poor child went about in fear, and had no peace from the time he left school to the time he went back.

One day the little daughter came running to her mother in the store-room, and said, 'Mother, give me an apple.' 'Yes, my child,' said the wife, and she gave her a beautiful apple out of the chest; the chest had a very heavy lid and a large iron lock.

'Mother,' said the little daughter again, 'may not brother have one too?' The mother was angry at this, but she answered, 'Yes, when he comes out of school.'

Just then she looked out of the window and saw him coming, and it seemed as if an evil spirit entered into her, for she snatched the apple out of her little daughter's hand, and said, 'You shall not have one before your brother.' She threw the apple into the chest and shut it to. The little boy now came in, and the evil spirit in the wife made her say kindly to him, 'My son, will you have an apple?' but she gave him a wicked look. 'Mother,' said the boy, 'how dreadful you look! Yes, give me an apple.' The thought came to her that she would kill him. 'Come with me,' she said, and she lifted up the lid of the chest; 'take one out for yourself.' And as he bent over to do so, the evil spirit urged her, and crash! Down went the lid, and off went the little boy's head. Then she was overwhelmed with fear at the thought of what she had done. 'If only I can prevent anyone knowing that I did it,' she thought. So she went upstairs to her room, and took a white handkerchief out of her top drawer; then she set the boy's head again on his shoulders, and bound it with the handkerchief so that nothing could be seen, and placed him on a chair by the door with an apple in his hand.

Soon after this, little Marleen came up to her mother who was stirring a pot of boiling water over the fire, and said, 'Mother, brother is sitting by the door with an apple in his hand, and he looks so pale; and when I asked him to give me the apple, he did not answer, and that frightened me.'

'Go to him again,' said her mother, 'and if he does not answer, give him a box on the ear.' So little Marleen went, and said, 'Brother, give me that apple,' but he did not say a word; then she gave him a box on the ear, and his head rolled off. She was so terrified at this, that she ran crying and screaming to her mother. 'Oh!' she said, 'I have knocked off brother's head,' and then she wept and wept, and nothing would stop her.

'What have you done!' said her mother, 'but no one must know about it, so you must keep silence; what is done can't be undone; we will make him into puddings.' And she took the little boy and cut him up, made him into puddings, and put him in the pot. But Marleen stood looking on, and wept and wept, and her tears fell into the pot, so that there was no need of salt.

Presently the father came home and sat down to his dinner; he asked, 'Where is my son?' The mother said nothing, but gave him a large dish of black pudding, and Marleen still wept without ceasing.

The father again asked, 'Where is my son?'

'Oh,' answered the wife, 'he is gone into the country to his mother's great uncle; he is going to stay there some time.'

'What has he gone there for, and he never even said goodbye to me!'

'Well, he likes being there, and he told me he should be away quite six weeks; he is well looked after there.'

'I feel very unhappy about it,' said the husband, 'in

case it should not be all right, and he ought to have said goodbye to me.'

With this he went on with his dinner, and said, 'Little Marleen, why do you weep? Brother will soon be back.' Then he asked his wife for more pudding, and as he ate, he threw the bones under the table.

Little Marleen went upstairs and took her best silk handkerchief out of her bottom drawer, and in it she wrapped all the bones from under the table and carried them outside, and all the time she did nothing but weep. Then she laid them in the green grass under the juniper-tree, and she had no sooner done so, then all her sadness seemed to leave her, and she wept no more. And now the juniper-tree began to move, and the branches waved backwards and forwards, first away from one another, and then together again, as it might be someone clapping their hands for joy. After this a mist came round the tree, and in the midst of it there was a burning as of fire, and out of the fire there flew a beautiful bird, that rose high into the air, singing magnificently, and when it could no more be seen, the juniper-tree stood there as before, and the silk handkerchief and the bones were gone.

Little Marleen now felt as lighthearted and happy as if her brother were still alive, and she went back to the house and sat down cheerfully to the table and ate.

The bird flew away and alighted on the house of a goldsmith and began to sing:

'My mother killed her little son;
My father grieved when I was gone;

My sister loved me best of all;
She laid her kerchief over me,
And took my bones that they might lie
Underneath the juniper-tree
Kywitt, Kywitt, what a beautiful bird am I!'

The goldsmith was in his workshop making a gold chain, when he heard the song of the bird on his roof. He thought it so beautiful that he got up and ran out, and as he crossed the threshold he lost one of his slippers. But he ran on into the middle of the street, with a slipper on one foot and a sock on the other; he still had on his apron, and still held the gold chain and the pincers in his hands, and so he stood gazing up at the bird, while the sun came shining brightly down on the street.

'Bird,' he said, 'how beautifully you sing! Sing me that song again.'

'Nay,' said the bird, 'I do not sing twice for nothing. Give that gold chain, and I will sing it you again.'

'Here is the chain, take it,' said the goldsmith. 'Only sing me that again.'

The bird flew down and took the gold chain in his right claw, and then he alighted again in front of the goldsmith and sang:

'My mother killed her little son;
My father grieved when I was gone;
My sister loved me best of all;
She laid her kerchief over me,
And took my bones that they might lie
Underneath the juniper-tree
Kywitt, Kywitt, what a beautiful bird am I!'

Then he flew away, and settled on the roof of a shoemaker's house and sang:

'My mother killed her little son;
My father grieved when I was gone;
My sister loved me best of all;
She laid her kerchief over me,
And took my bones that they might lie
Underneath the juniper-tree
Kywitt, Kywitt, what a beautiful bird am I!'

The shoemaker heard him, and he jumped up and ran out in his shirt-sleeves, and stood looking up at the bird on the roof with his hand over his eyes to keep himself from being blinded by the sun.

'Bird,' he said, 'how beautifully you sing!' Then he called through the door to his wife: 'Wife, come out; here is a bird, come and look at it and hear how beautifully it sings.' Then he called his daughter and the children, then the apprentices, girls and boys, and they all ran up the street to look at the bird, and saw how splendid it was with its red and green feathers, and its neck like burnished gold, and eyes like two bright stars in its head.

'Bird,' said the shoemaker, 'sing me that song again.'

'Nay,' answered the bird, 'I do not sing twice for nothing; you must give me something.'

'Wife,' said the man, 'go into the garret; on the upper shelf you will see a pair of red shoes; bring them to me.' The wife went in and fetched the shoes.

'There, bird,' said the shoemaker, 'now sing me that song again.'

The bird flew down and took the red shoes in his left claw, and then he went back to the roof and sang:

'My mother killed her little son;
My father grieved when I was gone;
My sister loved me best of all;
She laid her kerchief over me,
And took my bones that they might lie
Underneath the juniper-tree
Kywitt, Kywitt, what a beautiful bird am I!'

When he had finished, he flew away. He had the chain in his right claw and the shoes in his left, and he flew right away to a mill, and the mill went 'Click clack, click clack, click clack.' Inside the mill were twenty of the miller's men hewing a stone, and as they went 'Hick hack, hick hack, hick hack,' the mill went 'Click clack, click clack, click clack.'

The bird settled on a lime-tree in front of the mill and sang:

'My mother killed her little son;

then one of the men left off,

My father grieved when I was gone;

two more men left off and listened,

My sister loved me best of all;

then four more left off,

She laid her kerchief over me,
And took my bones that they might lie

now there were only eight at work,

Underneath

And now only five,

the juniper-tree.

and now only one,

Kywitt, Kywitt, what a beautiful bird am I!'

then he looked up and the last one had left off work.

'Bird,' he said, 'what a beautiful song that is you sing! Let me hear it too; sing it again.'

'Nay,' answered the bird, 'I do not sing twice for nothing; give me that millstone, and I will sing it again.'

'If it belonged to me alone,' said the man, 'you should have it.'

'Yes, yes,' said the others: 'if he will sing again, he can have it.'

The bird came down, and all the twenty millers set to and lifted up the stone with a beam; then the bird put his head through the hole and took the stone round his neck like a collar, and flew back with it to the tree and sang —

'My mother killed her little son;
My father grieved when I was gone;
My sister loved me best of all;
She laid her kerchief over me,
And took my bones that they might lie
Underneath the juniper-tree
Kywitt, Kywitt, what a beautiful bird am I!'

And when he had finished his song, he spread his wings, and with the chain in his right claw, the shoes in his left, and the millstone round his neck, he flew right away to his father's house.

The father, the mother, and little Marleen were having their dinner.

'How lighthearted I feel,' said the father, 'so pleased and cheerful.'

'And I,' said the mother, 'I feel so uneasy, as if a heavy thunderstorm were coming.'

But little Marleen sat and wept and wept.

Then the bird came flying towards the house and settled on the roof.

'I do feel so happy,' said the father, 'and how beautifully the sun shines; I feel just as if I were going to see an old friend again.'

'Ah!' said the wife, 'and I am so full of distress and uneasiness that my teeth chatter, and I feel as if there were a fire in my veins,' and she tore open her dress; and all the while little Marleen sat in the corner and wept, and the plate on her knees was wet with her tears.

The bird now flew to the juniper-tree and began singing:

'My mother killed her little son;

The mother shut her eyes and her ears, that she might see and hear nothing, but there was a roaring sound in her ears like that of a violent storm, and in her eyes a burning and flashing like lightning:

My father grieved when I was gone;

'Look, mother,' said the man, 'at the beautiful bird that is singing so magnificently; and how warm and bright the sun is, and what a delicious scent of spice in the air!'

My sister loved me best of all;

Then little Marleen laid her head down on her knees and sobbed.

'I must go outside and see the bird nearer,' said the man.

'Ah, do not go!' cried the wife. 'I feel as if the whole house were in flames!'

But the man went out and looked at the bird.

She laid her kerchief over me,
And took my bones that they might lie
Underneath the juniper-tree
Kywitt, Kywitt, what a beautiful bird am I!'

With that the bird let fall the gold chain, and it fell just round the man's neck, so that it fitted him exactly.

He went inside, and said, 'See, what a splendid bird

that is; he has given me this beautiful gold chain, and looks so beautiful himself.'

But the wife was in such fear and trouble, that she fell on the floor, and her cap fell from her head.

Then the bird began again:

'My mother killed her little son;

'Ah me!' cried the wife, 'if I were but a thousand feet beneath the earth, that I might not hear that song.'

My father grieved when I was gone;

then the woman fell down again as if dead.

My sister loved me best of all;

'Well,' said little Marleen, 'I will go out too and see if the bird will give me anything.'

So she went out.

She laid her kerchief over me,
And took my bones that they might lie

and he threw down the shoes to her,

Underneath the juniper-tree
Kywitt, Kywitt, what a beautiful bird am I!'

And she now felt quite happy and lighthearted; she put on the shoes and danced and jumped about in them. 'I was so miserable,' she said, 'when I came out, but that has all passed away; that is indeed a splendid bird, and he has given me a pair of red shoes.'

The wife sprang up, with her hair standing out from her head like flames of fire. 'Then I will go out too,' she said, 'and see if it will lighten my misery, for I feel as if the world were coming to an end.'

But as she crossed the threshold, crash! the bird threw the millstone down on her head, and she was crushed to death.

The father and little Marleen heard the sound and ran out, but they only saw mist and flame and fire rising from the spot, and when these had passed, there stood the little brother, and he took the father and little Marleen by the hand; then they all three rejoiced, and went inside together and sat down to their dinners and ate.

# *The Turnip*

There were two brothers who were both soldiers; the one was rich and the other poor. The poor man thought he would try to better himself; so, pulling off his red coat, he became a gardener, and dug his ground well, and sowed turnips.

When the seed came up, there was one plant bigger than all the rest; and it kept getting larger and larger, and seemed as if it would never cease growing; so that it might have been called the prince of turnips for there never was such a one seen before, and never will again. At last it was so big that it filled a cart, and two oxen could hardly draw it; and the gardener knew not what in the world to do with it, nor whether it would be a blessing or a curse to him. One day he said to himself, 'What shall I do with it? if I sell it, it will bring no more than another; and for eating, the little turnips are better than this; the best thing perhaps is to carry it and give it to the king as a mark of respect.'

Then he yoked his oxen, and drew the turnip to the court, and gave it to the king. 'What a wonderful thing!' said the king; 'I have seen many strange things, but such a monster as this I never saw. Where did you get the seed? or is it only your good luck? If so, you are a true child of fortune.' 'Ah, no!' answered the gardener, 'I am no child of fortune; I am a poor soldier, who never could get enough to live upon; so I laid aside my red coat, and set to work, tilling the ground. I have a brother, who is rich, and your majesty knows him well, and all the world knows him; but because I am poor, everybody forgets me.'

The king then took pity on him, and said, 'You shall be poor no longer. I will give you so much that you shall be even richer than your brother.' Then he gave him gold and lands and flocks, and made him so rich that his brother's fortune could not at all be compared with his.

When the brother heard of all this, and how a turnip had made the gardener so rich, he envied him sorely, and bethought himself how he could contrive to get the same good fortune for himself. However, he determined to manage more cleverly than his brother, and got together a rich present of gold and fine horses for the king; and thought he must have a much larger gift in return; for if his brother had received so much for only a turnip, what must his present be worth?

The king took the gift very graciously, and said he knew not what to give in return more valuable and wonderful than the great turnip; so the soldier was forced to put it into a cart, and drag it home with him. When he reached home, he knew not upon whom to vent his rage and spite; and at length wicked thoughts came into his head, and he resolved to kill his brother.

So he hired some villains to murder him; and having shown them where to lie in ambush, he went to his brother, and said, 'Dear brother, I have found a hidden treasure; let us go and dig it up, and share it between us.' The other had no suspicions of his roguery: so they went out together, and as they were travelling along, the murderers rushed out upon him, bound him, and were going to hang him on a tree.

But whilst they were getting all ready, they heard the trampling of a horse at a distance, which so frightened them that they pushed their prisoner neck and shoulders together into a sack, and swung him up by a cord to the tree, where they left him dangling, and ran away. Meantime he worked and worked away, till he made a hole large enough to put out his head.

When the horseman came up, he proved to be a student, a merry fellow, who was journeying along on his nag, and singing as he went. As soon as the man in the sack saw him passing under the tree, he cried out, 'Good morning! good morning to thee, my friend!' The student looked about everywhere; and seeing no one, and not knowing where the voice came from, cried out, 'Who calls me?'

Then the man in the tree answered, 'Lift up thine eyes, for behold here I sit in the sack of wisdom; here have I, in a short time, learned great and wondrous things. Compared to this seat, all the learning of the schools is as empty air. A little longer, and I shall know all that man can know, and shall come forth wiser than the wisest of mankind. Here I discern the signs and motions of the heavens and the stars; the laws that control the winds; the number of the sands on the seashore; the healing of the sick; the virtues of all simples, of birds, and of precious stones. Wert thou but once here, my friend, though wouldst feel and own the power of knowledge.

The student listened to all this and wondered much; at last he said, 'Blessed be the day and hour when I found you; cannot you contrive to let me into the sack for a little while?' Then the other answered, as if very unwillingly, 'A little space I may allow thee to sit here, if thou wilt reward me well and entreat me kindly; but thou must tarry yet an hour below, till I have learnt some little matters that are yet unknown to me.'

So the student sat himself down and waited a while; but the time hung heavy upon him, and he begged earnestly that he might ascend forthwith, for his thirst for knowledge was great. Then the other pretended to give way, and said, 'Thou must let the sack of wisdom descend, by untying yonder cord, and then thou shalt enter.' So the student let him down, opened the sack, and set him free. 'Now then,' cried he, 'let me ascend quickly.' As he began to put himself into the sack heels first, 'Wait a while,' said the gardener, 'that is not the way.' Then he pushed him in head first, tied up the sack, and soon swung up the searcher after wisdom dangling in the air. 'How is it with thee, friend?' said he, 'dost thou not feel that wisdom comes unto thee? Rest there in peace, till thou art a wiser man than thou wert.'

So saying, he trotted off on the student's nag, and left the poor fellow to gather wisdom till somebody should come and let him down.

# *The Water Of Life*

Long before you or I were born, there reigned, in a country a great way off, a king who had three sons. This king once fell very ill — so ill that nobody thought he could live. His sons were very much grieved at their father's sickness; and as they were walking together very mournfully in the garden of the palace, a little old man met them and asked what was the matter. They told him that their father was very ill, and that they were afraid nothing could save him. 'I know what would,' said the little old man; 'it is the Water of Life. If he could have a draught of it he would be well again; but it is very hard to get.' Then the eldest son said, 'I will soon find it': and he went to the sick king, and begged that he might go in search of the Water of Life, as it was the only thing that could save him. 'No,' said the king. 'I had rather die than place you in such great danger as you must meet with in your journey.' But he begged so hard that the king let him go; and the prince thought to himself, 'If I bring my father this water, he will make me sole heir to his kingdom.'

Then he set out: and when he had gone on his way

some time he came to a deep valley, overhung with rocks and woods; and as he looked around, he saw standing above him on one of the rocks a little ugly dwarf, with a sugarloaf cap and a scarlet cloak; and the dwarf called to him and said, 'Prince, whither so fast?' 'What is that to thee, you ugly imp?' said the prince haughtily, and rode on.

But the dwarf was enraged at his behaviour, and laid a fairy spell of ill-luck upon him; so that as he rode on the mountain pass became narrower and narrower, and at last the way was so straitened that he could not go to step forward: and when he thought to have turned his horse round and go back the way he came, he heard a loud laugh ringing round him, and found that the path was closed behind him, so that he was shut in all round. He next tried to get off his horse and make his way on foot, but again the laugh rang in his ears, and he found himself unable to move a step, and thus he was forced to abide spellbound.

Meantime the old king was lingering on in daily hope of his son's return, till at last the second son said, 'Father, I will go in search of the Water of Life.' For he thought to himself, 'My brother is surely dead, and the kingdom will fall to me if I find the water.' The king was at first very unwilling to let him go, but at last yielded to his wish. So he set out and followed the same road which his brother had done, and met with the same elf, who stopped him at the same spot in the mountains, saying, as before, 'Prince, prince, whither so fast?' 'Mind your own affairs, busybody!' said the prince scornfully, and rode on.

But the dwarf put the same spell upon him as he put on his elder brother, and he, too, was at last obliged to take up his abode in the heart of the mountains. Thus it is with proud silly people, who think themselves above everyone else, and are too proud to ask or take advice.

When the second prince had thus been gone a long time, the youngest son said he would go and search for the Water of Life, and trusted he should soon be able to make his father well again. So he set out, and the dwarf met him too at the same spot in the valley, among the mountains, and said, 'Prince, whither so fast?' And the prince said, 'I am going in search of the Water of Life, because my father is ill, and like to die: can you help me? Pray be kind, and aid me if you can!' 'Do you know where it is to be found?' asked the dwarf. 'No,' said the prince, 'I do not. Pray tell me if you know.' 'Then as you have spoken to me kindly, and are wise enough to seek for advice, I will tell you how and where to go. The water you seek springs from a well in an enchanted castle; and, that you may be able to reach it in safety, I will give you an iron wand and two little loaves of bread; strike the iron door of the castle three times with the wand, and it will open: two hungry lions will be lying down inside gaping for their prey, but if you throw them the bread they will let you pass; then hasten on to the well, and take some of the Water of Life before the clock strikes twelve; for if you tarry longer the door will shut upon you for ever.'

Then the prince thanked his little friend with the scarlet cloak for his friendly aid, and took the wand

and the bread, and went travelling on and on, over sea and over land, till he came to his journey's end, and found everything to be as the dwarf had told him. The door flew open at the third stroke of the wand, and when the lions were quieted he went on through the castle and came at length to a beautiful hall. Around it he saw several knights sitting in a trance; then he pulled off their rings and put them on his own fingers. In another room he saw on a table a sword and a loaf of bread, which he also took. Further on he came to a room where a beautiful young lady sat upon a couch; and she welcomed him joyfully, and said, if he would set her free from the spell that bound her, the kingdom should be his, if he would come back in a year and marry her. Then she told him that the well that held the Water of Life was in the palace gardens; and bade him make haste, and draw what he wanted before the clock struck twelve.

He walked on; and as he walked through beautiful gardens he came to a delightful shady spot in which stood a couch; and he thought to himself, as he felt tired, that he would rest himself for a while, and gaze on the lovely scenes around him. So he laid himself down, and sleep fell upon him unawares, so that he did not wake up till the clock was striking a quarter to twelve. Then he sprang from the couch dreadfully frightened, ran to the well, filled a cup that was standing by him full of water, and hastened to get away in time. Just as he was going out of the iron door it struck twelve, and the door fell so quickly upon him that it snapped off a piece of his heel.

When he found himself safe, he was overjoyed to think that he had got the Water of Life; and as he was going on his way homewards, he passed by the little dwarf, who, when he saw the sword and the loaf, said, 'You have made a noble prize; with the sword you can at a blow slay whole armies, and the bread will never fail you.' Then the prince thought to himself, 'I cannot go home to my father without my brothers'; so he said, 'My dear friend, cannot you tell me where my two brothers are, who set out in search of the Water of Life before me, and never came back?' 'I have shut them up by a charm between two mountains,' said the dwarf, 'because they were proud and ill-behaved, and scorned to ask advice.' The prince begged so hard for his brothers, that the dwarf at last set them free, though unwillingly, saying, 'Beware of them, for they have bad hearts.' Their brother, however, was greatly rejoiced to see them, and told them all that had happened to him; how he had found the Water of Life, and had taken a cup full of it; and how he had set a beautiful princess free from a spell that bound her; and how she had engaged to wait a whole year, and then to marry him, and to give him the kingdom.

Then they all three rode on together, and on their way home came to a country that was laid waste by war and a dreadful famine, so that it was feared all must die for want. But the prince gave the king of the land the bread, and all his kingdom ate of it. And he lent the king the wonderful sword, and he slew the enemy's army with it; and thus the kingdom was once more in peace and plenty. In the same manner he befriended two other countries through which they passed on their way.

When they came to the sea, they got into a ship and during their voyage the two eldest said to themselves, 'Our brother has got the water which we could not find, therefore our father will forsake us and give him the kingdom, which is our right'; so they were full of envy and revenge, and agreed together how they could ruin him. Then they waited till he was fast asleep, and poured the Water of Life out of the cup, and took it for themselves, giving him bitter sea-water instead.

When they came to their journey's end, the youngest son brought his cup to the sick king, that he might drink and be healed. Scarcely, however, had he tasted the bitter sea-water when he became worse even than he was before; and then both the elder sons came in, and blamed the youngest for what they had done; and said that he wanted to poison their father, but that they had found the Water of Life, and had brought it with them. He no sooner began to drink of what they brought him, than he felt his sickness leave him, and was as strong and well as in his younger days. Then they went to their brother, and laughed at him, and said, 'Well, brother, you found the Water of Life, did you? You have had the trouble and we shall have the reward. Pray, with all your cleverness, why did not you manage to keep your eyes open? Next year one of us will take away your beautiful princess, if you do not take care. You had better say nothing about this to our father, for he does not believe a word you say; and if you tell tales, you shall lose your life into the bargain: but be quiet, and we will let you off.'

The old king was still very angry with his youngest son, and thought that he really meant to have taken away his life; so he called his court together, and asked what should be done, and all agreed that he ought to be put to death. The prince knew nothing of what was going on, till one day, when the king's chief huntsmen went a-hunting with him, and they were alone in the wood together, the huntsman looked so sorrowful that the prince said, 'My friend, what is the matter with you?' 'I cannot and dare not tell you,' said he. But the prince begged very hard, and said, 'Only tell me what it is, and do not think I shall be angry, for I will forgive you.' 'Alas!' said the huntsman; 'the king has ordered me to shoot you.' The prince started at this, and said, 'Let me live, and I will change dresses with you; you shall take my royal coat to show to my father, and do you give me your shabby one.' 'With all my heart,' said the huntsman; 'I am sure I shall be glad to save you, for I could not have shot you.' Then he took the prince's coat, and gave him the shabby one, and went away through the wood.

Some time after, three grand embassies came to the old king's court, with rich gifts of gold and precious stones for his youngest son; now all these were sent from the three kings to whom he had lent his sword and loaf of bread, in order to rid them of their enemy and feed their people. This touched the old king's heart, and he thought his son might still be guiltless, and said to his court, 'O that my son were still alive!

How it grieves me that I had him killed!' 'He is still alive,' said the huntsman; 'and I am glad that I had pity on him, but let him go in peace, and brought home his royal coat.' At this the king was overwhelmed with joy, and made it known thoughout all his kingdom, that if his son would come back to his court he would forgive him.

Meanwhile the princess was eagerly waiting till her deliverer should come back; and had a road made leading up to her palace all of shining gold; and told her courtiers that whoever came on horseback, and rode straight up to the gate upon it, was her true lover; and that they must let him in: but whoever rode on one side of it, they must be sure was not the right one; and that they must send him away at once.

The time soon came, when the eldest brother thought that he would make haste to go to the princess, and say that he was the one who had set her free, and that he should have her for his wife, and the kingdom with her. As he came before the palace and saw the golden road, he stopped to look at it, and he thought to himself, 'It is a pity to ride upon this beautiful road'; so he turned aside and rode on the right-hand side of it. But when he came to the gate, the guards, who had seen the road he took, said to him he could not be what he said he was, and must go about his business.

The second prince set out soon afterwards on the same errand; and when he came to the golden road, and his horse had set one foot upon it, he stopped to look at it, and thought it very beautiful, and said to himself, What a pity it is that anything should tread here!' Then he too turned aside and rode on the left side of it. But when he came to the gate the guards said he was not the true prince, and that he too must go away about his business; and away he went.

Now when the full year was come round, the third brother left the forest in which he had lain hid for fear of his father's anger, and set out in search of his betrothed bride. So he journeyed on, thinking of her all the way, and rode so quickly that he did not even see what the road was made of, but went with his horse straight over it; and as he came to the gate it flew open, and the princess welcomed him with joy, and said he was her deliverer, and should now be her husband and lord of the kingdom. When the first joy at their meeting was over, the princess told him she had heard of his father having forgiven him, and of his wish to have him home again: so, before his wedding with the princess, he went to visit his father, taking her with him. Then he told him everything; how his brothers had cheated and robbed him, and yet that he had borne all those wrongs for the love of his father. And the old king was very angry, and wanted to punish his wicked sons; but they made their escape, and got into a ship and sailed away over the wide sea, and where they went to nobody knew and nobody cared.

And now the old king gathered together his court, and asked all his kingdom to come and celebrate the wedding of his son and the princess. And young and old, noble and squire, gentle and simple, came at once on the summons; and among the rest came the friendly dwarf, with the sugarloaf hat, and a new scarlet cloak.

And the wedding was held, and the merry bells run.
And all the good people they danced and they sung,
And feasted and frolick'd I can't tell how long.

# *Cat-Skin*

There was once a king, whose queen had hair of the purest gold, and was so beautiful that her match was not to be met with on the whole face of the earth. But this beautiful queen fell ill, and when she felt that her end drew near she called the king to her and said, 'Promise me that you will never marry again, unless you meet with a wife who is as beautiful as I am, and who has golden hair like mine.' Then when the king in his grief promised all she asked, she shut her eyes and died. But the king was not to be comforted, and for a long time never thought of taking another wife. At last, however, his wise men said, 'this will not do; the king must marry again, that we may have a queen.' So messengers were sent far and wide, to seek for a bride as beautiful as the late queen. But there was no princess in the world so beautiful; and if there had been, still there was not one to be found who had golden hair. So the messengers came home, and had had all their trouble for nothing.

Now the king had a daughter, who was just as beautiful as her mother, and had the same golden hair. And when she was grown up, the king looked at her and saw that she was just like this late queen: then he said to his courtiers, 'May I not marry my daughter? She is the very image of my dead wife: unless I have her, I shall not find any bride upon the whole earth, and you say there must be a queen.' When the courtiers heard this they were shocked, and said, 'Heaven forbid that a father should marry his daughter! Out of so great a sin no good can come.' And his daughter was also shocked, but hoped the king would soon give up such thoughts; so she said to him, 'Before I marry anyone I must have three dresses: one must be of gold, like the sun; another must be of shining silver, like the moon; and a third must be dazzling as the stars: besides this, I want a mantle of a thousand different kinds of fur put together, to which every beast in the kingdom must give a part of his skin.' And thus she though he would think of the matter no more. But the king made the most skilful workmen in his kingdom weave the three dresses: one golden, like the sun; another silvery, like the moon; and a third sparkling, like the stars: and his hunters were told to hunt out all the beasts in his kingdom, and to take the finest fur out of their skins: and thus a mantle of a thousand furs was made.

When all were ready, the king sent them to her; but she got up in the night when all were asleep, and took three of her trinkets, a golden ring, a golden necklace, and a golden brooch, and packed the three dresses — of the sun, the moon, and the stars — up in a nutshell, and wrapped herself up in the mantle made of all sorts of fur, and besmeared her face and hands with soot. Then she threw herself upon Heaven for help in her need, and went away, and journeyed on the whole night, till at last she came to a large wood. As she was very tired, she sat herself down in the hollow of a tree and soon fell asleep: and there she slept on till it was midday.

Now as the king to whom the wood belonged was hunting in it, his dogs came to the tree, and began to snuff about, and run round and round, and bark. 'Look sharp!' said the king to the huntsmen, 'and see what sort of game lies there.' And the huntsmen went up to the tree, and when they came back again said, 'In the hollow tree there lies a most wonderful beast, such as we never saw before; its skin seems to be of a thousand kinds of fur, but there it lies fast asleep.' 'See,' said the king, 'if you can catch it alive, and we will take it with us.' So the huntsmen took it up, and the maiden awoke and was greatly frightened, and said, 'I am a poor child that has neither father nor mother left; have pity on me and take me with you.' Then they said, 'Yes, Miss Cat-skin, you will do for the kitchen; you can sweep up the ashes, and do things of that sort.' So they put her into the coach, and took her home to the king's palace. Then they showed her a little corner under the staircase, where no light of day ever peeped in, and said, 'Cat-skin, you may lie and sleep there.' And she was sent into the kitchen, and made to fetch wood and water, to blow the fire, pluck the poultry, pick the herbs, sift the ashes, and do all the dirty work.

Thus Cat-skin lived for a long time very sorrowfully. 'Ah! pretty princess!' thought she, 'what will now become of thee?' But it happened one day that a feast was to be held in the king's castle, so she said to the cook, 'May I go up a little while and see what is going on? I will take care and stand behind the door.' And the cook said, 'Yes, you may go, but be back again in half an hour's time, to rake out the ashes.' Then she took her little lamp, and went into her cabin, and took off the fur skin, and washed the soot from off her face and hands, so that her beauty shone forth like the sun from behind the clouds. She next opened her nutshell, and brought out of it the dress that shone like the sun, and so went to the feast. Everyone made way for her, for nobody knew her, and they thought she could be no less than a king's daughter. But the king came up to her, and held out his hand and danced with her; and he thought in his heart, 'I never saw anyone half so beautiful.'

When the dance was at an end she curtsied; and when the king looked round for her, she was gone, no one knew wither. The guards that stood at the castle gate were called in: but they had seen no one. The truth was, that she had run into her little cabin, pulled off her dress, blackened her face and hands, put on the fur-skin cloak, and was Cat-skin again. When she went into the kitchen to her work, and began to rake the ashes, the cook said, 'Let that alone till the morning, and heat the king's soup; I should like to run up now and give a peep: but take care you don't let a hair fall into it, or you will run a chance of never eating again.'

As soon as the cook went away, Cat-skin heated the king's soup, and toasted a slice of bread first, as nicely as ever she could; and when it was ready, she went and looked in the cabin for her little golden ring, and put it into the dish in which the soup was. When the dance was over, the king ordered his soup to be brought in; and it pleased him so well, that he thought he had never tasted any so good before. At the bottom he saw a gold ring lying; and as he could not make out how it had got there, he ordered the cook to be sent for. The cook was frightened when he heard the order, and said to Cat-skin, 'You must have let a hair fall into the soup; if it be so, you will have a good beating.' Then he went before the king, and he asked him who had cooked the soup. 'I did,' answered the cook. But the king said, 'That is not true; it was better done than you could do it.' Then he answered, 'To tell the truth I did not cook it, but Cat-skin did.' 'Then let Cat-skin come up,' said the king: and when she came he said to her, 'Who are you?' 'I am a poor child,' said she, 'that has lost both father and mother.' 'How came you in my palace?' asked he. 'I am good for nothing,' said she, 'but to be scullion-girl, and to have boots and shoes thrown at my head.' 'But how did you get the ring that was in the soup?' asked the king. Then she would not own that she knew anything about the ring; so the king sent her away again about her business.

After a time there was another feast, and Cat-skin asked the cook to let her go up and see it as before. 'Yes,' said he, 'but come again in half an hour, and cook the king the soup that he likes so much.' Then she ran to her little cabin, washed herself quickly, and took her dress out which was silvery as the moon, and put it on; and when she went in, looking like a king's daughter, the king went up to her, and rejoiced at seeing her again, and when the dance began he danced with her. After the dance was at an end she managed to slip out, so slyly that the king did not see where she was gone; but she sprang into her little cabin, and made herself into Cat-skin again, and went into the kitchen to cook the soup. Whilst the cook was above stairs, she got the golden necklace and dropped it into the soup; then it was brought to the king, who ate it, and it pleased him as well as before; so he sent for the cook, who was again forced to tell him that Cat-skin had cooked it. Cat-skin was brought again before the king, but she still told him that she was only fit to have boots and shoes thrown at her head.

But when the king had ordered a feast to be got ready for the third time, it happened just the same as before. 'You must be a witch, Cat-skin,' said the cook; 'for you always put something into your soup, so that it pleases the king better than mine.' However, he let her go up as before. Then she put on her dress which sparkled like the stars, and went into the ball-room in it; and the king danced with her again, and thought she had never looked so beautiful as she did then. So whilst he was dancing with her, he put a gold ring on her finger without her seeing it, and ordered that the dance should be kept up a long time. When it was at an end, he would have held her fast by the hand, but she slipped away, and sprang so quickly through the crowd that he lost sight of her: and she ran as fast as she could into her little cabin under the stairs. But this time she kept away too long, and stayed beyond the half-hour; so she had not time to take off her fine dress, and threw her fur mantle over it, and in her haste did not blacken herself all over with soot, but left one of her fingers white.

Then she ran into the kitchen, and cooked the king's soup; and as soon as the cook was gone, she put the golden brooch into the dish. When the king got to the bottom, he ordered Cat-skin to be called once more, and soon saw the white finger, and the ring that he had put on it whilst they were dancing: so he seized her hand, and kept fast hold of it, and when she wanted to loose herself and spring away, the fur cloak fell off a little on one side, and the starry dress sparkled underneath it.

Then he got hold of the fur and tore it off, and her golden hair and beautiful form were seen, and she could no longer hide herself: so she washed the soot and ashes from her face, and showed herself to be the most beautiful princess upon the face of the earth. But the king said, 'You are my beloved bride, and we will never more be parted from each other.' And the wedding feast was held, and a merry day it was, as ever was heard of or seen in that country, or indeed in any other.

# *The Twelve Dancing Princesses*

There was a king who had twelve beautiful daughters. They slept in twelve beds all in one room; and when they went to bed, the doors were shut and locked up; but every morning their shoes were found to be quite worn through as if they had been danced in all night; and yet nobody could find out how it happened, or where they had been.

Then the king made it known to all the land, that if any person could discover the secret, and find out where it was that the princesses danced in the night, he should have the one he liked best for his wife, and should be king after his death; but whoever tried and did not succeed, after three days and nights, should be put to death.

A king's son soon came. He was well entertained, and in the evening was taken to the chamber next to the one where the princesses lay in their twelve beds. There he was to sit and watch where they went to dance; and, in order that nothing might pass without his hearing it, the door of his chamber was left open. But the king's son soon fell asleep; and when he awoke in the morning he found that the princesses had all been dancing, for the soles of their shoes were full of holes. The same thing happened the second and third night: so the king ordered his head to be cut off. After him came several others; but they had all the same luck, and all lost their lives in the same manner.

Now it chanced that an old soldier, who had been wounded in battle and could fight no longer, passed through the country where this king reigned: and as he was travelling through a wood, he met an old woman, who asked him where he was going. 'I hardly know where I am going, or what I had better do,' said the soldier; 'but I think I should like very well to find out where it is that the princesses dance, and then in time I might be a king.' 'Well,' said the old dame, 'that is no very hard task: only take care not to drink any of the wine which one of the princesses will bring to you in the evening; and as soon as she leaves you pretend to be fast asleep.'

Then she gave him a cloak, and said, 'As soon as you put that on you will become invisible, and you will then be able to follow the princesses wherever they go.' When the soldier heard all this good counsel, he determined to try his luck: so he went to the king, and said he was willing to undertake the task.

He was as well received as the others had been, and the king ordered fine royal robes to be given him; and when the evening came he was led to the outer chamber. Just as he was going to lie down, the eldest of the princesses brought him a cup of wine; but the soldier threw it all away secretly, taking care not to drink a drop. Then he laid himself down on his bed, and in a little while began to snore very loud as if he was fast asleep. When the twelve princesses heard this they laughed heartily; and the eldest said, 'This fellow too might have done a wiser thing than lose his life in this way!' Then they rose up and opened their drawers and boxes, and took out all their fine clothes, and dressed themselves at the glass, and skipped about as if they were eager to begin dancing. But the youngest said, 'I don't know how it is, while you are so happy I feel very uneasy; I am sure some mischance will befall us.' 'You simpleton,' said the eldest, 'you are always afraid; have you forgotten how many kings' sons have already watched in vain? And as for this soldier, even if I had not given him his sleeping draught, he would have slept soundly enough.'

When they were all ready, they went and looked at the soldier; but he snored on, and did not stir hand or foot: so they thought they were quite safe; and the eldest went up to her own bed and clapped her hands, and the bed sank into the floor and a trap-door flew open. The soldier saw them going down through the trap-door one after another, the eldest leading the way; and thinking he had no time to lose, he jumped up, put on the cloak which the old woman had given him, and followed them; but in the middle of the stairs he trod on the gown of the youngest princess, and she cried out to her sisters, 'All is not right; someone took hold of my gown.' 'You silly creature!' said the eldest, 'it is nothing but a nail in the wall.' Then down they all went, and at the bottom they found themselves in a most delightful grove of trees; and the leaves were all of silver, and glittered and sparkled beautifully. The soldier wished to take away some token of the place; so he broke off a little branch, and there came a loud noise from the tree. Then the youngest daughter said again, 'I am sure all is not right — did not you hear that noise? That never happened before.' But the eldest said, 'It is only our princes, who are shouting for joy at our approach.'

Then they came to another grove of trees, where all the leaves were of gold; and afterwards to a third, where the leaves were all glittering diamonds. And the soldier broke a branch from each; and every time there was a loud noise, which made the youngest sister tremble with fear; but the eldest still said it was only the princes, who were crying for joy. So they went on till they came to a great lake; and at the side of the lake there lay twelve little boats with twelve handsome princes in them, who seemed to be waiting there for the princesses.

One of the princesses went into each boat, and the soldier stepped into the same boat with the youngest. As they were rowing over the lake, the prince who was in the boat with the youngest princess and the soldier said, I do not know why it is, but though I am rowing with all my might we do not get on so fast as usual, and I am quite tired: the boat seems very heavy today.' 'It is only the heat of the weather,' said the princess: 'I feel it very warm too.'

On the other side of the lake stood a fine illuminated castle, from which came the merry music of horns and trumpets. There they all landed, and went into the castle, and each prince danced with his princess; and the soldier, who was all the time invisible, danced with them too; and when any of the princesses had a cup of wine set by her, he drank it all up, so that when she put the cup to her mouth it was empty. At this, too, the youngest sister was terribly frightened, but the eldest always silenced her. They danced on till three o'clock in the morning, and then all their shoes were worn out, so that they were obliged to leave off. The princes rowed them back again over the lake (but this time the soldier placed himself in the boat with the eldest princess); and on the opposite shore they took leave of each other, the princesses promising to come again the next night.

When they came to the stairs, the soldier ran on before the princesses, and laid himself down; and as the twelve sisters slowly came up very much tired, they heard him snoring in his bed; so they said, 'Now all is quite safe'; then they undressed themselves, put away their fine clothes, pulled off their shoes, and went to bed. In the morning the soldier said nothing about what had happened, but determined to see more of this strange adventure, and went again the second and third night; and everything happened just as before; the princesses danced each time till their shoes were worn to pieces, and then returned home. However, on the third night the soldier carried away one of the golden cups as a token of where he had been.

As soon as the time came when he was to declare the secret, he was taken before the king with the three branches and the golden cup; and the twelve princesses stood listening behind the door to hear what he would say. And when the king asked him. 'Where do my twelve daughters dance at night?' he answered, 'With twelve princes in a castle under ground.' And then he told the king all that had happened, and showed him the three branches and the golden cup which he had brought with him. Then the king called for the princesses, and asked them whether what the soldier said was true: and when they saw that they were discovered, and that it was of no use to deny what had happened, they confessed it all. And the king asked the soldier which of them he would choose for his wife; and he answered, 'I am not very young, so I will have the eldest.' — And they were married that very day, and the soldier was chosen to be the king's heir.

## *Briar Rose*

A king and queen once upon a time reigned in a country a great way off, where there were in those days fairies. Now this king and queen had plenty of money, and plenty of fine clothes to wear, and plenty of good things to eat and drink, and a coach to ride out in every day: but though they had been married many years they had no children, and this grieved them very much indeed. But one day as the queen was walking by the side of the river, at the bottom of the garden, she saw a poor little fish, that had thrown itself out of the water, and lay gasping and nearly dead on the bank. Then the queen took pity on the little fish, and threw it back again into the river; and before it swam away it lifted its head out of the water and said, 'I know what your wish is, and it shall be fulfilled, in return for your kindness to me — you will soon have a daughter.' What the little fish had foretold soon came to pass; and the queen had a little girl, so very beautiful that the king could not cease looking on it for joy, and said he would hold a great feast and make merry, and show the child to all the land. So he asked his kinsmen, and nobles, and friends, and neighbours. But the queen said, 'I will have the fairies also, that they might be kind and good to our little daughter.' Now there were thirteen fairies in the kingdom; but as the king and queen had only twelve golden dishes for them to eat out of, they were forced to leave one of the fairies without asking her. So twelve fairies came, each with a high red cap on her head, and red shoes with high heels on her feet, and a long white wand in her hand: and after the feast was over they gathered round in a ring and gave all their best gifts to the little princess. One gave her goodness, another beauty, another riches, and so on till she had all that was good in the world.

Just as eleven of them had done blessing her, a great noise was heard in the courtyard, and word was brought that the thirteenth fairy was come, with a black cap on her head, and black shoes on her feet, and a broomstick in her hand: and presently up she came into the dining-hall. Now, as she had not been asked to the feast she was very angry, and scolded the king and queen very much, and set to work to take her revenge. So she cried out, 'The king's daughter shall, in her fifteenth year, be wounded by a spindle, and fall down dead.' Then the twelfth of the friendly fairies, who had not yet given her gift, came forward, and said that the evil wish must be fulfilled, but that she could soften its mischief; so her gift was, that the king's daughter, when the spindle wounded her, should not really die, but should only fall asleep for a hundred years.

However, the king hoped still to save his dear child altogether from the threatened evil; so he ordered that all the spindles in the kingdom should be bought up and burnt. But all the gifts of the first eleven fairies were in the meantime fulfilled; for the princess was so beautiful, and well behaved, and good, and wise, that everyone who knew her loved her.

It happened that, on the very day she was fifteen years old, the king and queen were not at home, and she was left alone in the palace. So she roved about by herself, and looked at all the rooms and chambers, till at last she came to an old tower, to which there was a narrow staircase ending with a little door. In the door there was a golden key, and when she turned it the door sprang open, and there sat an old lady spinning away very busily. 'Why, how now, good mother,' said the princess; 'what are you doing there?' 'Spinning,' said the old lady, and nodded her head, humming a tune, while buzz! went the wheel. 'How prettily that little thing turns round!' said the princess, and took the spindle and began to try and spin. But scarcely had she touched it, before the fairy's prophecy was fulfilled; the spindle wounded her, and she fell down lifeless on the ground.

However, she was not dead, but had only fallen into a deep sleep; and the king and the queen, who had just come home, and all their court, fell asleep too; and the horses slept in the stables, and the dogs in the court, the pigeons on the house-top, and the very flies slept upon the walls. Even the fire on the hearth left off blazing, and went to sleep; the jack stopped, and the spit that was turning about with a goose upon it for the king's dinner stood still; and the cook, who was at that moment pulling the kitchen-boy by the hair to give him a box on the ear for something he had done amiss, let him go, and both fell asleep; the butler, who was slyly tasting the ale, fell asleep with the jug at his lips: and thus everything stood still, and slept soundly.

A large hedge of thorns soon grew round the palace, and every year it became higher and thicker; till at last the old palace was surrounded and hidden, so that not even the roof or the chimneys could be seen. But there went a report through all the land of the beautiful sleeping Briar Rose (for so the king's daughter was called): so that, from time to time, several kings' sons came, and tried to break through the thicket into the palace. This, however, none of them could ever do; for the thorns and bushes laid hold of them, as it were with hands; and there they stuck fast, and died wretchedly.

After many, many years there came a king's son into that land: and an old man told him the story of the thicket of thorns; and how a beautiful palace stood behind it, and how a wonderful princess, called Briar Rose, lay in it asleep, with all her court. He told, too, how he had heard from his grandfather that many, many princes had come, and had tried to break through the thicket, but that they had all stuck fast in it, and died. Then the young prince said, 'All this shall not frighten me; I will go and see this Briar Rose.' The old man tried to hinder him, but he was bent upon going.

Now that very day the hundred years were ended;

and as the prince came to the thicket he saw nothing but beautiful flowering shrubs, through which he went with ease, and they shut in after him as thick as ever. Then he came at last to the palace, and there in the court lay the dogs asleep; and the horses were standing in the stables; and on the roof sat the pigeons fast asleep, with their heads under their wings. And when he came into the palace, the flies were sleeping on the walls; the spit was standing still; the butler had the jug of ale at his lips, going to drink a draught; the maid sat with a fowl in her lap ready to be plucked; and the cook in the kitchen was still holding up her hand, as if she was going to beat the boy.

Then he went on still farther, and all was so still that he could hear every breath he drew; till at last he came to the old tower, and opened the door of the little room in which Briar Rose was; and there she lay, fast asleep on a couch by the window. She looked so beautiful that he could not take his eyes off her, so he stooped down and gave her a kiss. But the moment he kissed her she opened her eyes and awoke, and smiled upon him; and they went out together; and soon the king and queen also awoke, and all the court, and gazed on each other with great wonder. And the horses shook themselves, and the dogs jumped up and barked; the pigeons took their heads from under their wings, and looked about and flew into the fields; the flies on the walls buzzed again; the fire in the kitchen blazed up; round went the jack, and round went the spit, with the goose for the king's dinner upon it; the butler finished his draught of ale; the maid went on plucking the fowl; and the cook gave the boy the box on his ear.

And then the prince and Briar Rose were married, and the wedding feast was given; and they lived happily together all their lives long.

# *Cinderella*

The wife of a rich man fell sick, and as she felt that her end was drawing near, she called her only daughter to her bedside and said, 'Dear child, be good and pious, and then the good God will always protect you, and I will look down on you from heaven and be near you.'

Thereupon she closed her eyes and departed. Every day the maiden went out to her mother's grave, and wept, and she remained pious and good. When winter came the snow spread a white sheet over the grave, and by the time the spring sun had drawn it off again, the man had taken another wife.

The woman had brought with her into the house two daughters, who were beautiful and fair of face, but vile and black of heart. Now began a bad time for the poor step-child. 'Is the stupid goose to sit in the parlor with us,' they said. 'He who wants to eat bread must earn it. Out with the kitchen-wench.' They took her pretty clothes away from her, put an old grey bedgown on her, and gave her wooden shoes.

'Just look at the proud princess, how decked out she is,' they cried, and laughed, and led her into the kitchen. There she had to do hard work from morning till night, get up before daybreak, carry water, light fires, cook and wash. Besides this, the sisters did her every imaginable injury – they mocked her and emptied her peas and lentils into the ashes, so that she was forced to sit and pick them out again. In the evening when she had worked till she was weary she had no bed to go to, but had to sleep by the hearth in the cinders. And as on that account she always looked dusty and dirty, they called her Cinderella.

It happened that the father was once going to the fair, and he asked his two step-daughters what he should bring back for them.

'Beautiful dresses,' said one, 'Pearls and jewels,' said the second.

'And you, Cinderella,' said he, 'what will you have?'

'Father break off for me the first branch which knocks against your hat on your way home.'

So he bought beautiful dresses, pearls and jewels for his two step-daughters, and on his way home, as he was riding through a green thicket, a hazel twig brushed against him and knocked off his hat. Then he broke off the branch and took it with him. When he reached home he gave his step-daughters the things which they had wished for, and to Cinderella he gave the branch from the hazel-bush. Cinderella thanked him, went to her mother's grave and planted the branch on it, and wept so much that the tears fell down on it and watered it. And it grew and became a handsome tree. Thrice a day Cinderella went and sat beneath it, and wept and prayed, and a little white bird always came on the tree, and if Cinderella expressed a wish, the bird threw down to her what she had wished for.

It happened, however, that the king gave orders for a festival which was to last three days, and to which all the beautiful young girls in the country were invited, in order that his son might choose himself a bride. When the two step-sisters heard that they too were to appear among the number, they were delighted, called Cinderella and said, 'comb our hair for us, brush our shoes and fasten our buckles, for we are going to the wedding at the king's palace.'

Cinderella obeyed, but wept, because she too would have liked to go with them to the dance, and begged her step-mother to allow her to do so.

'You go, Cinderella,' said she, 'covered in dust and dirt as you are, and would go to the festival. You have no clothes and shoes, and yet would dance.' As, however, Cinderella went on asking, the step-mother said at last, 'I have emptied a dish of lentils into the ashes for you, if you have picked them out again in two hours, you shall go with us.'

The maiden went through the back-door into the garden, and called, 'You tame pigeons, you turtle-doves, and all you birds beneath the sky, come and help me to pick

the good into the pot,
the bad into the crop.'

Then two white pigeons came in by the kitchen window, and afterwards the turtle-doves, and at last all the birds beneath the sky, came whirring and crowding in, and alighted amongst the ashes. And the pigeons nodded with their heads and began pick, pick, pick, pick, and the rest began also pick, pick, pick, pick, and gathered all the good grains into the dish. Hardly had one hour passed before they had finished, and all flew out again.

Then the girl took the dish to her step-mother, and was glad, and believed that now she would be allowed to go with them to the festival.

But the step-mother said, 'No, Cinderella, you have no clothes and you cannot dance. You would only be laughed at.' And as Cinderella wept at this, the step-mother said, if you can pick two dishes of lentils out of the ashes for me in one hour, you shall go with us. And she thought to herself, that she most certainly cannot do it again.

When the step-mother had emptied the two dishes of lentils amongst the ashes, the maiden went through the back-door into the garden and cried, 'You tame pigeons, you turtle-doves, and all you birds beneath the sky, come and help me to pick

the good into the pot,
the bad into the crop.'

Then two white pigeons came in by the kitchen-window, and afterwards the turtle-doves, and at length all the birds beneath the sky, came whirring and crowding in, and alighted amongst the ashes. And the doves nodded with their heads and began pick, pick,

pick, pick, and the others began also pick, pick, pick, pick, and gathered all the good seeds into the dishes, and before half an hour was over they had already finished, and all flew out again. Then the maiden was delighted, and believed that she might now go with them to the wedding.

But the step-mother said, 'All this will not help. You cannot go with us, for you have no clothes and cannot dance. We should be ashamed of you.' On this she turned her back on Cinderella, and hurried away with her two proud daughters.

As no one was now at home, Cinderella went to her mother's grave beneath the hazel-tree, and cried,

> 'Shiver and quiver, little tree,
> Silver and gold throw down over me.'

Then the bird threw a gold and silver dress down to her, and slippers embroidered with silk and silver. She put on the dress with all speed, and went to the wedding. Her step-sisters and the step-mother however did not know her, and thought she must be a foreign princess, for she looked so beautiful in the golden dress. They never once thought of Cinderella, and believed that she was sitting at home in the dirt, picking lentils out of the ashes. The prince approached her, took her by the hand and danced with her. He would dance with no other maiden, and never let loose of her hand, and if any one else came to invite her, he said, 'This is my partner.'

She danced till it was evening, and then she wanted to go home. But the king's son said, 'I will go with you and bear you company,' for he wished to see to whom the beautiful maiden belonged. She escaped from him, however, and sprang into the pigeon-house. The king's son waited until her father came, and then he told him that the unknown maiden had leapt into the pigeon-house. The old man thought, 'can it be Cinderella.' And they had to bring him an axe and a pickaxe that he might hew the pigeon-house to pieces, but no one was inside it. And when they got home Cinderella lay in her dirty clothes among the ashes, and a dim little oil-lamp was burning on the mantle-piece, for Cinderella had jumped quickly down from the back of the pigeon-house and had run to the little hazel-tree, and there she had taken off her beautiful clothes and laid them on the grave, and the bird had taken them away again, and then she had seated herself in the kitchen amongst the ashes in her grey gown.

Next day when the festival began afresh, and her parents and the step-sisters had gone once more, Cinderella went to the hazel-tree and said,

> 'Shiver and quiver, my little tree,
> Silver and gold throw down over me.'

Then the bird threw down a much more beautiful dress than on the preceding day. And when Cinderella appeared at the wedding in this dress, every one was astonished at her beauty. The king's son had waited until she came, and instantly took her by the hand and danced with no one but her. When others came and invited her, he said, 'This is my partner.' When evening came she wished to leave, and the king's son followed her and wanted to see into which house she went. But she sprang away from him, and into the garden behind the house. Therein stood a beautiful tall tree on which hung the most magnificent pears. She clambered so nimbly between the branches like a squirrel that the king's son did not know where she was gone. He waited until her father came, and said to him, 'The unknown maiden has escaped from me, and I believe she has climbed up the pear-tree.' The father thought, 'can it be Cinderella.' And had an axe brought and cut the tree down, but no one was on it. And when they got into the kitchen, Cinderella lay there among the ashes, as usual, for she had jumped down on the other side of the tree, had taken the beautiful dress to the bird on the little hazel-tree, and put on her grey gown.

On the third day, when the parents and sisters had gone away, Cinderella went once more to her mother's grave and said to the little tree,

> 'Shiver and quiver, my little tree,
> silver and gold throw down over me.'

And now the bird threw down to her a dress which was more splendid and magnificent than any she had yet had, and the slippers were golden. And when she went to the festival in the dress, no one knew how to speak for astonishment. The king's son danced with her only, and if any one invited her to dance, he said, 'This is my partener.'

When evening came, Cinderella wished to leave, and the king's son was anxious to go with her, but she escaped from him so quickly that he could not follow her. The king's son, however, had employed a ruse, and had caused the whole staircase to be smeared with pitch, and there, when she ran down, had the maiden's left slipper remained stuck. The king's son picked it up, and it was small and dainty, and all golden.

Next morning, he went with it to the father, and said to him, no one shall be my wife but she whose foot this golden slipper fits. Then were the two sisters glad, for they had pretty feet. The eldest went with the shoe into her room and wanted to try it on, and her mother stood by. But she could not get her big toe into it, and the shoe was too small for her. Then her mother gave her a knife and said, 'Cut the toe off, when you are queen you will have no more need to go on foot.' The maiden cut the toe off, forced the foot into the shoe, swallowed the pain, and went out to the king's son. Then he took her on his horse as his bride and rode away with her. They were obliged, however, to pass the grave, and there, on the hazel-tree, sat the two pigeons and cried,

'Turn and peep, turn and peep,
there's blood within the shoe,
the shoe it is too small for her,
the true bride waits for you.'

Then he looked at her foot and saw how the blood was trickling from it. He turned his horse round and took the false bride home again, and said she was not the true one, and that the other sister was to put the shoe on. Then this one went into her chamber and got her toes safely into the shoe, but her heel was too large.

So her mother gave her a knife and said, 'Cut a bit off your heel, when you are queen you will have no more need to go on foot.' The maiden cut a bit off her heel, forced her foot into the shoe, swallowed the pain, and went out to the king's son. He took her on his horse as his bride, and rode away with her, but when they passed by the hazel-tree, the two pigeons sat on it and cried,

'Turn and peep, turn and peep,
there's blood within the shoe,
the shoe it is too small for her,
the true bride waits for you.'

He looked down at her foot and saw how the blood was running out of her shoe, and how it had stained her white stocking quite red. Then he turned his horse and took the false bride home again. 'This also is not the right one,' said he, 'have you no other daughter.' 'No,' said the man, 'there is still a little stunted kitchen-wench which my late wife left behind her, but she cannot possibly be the bride.' The king's son said he was to send her up to him, but the mother answered, 'oh, no, she is much too dirty, she cannot show herself'. But he absolutely insisted on it, and Cinderella had to be called.

She first washed her hands and face clean, and then went and bowed down before the king's son, who gave her the golden shoe. Then she seated herself on a stool, drew her foot out of the heavy wooden shoe, and put it into the slipper, which fitted like a glove. And when she rose up and the king's son looked at her face he recognized the beautiful maiden who had danced with him and cried, 'That is the true bride.' The stepmother and the two sisters were horrified and became pale with rage. He, however, took Cinderella on his horse and rode away with her. As they passed by the hazel-tree, the two white doves cried,

> 'Turn and peep, turn and peep,
> there's blood within the shoe,
> the shoe it is too small for her,
> the true bride waits for you.'

And when they had cried that, the two came flying down and placed themselves on Cinderella's shoulders, one on the right, the other on the left, and remained sitting there. When the wedding with the king's son was to be celebrated, the two false sisters came and wanted to get into favour with Cinderella and share her good fortune. When the betrothed couple went to church, the elder was at the right side and the younger at the left, and the pigeons pecked out one eye from each of them. Afterwards as they came back the elder was at the left, and the younger at the right, and then the pigeons pecked out the other eye from each. And thus, for their wickedness and falsehood, they were punished with blindness all their days.

# *Little Snow-White*

Once upon a time in the middle of winter, when the flakes of snow were falling like feathers from the sky, a queen sat at a window sewing, and the frame of the window was made of black ebony. And whilst she was sewing and looking out of the window at the snow, she pricked her finger with the needle, and three drops of blood fell upon the snow. And the red looked pretty upon the white snow, and she thought to herself, 'Would that I had a child as white as snow, as red as blood, and as black as the wood of the window frame.'

Soon after that she had a little daughter, who was as white as snow, and as red as blood, and her hair was as black as ebony; and she was therefore called Little Snow-white. And when the child was born, the Queen died.

After a year had passed, the King took to himself another wife. She was a beautiful woman, but proud and haughty, and she could not bear that anyone else should surpass her in beauty. She had a wonderful looking-glass, and when she stood in front of it and looked at herself in it, and said –

'Looking-glass, Looking-glass, on the wall,
Who in this land is the fairest of all?'

The looking-glass answered –

'Thou, O Queen, art the fairest of all!'

Then she was satisfied, for she knew that the looking-glass spoke the truth.

But Snow-white was growing up, and grew more and more beautiful; and when she was seven years old she was as beautiful as the day, and more beautiful than the Queen herself. And once when the Queen asked her looking-glass –

'Looking-glass, Looking-glass, on the wall,
Who in this land is the fairest of all?'

It answered –

'Thou art fairer than all who are here, Lady Queen,
But more beautiful still is Snow-white, as I ween.'

Then the Queen was shocked, and turned yellow and green with envy. From that hour, whenever she looked at Snow-white, her heart heaved in her breast, she hated the girl so much.

And envy and pride grew higher and higher in her heart like a weed, so that she had no peace day or night. She called a huntsman, and said, 'Take the child away into the forest; I will no longer have her in my sight.

Kill her, and bring me back her heart as a token.' The huntsman obeyed, and took her away; but when he had drawn his knife, and was about to pierce Snow-white's innocent heart, she began to weep, and said, 'Ah, dear huntsman, leave me my life! I will run away into the wild forest and never come home again.'

And as she was so beautiful the huntsman had pity on her and said, 'Run away, then, you poor child.' 'The wild beasts will soon have devoured you,' thought he, and yet it seemed as if a stone had been rolled from his heart since it was no longer needful for him to kill her. And as a young boar just then came running by he stabbed it and cut out its heart and took it to the Queen as a proof that the child was dead. The cook had to salt this, and the wicked Queen ate it, and thought she had eaten the heart of Snow-white.

But now the poor child was all alone in the great forest, and so terrified that she looked at every leaf of every tree, and did not know what to do. Then she began to run, and ran over sharp stones and through thorns, and the wild beasts ran past her, but did her no harm.

She ran as long as her feet would go until it was almost evening; then she saw a little cottage and went into it to rest herself. Everything in the cottage was small, but neater and cleaner than can be told. There was a table on which was a white cover, and seven little plates, and on each plate a little spoon; moreover, there were seven little knives and forks, and seven little mugs. Against the wall stood seven little beds side by side, and covered with Snow-white counterpanes.

Little Snow-white was so hungry and thirsty that she

ate some vegetables and bread from each plate and drank a drop of wine out of each mug, for she did not wish to take all from one only. Then, as she was so tired, she laid herself down on one of the little beds, but none of them suited her; one was too long, another too short, but at last she found that the seventh one was right, and so she remained in it, said a prayer and went to sleep.

When it was quite dark the owners of the cottage came back; they were seven dwarfs who dug and delved in the mountains for ore. They lit their seven candles, and as it was not light within the cottage they saw that some one had been there, for everything was not in the same order in which they had left it.

The first said, 'Who has been sitting on my chair?'

The second, 'Who has been eating off my plate?'

The third, 'Who has been taking some of my bread?'

The fourth, 'Who has been eating my vegetables?'

The fifth, 'Who has been using my fork?'

The sixth, 'Who has been cutting with my knife?'

The seventh, 'Who has been drinking out of my mug?'

Then the first looked round and saw that there was a little hole on his bed, and he said, 'Who has been getting into my bed?' The others came up and each called out, 'Somebody has been lying in my bed too.' But the seventh when he looked at his bed saw little Snow-white, who was lying asleep therein. And he called the others, who came running up, and they cried out with astonishment, and brought their seven little candles and let the light fall on little Snow-white. 'Oh, heavens! oh, heavens!' cried they, 'what a lovely child!' and they were so glad that they did not wake her up, but let her sleep on in the bed. And the seventh dwarf slept with his companions, one hour with each, and so got through the night.

When it was morning little Snow-white awoke, and was frightened when she saw the seven dwarfs. But they were friendly and asked her what her name was. 'My name is Snow-white,' she answered. 'How have you come to our house?' said the dwarfs. Then she told them that her step-mother had wished to have her killed, but that the huntsman had spared her life, and that she had run for the whole day, until at last she had found their dwelling. The dwarfs said, 'If you will take care of our house, cook, make the beds, wash, sew and knit, and if you will keep everything neat and clean, you can stay with us and you shall want for nothing.' 'Yes,' said Snow-white, 'with all my heart,' and she stayed with them. She kept the house in order for them; in the mornings they went to the mountains and looked for copper and gold, in the evenings they came back, and then their supper had to be ready. The girl was alone the whole day, so the good dwarfs warned her and said, 'Beware of your step-mother, she will soon know that you are here; be sure to let no one come in.'

But the Queen, believing that she had eaten Snow-white's heart, could not but think that she was again the first and most beautiful of all; and she went to her looking-glass and said –

'Looking-glass, Looking-glass, on the wall,
Who in this land is the fairest of all?'

And the glass answered –

'Oh, Queen, thou art fairest of all I see,
But over the hills, where the seven dwarfs dwell,
Snow-white is still alive and well,
And none is so fair as she.'

Then she was astounded, for she knew that the looking-glass never spoke falsely, and she knew that the huntsman had betrayed her, and that little Snow-white was still alive.

And so she thought and thought again how she might kill her, for so long as she was not the fairest in the whole land, envy let her have no rest. And when she had at last thought of something to do, she painted her face, and dressed herself like an old peddler-woman, and no one could have known her. In this disguise she went over the seven mountains to the seven dwarfs, and knocked at the door and cried, 'Pretty things to sell, very cheap, very cheap.' Little Snow-white looked out of the window and called out, 'Good – day, my good woman, what have you to sell?' 'Good things, pretty things," she answered; 'stay-laces of all colours,' and she pulled out one which was woven of bright-coloured silk. 'I may let the worthy old woman in,' thought Snow-white, and she unbolted the door and bought the pretty laces. 'Child,' said the old woman, 'what a fright you look; come, I will lace you properly for once.' Snow-white had no suspicion, but stood before her, and let herself be laced with the new laces. But the old woman laced so quickly and laced so tightly that Snow-white lost her breath and fell down as if dead. 'Now I am the most beautiful,' said the Queen to herself, and ran away.

Not long afterwards, in the evening, the seven dwarfs came home, but how shocked they were when they saw their dear little Snow-white lying on the ground, and that she neither stirred nor moved, and seemed to be dead. They lifted her up, and, as they saw that she was laced too tightly, they cut the laces; then she began to breathe a little, and after a while came to life again. When the dwarfs heard what had happened they said, 'The old peddler-woman was no one else than the wicked Queen; take care and let no one come in when we are not with you.'

But the wicked woman when she had reached home went in front of the glass and asked –

> 'Looking-glass, Looking-glass, on the wall,
> Who in this land is the fairest of all?'

And it answered as before –

> 'Oh, Queen, thou art fairest of all I see,
> But over the hills, where the seven dwarfs dwell,
> Snow-white is still alive and well,
> And none is so fair as she.'

When she heard that, all her blood rushed to her

heart with fear, for she saw plainly that little Snow-white was again alive. 'But now,' she said, 'I will think of something that shall put an end to you,' and by the help of witchcraft, which she understood, she made a poisonous comb. The she disguised herself and took the shape of another old woman. So she went over the seven mountains to the seven dwarfs, knocked at the door, and cried, 'Good things to sell cheap, cheap!' Little Show-white looked out and said, 'Go away; I cannot let anyone come in.' 'I suppose you can look,' said the old woman, and pulled the poisonous comb out and held it up. It pleased the girl so well that she let herself be beguiled, and opened the door. When they had made a bargain the old woman said, 'Now I will comb you properly for once.' Poor little Snow-white had no suspicion, and let the old woman do as she pleased, but hardly had she put the comb in her hair than the poison in it took effect, and the girl fell down senseless. 'You paragon of beauty,' said the wicked woman, 'you are done for now,' and she went away.

But fortunately it was almost evening, when the seven dwarfs came home. When they saw Snow-white lying as if dead upon the ground, they at once suspected the step-mother, and they looked and found the poisoned comb. Scarcely had they taken it out when Snow-white came to herself, and told them what had happened. Then they warned her once more to be upon her guard and to open the door to no one.

The Queen, at home, went in front of the glass and said –

'Looking-glass, Looking-glass, on the wall,
Who in this land is the fairest of all?'

Then it answered as before –

'Oh, Queen, thou art fairest of all I see,
But over the hills, where the seven dwarfs dwell,
Snow-white is still alive and well,
And none is so fair as she.'

When she heard the glass speak thus she trembled and shook with rage. 'Snow-white shall die,' she cried, 'even if it costs me my life!'

Thereupon she went into a quite secret, lonely room, where no one ever came, and there she made a very poisonous apple. Outside it looked pretty, white with a red cheek, so that every one who saw it longed for it; but whoever ate a piece of it must surely die.

When the apple was ready, she painted her face, and dressed herself up as a country-woman, and so she went over the seven mountains to the seven dwarfs. She knocked at the door. Snow-white put her head out of the window and said, 'I cannot let anyone in; the seven dwarfs have forbidden me.' 'It is all the same to me,' answered the woman, 'I shall soon get rid of my apples. There, I will give you one.'

'No,' said Snow-white, 'I dare not take anything.' 'Are you afraid of poison?' said the old woman; 'look, I will cut the apple in two pieces; you eat the red cheek, and I will eat the white.' The apple was so cunningly made that only the red cheek was poisoned.

Snow-white longed for the fine apple, and when she saw that the woman ate part of it she could resist no longer, and stretched out her hand and took the poisonous half. But hardly had she a bit of it in her mouth than she fell down dead. Then the Queen looked at her with a dreadful look, and laughed aloud and said, 'White as snow, red as blood, black as ebony-wood! This time the dwarfs cannot wake you up again.'

And when she asked of the Looking-glass at home –

> 'Looking-glass, Looking-glass, on the wall,
> Who in this land is the fairest of all?'

It answered at last –

> 'Oh, Queen, in this land thou art fairest of all.'

Then her envious heart had rest, so far as an envious heart can have rest.

The dwarfs, when they came home in the evening, found Snow-white lying upon the ground; she breathed no longer and was dead. They lifted her up, looked to see whether they could find anything poisonous, unlaced her, combed her hair, washed her with water and wine, but it was all of no use; the poor child was dead, and remained dead. They laid her upon a bier, and all seven of them sat round it and wept for her, and wept three days long.

Then they were going to bury her, but she still looked as if she were living, and still had her pretty red cheeks. They said, 'We could not bury her in the dark ground,' and they had a transparent coffin of glass made, so that she could be seen from all sides, and they laid her in it, and wrote her name upon it in golden letters, and that she was a king's daughter. Then they put the coffin out upon the mountain, and one of them always stayed by it and watched it. And birds came too, and wept for Snow-white, first an owl, then a raven, and last a dove.

And now Snow-white lay a long, long time in the coffin, and she did not change, but looked as if she were asleep; for she was as white as snow, as red as blood, and her hair was as black as ebony.

It happened, however, that a king's son came into the forest, and went to the dwarfs' house to spend the night. He saw the coffin on the mountain, and the beautiful Snow-white within it, and read what was written upon it in golden letters. Then he said to the dwarfs, 'Let me have the coffin, I will give you whatever you want for it.' But the dwarfs answered, 'We will not part with it for all the gold in the world.' Then he said, 'Let me have it as a gift, for I cannot live without seeing Snow-white. I will honour and prize her as my dearest possession.' As he spoke in this way the good dwarfs took pity upon him, and gave him the coffin.

And now the King's son had it carried away by his servants on their shoulders. And it happened that they stumbled over a treestump, and with the shock the poisonous piece of apple which Snow-white had bitten off came out of her throat. And before long she opened her eyes, lifted up the lid of the coffin, sat up, and was once more alive. 'Oh, heavens, where am I?' she cried. The King's son, full of joy, said, 'You are with me,' and told her what had happened, and said, 'I love you more than everything in the world; come with me to my father's palace, you shall be my wife.'

And Snow-white was willing, and went with him, and their wedding was held with great show and splendour. But Snow-white's wicked step-mother was also bidden to the feast. When she had arrayed herself in beautiful clothes she went before the Looking-glass, and said –

'Looking-glass, Looking-glass, on the wall,
Who in this land is the fairest of all?'

The glass answered –

'Oh, Queen, of all here the fairest art thou,
But the young Queen is fairer by far as I trow.'

Then the wicked woman uttered a curse, and was so wretched, so utterly wretched, that she knew not what to do. At first she would not go to the wedding at all, but she had no peace, and must go to see the young Queen. And when she went in she knew Snow-white; and she stood still with rage and fear, and could not stir. But iron slippers had already been put upon the fire, and they were brought in with tongs, and set before her. Then she was forced to put on the red-hot shoes, and dance until she dropped down dead.

# *Rapunzel*

There were once a man and a woman who had long in vain wished for a child. At length the woman hoped that God was about to grant her desire. These people had a little window at the back of their house from which a splendid garden could be seen, which was full of the most beautiful flowers and herbs. It was, however, surrounded by a high wall, and no one dared to go into it because it belonged to an enchantress, who had great power and was dreaded by all the world. One day the woman was standing by this window and looking down into the garden, when she saw a bed which was planted with the most beautiful rampion (rapunzel), and it looked so fresh and green that she longed for it, she quite pined away, and began to look pale and miserable. Then her husband was alarmed, and asked: 'What ails you, dear wife?' 'Ah,' she replied, 'if I can't eat some of the rampion, which is in the garden behind our house, I shall die.' The man, who loved her, thought: 'Sooner than let your wife die, bring her some of the rampion yourself, let it cost what it will.' At twilight, he clambered down over the wall into the garden of the enchantress, hastily clutched a handful of rampion, and took it to his wife. She at once made herself a salad of it, and ate it greedily. It tasted so good to her — so very good, that the next day she longed for it three times as much as before. If he was to have any rest, her husband must once more descend into the garden. In the gloom of evening therefore, he let himself down again; but when he had clambered down the wall he was terribly afraid, for he saw the enchantress standing before him. 'How can you dare,' said she with angry look, 'descend into my garden and steal my rampion like a thief? You shall suffer for it!' 'Ah,' answered he, 'let mercy take the place of justice, I only made up my mind to do it out of necessity. My wife saw your rampion from the window, and felt such a longing for it that she would have died if she had not got some to eat.' Then the enchantress allowed her anger to be softened, and said to him: 'If the case be as you say, I will allow you to take away with you as much rampion as you will, only I make one condition, you must give me the child which your wife will bring into the world; it shall be well treated, and I will care for it like a mother.' The man in his terror consented to everything, and when the woman was brought to bed, the enchantress appeared at once, gave the child the name of Rapunzel, and took it away with her.

Rapunzel grew into the most beautiful child under the sun. When she was twelve years old, the enchantress shut her into a tower, which lay in a forest, and had neither stairs nor door, but quite at the top was a little window. When the enchantress wanted to go in, she placed herself beneath it and cried:

'Rapunzel, Rapunzel,
Let down your hair to me.'

Rapunzel had magnificent long hair, fine as spun gold, and when she heard the voice of the enchantress she unfastened her braided tresses, wound them round one of the hooks of the window above, and then the hair fell twenty ells down, and the enchantress climbed up by it.

After a year or two, it came to pass that the king's son rode through the forest and passed by the tower. Then he heard a song, which was so charming that he stood still and listened. This was Rapunzel, who in her solitude passed her time in letting her sweet voice resound. The king's son wanted to climb up to her, and looked for the door of the tower, but none was to be found. He rode home, but the singing had so deeply touched his heart, that every day he went out into the forest and listened to it. Once when he was thus standing behind a tree, he saw that an enchantress came there, and he heard how she cried:

'Rapunzel, Rapunzel,
Let down your hair to me.'

Then Rapunzel let down the braids of her hair, and the enchantress climbed up to her. 'If that is the ladder by which one mounts, I too will try my fortune,' said he, and the next day when it began to grow dark, he went to the tower and cried:

'Rapunzel, Rapunzel,
Let down your hair to me.'

Immediately the hair fell down and the king's son climbed up.

At first Rapunzel was terribly frightened when a man, such as her eyes had never yet beheld, came to her; but the king's son began to talk to her quite like a friend, and told her that his heart had been so stirred that it had let him have no rest, and he had been forced to see her. Then Rapunzel lost her fear, and when he asked her if she would take him for her husband, and she saw that he was young and handsome, she thought: 'He will love me more than old Dame Gothel does'; and she said yes, and laid her hand in his. She said: 'I will willingly go away with you, but I do not know how to get down. Bring with you a skein of silk every time that you come, and I will weave a ladder with it, and when that is ready I will descend, and you will take me on your horse.' They agreed that until that time he should come to her every evening, for the old woman came by day. The enchantress remarked nothing of this, until once Rapunzel said to her: 'Tell me, Dame Gothel, how it happens that you are so much heavier for me to draw up than the young king's son — he is with me in a moment.' 'Ah! you wicked child,' cried the enchantress. 'What do I hear you say! I thought I had separated you from all the world, and yet you have deceived me!' In her anger she clutched Rapunzel's beautiful tresses, wrapped them twice round her left hand, seized a pair of scissors with the right, and snip, snap, they were cut off, and the lovely braids lay on the ground. And she was so pitiless that she took poor Rapunzel into a desert where she had to live in great grief and misery.

On the same day that she cast out Rapunzel, however, the enchantress fastened the braids of hair, which she had cut off, to the hook of the window, and when the king's son came and cried:

'Rapunzel, Rapunzel,
Let down your hair to me.'

she let the hair down. The king's son ascended, but instead of finding his dearest Rapunzel, he found the enchantress, who gazed at him with wicked and venomous looks. 'Aha!' she cried mockingly, 'you would fetch your dearest, but the beautiful bird sits no longer singing in the nest; the cat has got it, and will scratch out your eyes aswell. Rapunzel is lost to you; you will never see her again.' The king's son was beside himself with pain, and in his despair he leapt down from the tower. He escaped with his life, but the thorns into which he fell pierced his eyes. Then he wandered quite blind about the forest, ate nothing but roots and berries, and did naught but lament and weep over the loss of his dearest wife. Thus he roamed about in misery for some years, and at length came to the desert where Rapunzel, with the twins to which she had given birth, a boy and a girl, lived in wretchedness. He heard a voice, and it seemed so familiar to him that he went towards it, and when he approached, Rapunzel knew him and fell on his neck and wept. Two of her tears wetted his eyes and they grew clear again, and he could see with them as before. He led her to his kingdom where he was joyfully received, and they lived for a long time afterwards, happy and contented.

# *The Frog-King, Or Iron Henry*

In old times when wishing still helped one, there lived a king whose daughters were all beautiful, but the youngest was so beautiful that the sun itself, which has seen so much, was astonished whenever it shone in her face. Close by the King's castle lay a great dark forest, and under an old lime-tree in the forest was a well, and when the day was very warm, the King's child went out into the forest and sat down by the side of the cool fountain, and when she was dull she took a golden ball, and threw it up on high and caught it, and this ball was her favourite plaything.

Now it so happened that on one occasion the princess's golden ball did not fall into the little hand which she was holding up for it, but on to the ground beyond, and rolled straight into the water. The King's daughter followed it with her eyes, but it vanished, and the well was deep, so deep that the bottom could not be seen. On this she began to cry, and cried louder and louder, and could not be comforted. And as she thus lamented, some one said to her, 'What ails thee, King's daughter? Thou weepest so that even a stone would show pity.' She looked round to the side from whence the voice came, and saw a frog stretching forth its thick, ugly head from the water.

'Ah! old water-splasher, is it thou?' said she; 'I am weeping for my golden ball, which has fallen into the well.'

'Be quiet, and do not weep,' answered the frog. 'I can help thee, but what wilt thou give me if I bring thy plaything up again?' 'Whatever thou wilt have, dear frog,' said she – 'my clothes, my pearls and jewels, and even the golden crown which I am wearing.'

The frog answered, 'I do not care for thy clothes, thy pearls and jewels, or thy golden crown, but if thou wilt love me and let me be thy companion and play-fellow, and sit by thee at thy little table, and eat off thy little golden plate, and drink out of thy little cup, and sleep in thy little bed – if thou wilt promise me this I will go down below, and bring thee thy golden ball up again.'

'Oh, yes,' said she, 'I promise thee all thou wishest, if thou wilt but bring me my ball back again.' She, however, thought, 'How silly the frog does talk! He lives in the water with the other frogs and croaks, and can be no companion to any human being!'

But the frog when he had received this promise put his head into the water and sank down, and in a short time came swimming up again with the ball in his mouth, and threw it on the grass. The King's daughter was delighted to see her pretty plaything once more, and picked it up, and ran away with it.

'Wait, wait,' said the frog. 'Take me with thee. I can't run as thou canst.'

But what did it avail him to scream his croak, croak,

after her, as loudly as he could? She did not listen to it, but ran home and soon forgot the poor frog, who was forced to go back into his well again.

The next day when she had seated herself at table with the King and all the courtiers, and was eating from her little golden plate, something came creeping splish, splash, splish, splash, up the marble staircase, and when it had got to the top, it knocked at the door and cried, 'Princess, youngest princess, open the door for me.' She ran to see who was outside, but when she opened the door, there sat the frog in front of it. Then she slammed the door to, in great haste, sat down to dinner again, and was quite frightened. The King saw plainly that her heart was beating violently, and said, 'My child, what art thou so afraid of? Is there perchance a giant outside who wants to carry thee away?' 'Ah, no,' replied she, 'it is no giant, but a disgusting frog.'

'What does the frog want with thee?' 'Ah, dear father, yesterday when I was in the forest sitting by the well, playing, my golden ball fell into the water. And because I cried so, the frog brought it out again for me, and because he insisted so on it, I promised him he should be my companion, but I never thought he would be able to come out of his water! And now he is outside there, and wants to come in to me.'

In the meantime it knocked a second time, and cried,

> 'Princess! youngest princess!
> Open the door for me!

Dost thou not know what thou saidst to me
Yesterday by the cool waters of the fountain?
Princess, youngest princess!
Open the door for me!'

Then said the King, 'That which thou hast promised, must thou perform. Go and let him in.' She went and opened the door, and the frog hopped in and followed her, step by step, to her chair. There he sat still and cried, 'Lift me up beside thee.' She delayed, until at last the King commanded her to do it. When the frog was once on the chair he wanted to be on the table, and when he was on the table he said, 'Now, push thy little golden plate nearer to me that we may eat together.' She did this, but it was easy to see that she did not do it willingly. The frog enjoyed what he ate, but almost every mouthful she took choked her. At length he said, 'I have eaten and am satisfied; now I am tired, carry me into thy little room and make thy little silken bed ready, and we will both lie down and go to sleep.'

The King's daughter began to cry, for she was afraid of the cold frog which she did not like to touch, and which was now to sleep in her pretty, clean little bed. But the King grew angry and said, 'He who helped thee when thou went in trouble ought not afterwards to be despised by thee.' So she took hold of the frog with two fingers, carried him upstairs, and put him in a corner. But when she was in bed he crept to her and said, 'I am tired, I want to sleep as well as thou, lift me up or I will tell thy father.' Then she was terribly angry, and took him up and threw him with all her might against the wall. 'Now, thou wilt be quiet, odious frog,' said she. But when he fell down he was no frog but a king's son with beautiful, kind eyes. He by her father's will was now her dear companion and husband. Then he told her how he had been bewitched by a wicked witch, and how no one could have delivered him from the well but herself, and that to-morrow they would go together into his kingdom. Then they went to sleep, and next morning when the sun awoke them, a carriage came driving up with eight white horses, which had white ostrich feathers on their heads, and were harnessed with golden chains, and behind stood the young King's servant, faithful Henry. Faithful Henry had been so unhappy when his master was changed into a frog, that he had caused three iron bands to be laid round his heart, lest it should burst with grief and sadness.

The carriage was to conduct the young King into his kingdom. Faithful Henry helped them both in, and placed himself behind again, and was full of joy because of this deliverance. And when they had driven a part of the way, the King's son heard a cracking behind him as if something had broken. So he turned round and cried, 'Henry, the carriage is breaking.'

'No, master, it is not the carriage. It is a band from my heart, which was put there in my great pain when you were a frog and imprisoned in the well.' Again and once again while they were on their way something cracked, and each time the King's son thought the carriage was breaking; but it was only the bands which were springing from the heart of faithful Henry because his master was set free and was happy.

# *The Three Little Men In The Wood*

There was once a man whose wife died, and a woman whose husband died, and the man had a daughter, and the woman also had a daughter. The girls were acquainted with each other, and went out walking together, and afterwards came to the woman in her house. Then said she to the man's daughter, 'Listen, tell thy father that I would like to marry him, and then thou shalt wash thyself in milk every morning, and drink wine, but my own daughter shall wash herself in water and drink water.' The girl went home, and told her father what the woman had said. The man said, 'What shall I do? Marriage is a joy and also a torment.' At length as he could come to no decision, he pulled off his boot, and said, 'Take this boot, it has a hole in the sole of it. Go with it up to the loft, hang it on the big nail, and then pour water into it. If it hold the water, then I will again take a wife, but if it run through, I will not.' The girl did as she was ordered, but the water drew the hole together and the boot became full to the top. She informed her father how it had turned out. Then he himself went up, and when he saw that she was right, he went to the widow and wooed her, and the wedding was celebrated.

The next morning, when the two girls got up, there stood before the man's daughter milk for her to wash in and wine for her to drink, but before the woman's daughter stood water to wash herself with and water for drinking. On the second morning, stood water for washing and water for drinking before the man's daughter as well as before the woman's daughter. And on the third morning stood water for washing and water for drinking, before the man's daughter, and milk for washing and wine for drinking, before the woman's daughter, and so it continued. The woman became bitterly unkind to her step-daughter, and day by day did her best to treat her still worse. She was envious too because her step-daughter was beautiful and lovable, and her own daughter ugly and repulsive.

Once, in winter, when everything was frozen as hard as a stone, and hill and vale lay covered with snow, the woman made a frock of paper, called her step-daughter, and said, 'Here, put on this dress and go out into the wood, and fetch me a little basketful of strawberries, – I have a fancy for some.'

'Good heavens!' said the girl, 'no strawberries grow in winter! The ground is frozen, and besides the snow has covered everything. And why am I to go in this paper frock? It is so cold outside that one's very breath freezes! The wind will blow through the frock, and the thorns will tear it off my body.'

'Wilt thou contradict me again?' said the step-mother. 'See that thou goest, and do not show thy face again until thou hast the basketful of strawberries!' Then she gave her a little piece of hard bread, and said, 'This will last thee the day,' and thought, 'Thou wilt die of cold and hunger outside, and wilt never be seen again by me.'

Then the maiden was obedient, and put on the paper frock, and went out with the basket. Far and wide there was nothing but snow, and not a green blade to be seen. When she got into the wood she saw a small house out of which peeped three little dwarfs.[1] She wished them good day, and knocked modestly at the door. They cried, 'Come in,' and she entered the room and seated herself on the bench by the stove, where she began to warm herself and eat her breakfast. The elves said, 'Give us, too, some of it.' 'Willingly,' said she, and divided her bit of bread in two, and gave them the half. They asked, 'What dost thou here in the forest in the winter time, in thy thin dress?' 'Ah,' she answered, 'I am to look for a basketful of strawberries, and am not to go home until I can take them with me.' When she had eaten her bread, they gave her a broom and said, 'Sweep away the snow at the back door with it.' But when she was outside, the three little men said to each other, 'What shall we give her as she is so good, and has shared her bread with us?'

Then said the first, 'My gift is, that she shall every day grow more beautiful.' The second said, 'My gift is, that gold pieces shall fall out of her mouth every

1. In the original Haulemannerchen – i.e., Hohlen-Waldmannlein. They are so called because they live in eaves in the forests. They are little dwarfs with large heads, and are supposed to steal unbaptized children. – Tr.

time she speaks.' The third said, 'My gift is that a king shall come and take her to wife.'

The girl, however, did as the little men had bidden her, swept away the snow behind the little house with the broom, and what did she find but real ripe strawberries, which came up quite dark-red out of the snow! In her joy she hastily gathered her basket full, thanked the little men, shook hands with each of them, and ran home to take her step-mother what she had longed for so much. When she went in and said good-evening, a piece of gold at once fell out of her mouth. Thereupon she related what had happened to her in the wood, but with every word she spoke, gold pieces fell from her mouth, until very soon the whole room was covered with them. 'Now look at her arrogance,' cried the step-sister, 'to throw about gold in that way!' but she was secretly envious of it, and wanted to go into the forest also to seek strawberries. The mother said, 'No, my dear little daughter, it is too cold, thou mightest die of cold.' However, as her daughter let her have no peace, the mother at last yielded, made her a magnificent dress of fur, which she was obliged to put on, and gave her bread-and-butter and cake with her.

The girl went into the forest and straight up to the little house. The three little elves peeped out again, but she did not greet them, and without looking round at them and without speaking to them, she went awkwardly into the room, seated herself by the stove, and began to eat her bread-and-butter and cake. 'Give us some of it,' cried the little men; but she replied, 'There is not enough for myself, so how can I give it away to other people?' When she had done eating, they said, 'There is a broom for thee, sweep all clean for us outside by the back-door.' 'Humph! Sweep for yourselves,' she answered, 'I am not your servant.' When she saw that they were not going to give her anything she went out by the door. Then the little men said to each other, 'What shall we give her as she is so naughty, and has a wicked envious heart, that will never let her do a good turn to anyone?' The first said, 'I grant that she may grow uglier every day.' The second said, 'I grant that at every word she says, a toad shall spring out of her mouth.' The third said, 'I grant that she may die a miserable death.' The maiden looked for strawberries outside, but as she found none, she went angrily home. And when she opened her mouth, and was about to tell her mother what had happened to her in the wood, with every word she said, a toad sprang out of her mouth, so that everyone was seized with horror of her.

Then the step-mother was still more enraged, and thought of nothing but how to do every possible injury to the man's daughter, whose beauty, however, grew daily greater. At length she took a cauldron, set it on the fire, and boiled yarn in it. When it was boiled, she flung it on the poor girl's shoulder, and gave her an axe in order that she might go on the frozen river, cut a hole in the ice, and rinse the yarn. She was obedient, went thither and cut a hole in the ice; and while she was in the midst of her cutting, a splendid carriage came driving up, in which sat the King. The carriage stopped, and the King asked, 'My child, who art thou, and what art thou doing here?' 'I am a poor girl, and I am rinsing yarn.' Then the King felt compassion, and when he saw that she was so very beautiful, he said to her, 'Wilt thou go away with me?' 'Ah, yes, with all my heart,' she answered, for she was glad to get away from the mother and sister.

So she got into the carriage and drove away with the King, and when they arrived at his palace, the wedding was celebrated with great pomp, as the little men had granted to the maiden. When a year was over, the young Queen bore a son, and as the step-mother had heard of her great good-fortune, she came with her daughter to the palace and pretended that she wanted to pay her a visit. Once, however, when the King had gone out, and no one else was present, the wicked woman seized the Queen by the head, and her daughter seized her by the feet, and they lifted her out of the bed, and threw her out of the window into the stream which flowed by. Then the ugly daughter laid herself in the bed, and the old woman covered her up over her head. When the King came home again and wanted to speak to his wife, the old woman cried, 'Hush, hush, that can't be now, she is lying in a violent perspiration; you must let her rest to-day.' The King suspected no evil, and did not come back again till next morning; and as he talked with his wife and she answered him, with every word a toad leaped out, whereas formerly a piece of gold had fallen out. Then he asked what that could be, but the old woman said that she had got that from the violent perspiration, and would soon lose it again. During the night, however, the scullion saw a duck come swimming up the gutter, and it said,

'King, what art thou doing now?
Sleepest thou, or wakest thou?'

And as he returned no answer it said,

'And my guests, What may they do?'

The scullion said,

'They are sleeping soundly, too.'

Then it asked again,

'What does little baby mine?'

He answered,

'Sleepeth in her cradle fine.'

Then she went upstairs in the form of the Queen, nursed the baby, shook up its little bed, covered it over, and then swam away again down the gutter in the shape of a duck. She came thus for two nights; on the third, she said to the scullion, 'Go and tell the King to take his sword and swing it three times over me on the threshold.' Then the scullion ran and told this to the King, who came with his sword and swung it thrice over the spirit, and at the third time, his wife stood before him strong, living, and healthy as she had been before. Thereupon the King was full of great joy, but he kept the Queen hidden in a chamber until the Sunday when the baby was to be christened. And when it was christened he said, 'What does a person deserve who drags another out of bed and throws him in the water?' 'The wretch deserves nothing better,' answered the old woman, 'than to be taken and put in a barrel stuck full of nails, and rolled down hill into the water.' 'Then,' said the King, 'thou hast pronounced thine own sentence;' and he ordered such a barrel to be brought, and the old woman to be put into it with her daughter, and then the top was hammered on, and the barrel rolled down hill until it went into the river.

## *One-Eye, Two-Eyes, And Three-Eyes*

There was once a woman who had three daughters, the eldest of whom was called One-eye, because she had only one eye in the middle of her forehead, and the second, Two-eyes, because she had two eyes like other folks, and the youngest, Three-eyes, because she had three eyes; and her third eye was also in the centre of her forehead. However, as Two-eyes saw just as other human beings did, her sisters and her mother could not endure her. They said to her, 'Thou, with thy two eyes, art no better than the common people; thou dost not belong to us!' They pushed her about, and threw old clothes to her, and gave her nothing to eat but what they left, and did everything that they could to make her unhappy. It came to pass that Two-eyes had to go out into the fields and tend the goat, but she was still quite hungry, because her sisters had given her so little to eat. So she sat down on a ridge and began to weep, and so bitterly that two streams ran down from her eyes. And once when she looked up in her grief, a woman was standing beside her, who said, 'Why art thou weeping, little Two-eyes?' Two-eyes answered, 'Have I not reason to weep, when I have two eyes like other people, and my sisters and mother hate me for it, and push me from one corner to another, throw old clothes at me, and give me nothing to eat but the scraps they leave? To-day they have given me so little that I am still quite hungry.' Then the wise woman said, 'Wipe away thy tears, Two-eyes, and I will tell thee something to stop thee ever suffering from hunger again; just say to thy goat,

> 'Bleat, my little goat, bleat,
> Cover the table with something to eat,'

and then a clean well-spread little table will stand before thee, with the most delicious food upon it of which thou mayest eat as much as thou art inclined for, and when thou hast had enough, and hast no more need of the little table, just say,

> 'Bleat, bleat, my little goat, I pray,
> And take the table quite away,'

and then it will vanish again from thy sight.' Hereupon the wise woman departed. But Two-eyes thought, 'I must instantly make a trial, and see if what she said is true, for I am far too hungry,' and she said,

> 'Bleat, my little goat, bleat,
> Cover the table with something to eat,'

and scarcely had she spoken the words than a little table, covered with a white cloth, was standing there, and on it was a plate with a knife and fork, and a silver spoon; and the most delicious food was there also, warm and smoking as if it had just come out of the kitchen. Then Two-eyes said the shortest prayer she knew, 'Lord God, be with us always, Amen,' and helped herself to some food, and enjoyed it. And when she was satisfied, she said, as the wise woman had taught her,

'Bleat, bleat, my little goat, I pray,
And take the table quite away,'

and immediately the little table and everything on it was gone again. 'This is a delightful way of keeping house!' thought Two-eyes, and was quite glad and happy.

In the evening, when she went home with her goat, she found a small earthenware dish, with some food, which her sisters had set ready for her, but she did not touch it. Next day she again went out with her goat, and left the few bits of broken bread which had been handed to her, lying untouched. The first and second time that she did this, her sisters did not remark it at all, but as it happened every time, they did observe it, and said, 'There is something wrong about Two-eyes, she always leaves her food untasted, and she used to eat up everything that was given her; she must have discovered other ways of getting food.' In order that they might learn the truth, they resolved to send One-eye with Two-eyes when she went to drive her goat to the pasture, to observe what Two-eyes did when she was there, and whether any one brought her anything to eat and drink. So when Two-eyes set out the next time, One-eye went to her and said, 'I will go with you to the pasture, and see that the goat is well taken care of, and driven where there is food.' But Two-eyes knew what was in One-eye's mind, and drove the goat into high grass and said, 'Come, One-eye, we will sit down and I will sing something to you.' One-eye sat down and was tired with the unaccustomed walk and the heat of the sun, and Two-eyes sang constantly,

'One eye, wakest thou?
One eye, sleepest thou?'

until One-eye shut her one eye, and fell asleep, and as soon as Two-eyes saw that One-eye was fast asleep, and could discover nothing, she said,

'Bleat, my little goat, bleat,
Cover the table with something to eat,'

and seated herself at her table, and ate and drank until she was satisfied, and then she again cried,

'Bleat, bleat, my little goat, I pray,
And take the table quite away,'

and in an instant all was gone. Two-eyes now awakened One-eye, and said 'One-eye, you want to take care of the goat, and go to sleep while you are doing it, and in the meantime the goat might run all over the world. Come, let us go home again.' So they went home, and again Two-eyes let her little dish stand untouched, and One-eye could not tell her mother why she would not eat it, and to excuse herself said, 'I fell asleep when I was out.'

Next day the mother said to Three-eyes, 'This time thou shalt go and observe if Two-eyes eats anything when she is out, and if any one fetches her food and drink, for she must eat and drink in secret.' So Three-eyes went to Two-eyes, and said, 'I will go with you and see if the goat is taken proper care of, and driven where there is food.' But Two-eyes knew what was in Three-eyes' mind, and drove the goat into high-grass and said, 'We will sit down, and I will sing something to you, Three-eyes.' Three-eyes sat down and was tired with the walk and with the heat of the sun, and Two-eyes began the same song as before, and sang,

'Three eyes, are you waking?'

but then, instead of singing,

'Three eyes, are you sleeping?'

as she ought to have done, she thoughtlessly sang,

'Two eyes, are you sleeping?'

and sang all the time,

'Three eyes, are you waking?
Two eyes, are you sleeping?'

Then two of the eyes which Three-eyes had, shut and fell asleep, but the third, as it had not been named in the song, did not sleep. It is true that Three-eyes shut it, but only in her cunning, to pretend it was asleep too, but it blinked, and could see everything very well. And when Two-eyes thought that Three-eyes was fast asleep she used her little charm,

'Bleat, my little goat, bleat,
Cover the table with something to eat,'

and ate and drank as much as her heart desired, and then ordered the table to go away again,

'Bleat, bleat, my little goat, I pray,
And take the table quite away,'

and Three-eyes had seen everything. Then Two-eyes came to her, waked her and said, 'Have you been asleep, Three-eyes? You are a good care-taker! Come, we will go home.' And when they got home, Two-eyes again did not eat, and Three-eyes said to the mother, 'Now, I know why that high-minded thing there does not eat. When she is out, she says to the goat,

'Bleat, my little goat, bleat,
Cover the table with something to eat,'

and then a little table appears before her covered with the best of food, much better than any we have here, and when she has eaten all she wants, she says,

'Bleat, bleat, my little goat, I pray,
And take the table quite away,'

and all disappears. I watched everything closely. She put two of my eyes to sleep by using a certain form of words, but luckily the one in my forehead kept awake.' Then the envious mother cried, 'Dost thou want to fare better than we do? The desire shall pass away,' and she fetched a butcher's knife, and thrust it into the heart of the goat, which fell down dead.

When Two-eyes saw that, she went out full of trouble, seated herself on the ridge of grass at the edge of the field and wept bitter tears. Suddenly the wise woman once more stood by her side, and said, 'Two-eyes, why art thou weeping?' 'Have I not reason to weep?' she answered. 'The goat which covered the table for me every day when I spoke your charm, has been killed by my mother, and now I shall again have to bear hunger and want.' The wise woman said. 'Two-eyes, I will give thee a piece of good advice; ask the sisters to give thee the entrails of the slaughtered goat, and bury them in the ground in front of the house, and thy fortune will be made.' Then she vanished, and Two-eyes went home and said to her sisters, 'Dear sisters, do give me some part of my goat; I don't wish for what is good, but give me the entrails.' Then they laughed and said, 'If that's all you want, you can have it.' So Two-eyes took the entrails and buried them quietly in the evening, in front of the house-door, as the wise woman had counselled her to do.

Next morning, when they all awoke, and went to

the house-door, there stood a strangely magnificent tree with leaves of silver, and fruit of gold hanging among them, so that in all the wide world there was nothing more beautiful or precious. They did not know how the tree could have come there during the night, but Two-eyes saw that it had grown up out of the entrails of the goat, for it was standing on the exact spot where she had buried them. Then the mother said to One-eye, 'climb up, my child, and gather some of the fruit of the tree for us.' One-eye climbed up, but when she was about to get hold of one of the golden apples, the branch escaped from her hands, and that happened each time, so that she could not pluck a single apple, let her do what she might. Then said the mother, 'Three-eyes, do you climb up; you with your three eyes can look about you better than One-eye. One-eye slipped down, and Three-eyes climbed up. Three-eyes was not more skilful, and might search as she liked, but the golden apples always escaped her. At length the mother grew impatient, and climbed up herself, but could get hold of the fruit no better than One-eye and Three-eyes, for she always clutched empty air. Then said Two-eyes, 'I will just go up, perhaps I may succeed better.' The sisters cried, 'You indeed, with your two eyes, what can you do?' But Two-eyes climbed up, and the golden apples did not get out of her way, but came into her hand of their own accord, so that she could pluck them one after the other, and brought a whole apronful down with her. The mother took them away from her, and instead of treating poor Two-eyes any better for this, she and

One-eye and Three-eyes were only envious, because Two-eyes alone had been able to get the fruit, and they treated her still more cruelly.

It so befell that once when they were all standing together by the tree, a young knight came up. 'Quick, Two-eyes,' cried the two sisters, 'creep under this, and don't disgrace us!' and with all speed they turned an empty barrel which was standing close by the tree over poor Two-eyes, and they pushed the golden apples which she had been gathering, under it too. When the knight came nearer he was a handsome lord, who stopped and admired the magnificent gold and silver trees, and said to the two sisters, 'To whom does this fine tree belong? Anyone who would bestow one branch of it on me might in return for it ask whatsoever he desired.' Then One-eye and Three-eyes replied that the tree belonged to them, and that they would give him a branch. They both took great trouble, but they were not able to do it, for the branches and fruit both moved away from them every time. Then said the knight, 'It is very strange that the tree should belong to you, and that you should still not be able to break a piece off.' They again asserted that the tree was their property. Whilst they were saying so, Two-eyes rolled out a couple of golden apples from under the barrel to the feet of the knight, for she was vexed with One-eye and Three-eyes, for not speaking the truth. When the knight saw the apples he was astonished, and asked where they came from. One-eye and Three-eyes answered that they had another sister, who was not allowed to show herself, for she had only two eyes like any common person. The knight, however, desired to see her, and cried, 'Two-eyes, come forth.' Then Two-eyes, quite comforted, came from beneath the barrel, and the knight was surprised at her great beauty, and said, 'Thou, Two-eyes, canst certainly break off a branch from the tree for me.' 'Yes,' replied Two-eyes, 'that I certainly shall be able to do, for the tree belongs to me.' And she climbed up, and with the greatest ease broke off a branch with beautiful silver leaves and golden fruit, and gave it to the knight. Then said the knight, 'Two-eyes, what shall I give thee for it?' 'Alas!' answered Two-eyes, 'I suffer from hunger and thirst, grief and want, from early morning till late night; if you would take me with you, and deliver me from these things, I should be happy,' So the knight lifted Two-eyes on to his horse, and took her home with him to his father's castle, and there he gave her beautiful clothes and meat and drink to her heart's content, and as he loved her so much he married her, and the wedding was solemnized with great rejoicing. When Two-eyes was thus carried away by the handsome knight, her two sisters grudged her good fortune in downright earnest. 'The wonderful tree, however, still remains with us,' thought they, 'and even if we can gather no fruit from it, still every one will stand still and look at it, and come to us and admire it. Who knows what good things may be in store for us?' But next morning, the tree had vanished, and all their hopes were at an end. And when Two-eyes looked out of the window of her own little room to her great delight it was standing in front of it, and so it had followed her.

Two-eyes lived a long time in happiness. Once two poor women came to her in her castle, and begged for alms. She looked in their faces, and recognized her sisters, One-eye, and Three-eyes, who had fallen into such poverty that they had to wander about and beg their bread from door to door. Two-eyes, however, made them welcome, and was kind to them, and took care of them, so that they both with all their hearts repented the evil that they had done their sister in their youth.

# *The Spirit In The Bottle*

There was once a poor woodcutter who toiled from early morning till late night. When at last he had laid by some money he said to his boy, 'You are my only child, I will spend the money which I have earned with the sweat of my brow on your education; if you learn some honest trade you can support me in my old age, when my limbs have grown stiff and I am obliged to stay at home.' Then the boy went to a High School and learned diligently so that his masters praised him, and he remained there a long time. When he had worked through two classes, but was still not yet perfect in everything, the little pittance which the father had earned was all spent, and the boy was obliged to return home to him. 'Ah,' said the father, sorrowfully, 'I can give you no more, and in these hard times I cannot earn a farthing more than will suffice for our daily bread.' 'Dear father,' said the son, 'don't trouble yourself about it; if it is God's will it will turn to my advantage. I shall soon accustom myself to it.' When the father wanted to go into the forest to earn money by helping to pile and stack wood and also to chop it, the son said, 'I will go with you and help you.' 'Nay, my son,' said the father, 'that would be hard for you; you are not accustomed to rough work, and will not be able to bear it, besides I have only one axe and no money left wherewith to buy another.' 'Just go to the neighbour,' answered the son, 'he will lend you his axe until I have earned one for myself.' The father then borrowed an axe of the neighbour, and next morning at break of day they went into the forest together. The son helped his father and was quite merry and brisk about it. But when the sun was right over their heads, the father said, 'We will rest, and have our dinner, and then we shall work as well again.' The son took his bread in his hands, and said, 'Just you rest, father, I am not tired; I will walk up and down a little in the forest, and look for birds' nests.' 'Oh, you fool,' said the father, 'why should you want to run about there? Afterwards you will be tired, and no longer able to raise your arm; stay here, and sit down beside me.' The son, however, went into the forest, ate his bread, was very merry, peered in among the green branches to see if he could discover a bird's nest anywhere. So he went up and down to see if he could find a bird's nest, until at last he came to a great dangerous-looking oak, which certainly was already many hundred years old, and which five men could not have spanned. He stood still and looked at it, and thought, 'Many a bird must have built its nest in that.' Then all at once it seemed to him that he heard a voice. He listened and became aware that some one was crying in a very smothered voice, 'Let me out, let me out!' He looked around, but could discover nothing; nevertheless, he fancied that the voice came out of the ground. Then he cried, 'Where art thou?' The voice answered, 'I am down here amongst the roots of the oak-tree. Let me out! Let me out!' The scholar began to loosen the earth under the tree, and search among the roots, until at last he found a glass bottle in a little hollow. He lifted it up and held it against the light, and then saw a creature shaped like a frog springing up and down in it. 'Let me out! Let me out!' it cried anew, and the scholar thinking no evil, drew the cork out of the bottle. Immediately a spirit ascended from it, and began to grow, and grew so fast that in a very few moments he stood before the scholar, a terrible fellow as big as half the tree by which he was standing. 'Knowest thou,' he cried in an awful voice, 'what thy wages are for having let me out?' 'No,' replied the scholar fearlessly, 'how should I know that?' 'Then I will tell thee,' cried the spirit; 'I must strangle thee for it.' 'Thou shouldst have told me that sooner,' said the scholar, 'for I should then have left thee shut up, but my head shall stand fast for all thou canst do; more persons than one must be consulted about that.' 'More persons here, more persons there,' said the spirit. 'Thou shalt have the wages thou hast earned. Dost thou think that I was shut up there for such a long time as a favour? No, it was a punishment for me. I am the mighty Mercurius. Who so releases me, him must I strangle.' 'Softly,' answered the scholar, 'not so fast. I must first know that thou wert really shut up in that little bottle, and that thou art the right spirit. If indeed thou canst get in again, I will believe, and then thou mayst do as thou wilt with me. The spirit said haughtily, 'That is a very trifling feat,' drew himself together, and made himself as small and slender as he had been at first, so that he crept through the same opening, and right through the neck of the bottle in again. Scarcely was he within than the scholar thrust the cork he had drawn back into the bottle, and threw it among the roots of the oak into its old place, and the spirit was betrayed.

And now the scholar was about to return to his father, but the spirit cried very piteously. 'Ah, do let me out! Ah, do let me out!' 'No,' answered the scholar, 'not a second time! He who has once tried to take my life shall not be set free by me, now that I have caught him again.' 'If thou wilt set me free,' said the spirit, 'I will give thee so much that thou wilt have plenty all the days of thy life.' 'No,' answered the scholar, 'thou wouldst cheat me as thou didst the first time.' 'Thou art playing away thy own good luck,' said the spirit; 'I will do thee no harm, but will reward thee richly.' The scholar thought, 'I will venture it, perhaps he will keep his word, and anyhow he shall not get the better of me.' Then he took out the cork, and the spirit rose up from the bottle as he had done before, stretched himself out and became as big as a giant. 'Now thou shalt have thy reward,' said he, and handed the scholar a little bag just like a plaster, and said, 'If thou spreadest one end of this over a wound it will heal, and if thou rubbest steel or iron with the other end it will be changed into silver.' 'I must just try that,' said the scholar, and went to a tree, tore off the bark with his axe, and rubbed it with one end of the plaster. It immediately closed together and was healed. 'Now, it is all right,' he said to the spirit, 'and we can part.' The spirit thanked him for his release, and the scholar thanked the spirit for his present, and went back to his father.

'Where hast thou been racing about?' said the father; 'why hast thou forgotten thy work? I said at once that thou wouldst never get on with anything.' 'Be easy, father, I will make it up.' 'Make it up indeed,' said the father angrily, 'there's no art in that.' 'Take care, father, I will soon hew that tree there, so that it will split.' Then he took his plaster, rubbed the axe with it, and dealt a mighty blow, but as the iron had changed into silver, the edge turned: 'Hollo, father, just look what a bad axe you've given me, it has become quite crooked.' The father was shocked and said, 'Ah, what hast thou done? now I shall have to pay for that, and have not the wherewithal, and that is all the good I have got by thy work.' 'Don't get angry,' said the son, 'I will soon pay for the axe.' 'Oh, thou blockhead,' cried the father, 'wherewith wilt thou pay for it? Thou hast nothing but what I give thee. These are students' tricks that are sticking in thy head, but thou hast no idea of wood-cutting.' After a while the scholar said, 'Father, I can really work no more, we had better take a holiday.' 'Eh, what!' answered he. 'Dost thou think I will sit with my hands lying in my lap like thee? I must go on working, but thou mayst take thyself off home.' 'Father, I am here in this wood for the first time, I don't know my way alone. Do go with me.' As his anger had now abated, the father at last let himself be persuaded and went home with him. Then he said to the son, 'Go and sell thy damaged axe, and see what thou canst get for it, and I must earn the difference, in order to pay the neighbour.' The son took the axe, and carried it into town to a goldsmith, who tested it, laid it in the scales, and said, 'It is worth four hundred thalers, I have not so much as that by me.' The son said, 'Give me what you have, I will lend you the rest.' The goldsmith gave him three hundred thalers, and remained a hundred in his debt. The son thereupon went home and said, 'Father, I have got the money, go and ask the neighbour what he wants for the axe.' 'I know that already,' answered the old man, 'one thaler six groschen.' 'Then give him two thalers, twelve groschen, that is double and enough; see, I have money in plenty,' and he gave the father a hundred thalers, and said, 'You shall never know want, live as comfortably as you like.' 'Good heavens!' said the father, 'how hast thou come by these riches?' The scholar then told how all had come to pass, and how he, trusting in his luck, had made such a good hit. But with the money that was left, he went back to the High School and went on learning more, and as he could heal all wounds with his plaster, he became the mostfamous doctor in the whole world.

# *Wise Folks*

One day a peasant took his good hazel-stick out of the corner and said to his wife, 'Trina, I am going across country, and shall not return for three days. If during that time the cattle-dealer should happen to call and want to buy our three cows, you may strike a bargain at once, but not unless you can get two hundred thalers for them; nothing less, do you hear?' 'For heaven's sake just go in peace,' answered the woman, 'I will manage that.' 'You, indeed,' said the man. 'You once fell on your head when you were a little child, and that affects you even now; but let me tell you this, if you do anything foolish, I will make your back black and blue, and not with paint, I assure you, but with the stick which I have in my hand, and the colouring shall last a whole year, you may rely on that.' And having said that, the man went on his way.

Next morning the cattle-dealer came, and the woman had no need to say many words to him. When he had seen the cows and heard the price, he said, 'I am quite willing to give that; honestly speaking, they are worth it. I will take the beasts away with me at once.' He unfastened their chains and drove them out of the byre, but just as he was going out of the yard-door, the woman clutched him by the sleeve and said, 'You must give me the two hundred thalers now, or I cannot let the cows go. 'True,' answered the man, 'but I have forgotten to buckle on my money-belt. Have no fear, however, you shall have security for my paying. I will take two cows with me and leave one, and then you will have a good pledge.' The woman saw the force of this, and let the man go away with the cows, and thought to herself, 'How pleased Hans will be when he finds how cleverly I have managed it!' The peasant came home on the third day as he had said he would, and at once inquired if the cows were sold? 'Yes, indeed, dear Hans,' answered the woman, 'and as you said, for two hundred thalers. They are scarcely worth so much, but the man took them without making any objection.' 'Where is the money?' asked the peasant. 'Oh, I have not got the money,' replied the woman; 'he had happened to forget his money-belt, but he will soon bring it, and he left good security behind him.' 'What kind of security?' asked the man. 'One of the three cows, which he shall not have until he has paid for the other two. I have managed very cunningly, for I have kept the smallest, which eats the least.' The man was enraged and lifted up his stick, and was just going to give her the beating he had promised her. Suddenly he let the stick fall and said, 'You are the stupidest goose that ever waddled on God's earth, but I am sorry for you. I will go out into the highways and wait for three days to see if I find anyone who is still stupider than you. If I succeed in doing so, you shall go scot-free, but if I do not find him, you shall receive your well-deserved reward without any discount.'

He went out into the great highways, sat down on a stone, and waited for what would happen. Then he saw a peasant's waggon coming towards him, and a woman was standing upright in the middle of it, instead of sitting on the bundle of straw which was lying beside her, or walking near the oxen and leading them. The man thought to himself, 'That is certainly one of the kind I am in search of,' and jumped up and ran backwards and forwards in front of the waggon like one who is not very wise. 'What do you want, my friend?' said the woman to him; 'I don't know you, where do you come from?' 'I have fallen down from Heaven,' replied the man, 'and don't know how to get back again, couldn't you drive me up?' 'No,' said the woman, 'I don't know the way, but if you come from Heaven you can surely tell me how my husband, who has been there these three years, is. You must have seen him?' 'Oh, yes, I have seen him, but all men can't get on well. He keeps sheep, and the sheep give him a great deal to do. They run up the mountains and lose their way in the wilderness, and he has to run after them and drive them together again. His clothes are all torn to pieces too, and will soon fall off his body. There is no tailor there, for Saint Peter won't let any of them in, as you know by the story.' 'Who would have thought it?' cried the woman, 'I tell you what, I will fetch his Sunday coat which is still hanging at home in the cupboard, he can wear that and look respectable. You will be so kind as to take it with you.' 'That won't do very well,' answered the peasant; 'people are not allowed to take clothes into Heaven, they are taken away from one at the gate.' 'Then hark you,' said the woman, 'I sold my fine wheat yesterday and got a good lot of money for it, I will send that to him. If you hide the purse in your pocket, no one will know that you have it.' 'If you can't manage it any other way,' said the peasant, 'I will do you that favour.' 'Just sit still where you are,' said she, 'and I will drive home and fetch the purse, I shall soon be back again. I do not sit down on the bundle of straw, but stand up in the waggon, because it makes it lighter for the cattle.' She drove her oxen away, and the peasant thought, 'that woman has a perfect talent for folly, if she really brings the money, my wife may think herself fortunate, for she will get no beating.' It was not long before she came in a great hurry with the money, and with her own hands put it in his pocket. Before she went away, she thanked him again a thousand times for his courtesy.

When the woman got home again, she found her son who had come in from the field. She told him what unlooked-for things had befallen her, and then added, 'I am truly delighted at having found an opportunity of sending something to my poor husband. Who would ever have imagined that he could be suffering for want of anything up in Heaven?' The son was full of astonishment. 'Mother,' said he, 'it is not every day that a man comes from Heaven in this way, I will go out immediately, and see if he is still to be found; he must tell me what it is like up there, and how the work is done.' He saddled the horse and rode off with all speed. He found the peasant who was sitting under a willow tree, and was just going to count the money in the purse. 'Have you seen the man who has fallen down from Heaven?' cried the youth to him. 'Yes,' answered the peasant, 'he has set out on his way back there, and has gone up that hill, from whence it will be rather nearer; you could still catch him up, if you were to ride fast.' 'Alas,' said the youth, 'I have been doing tiring work all day, and the ride here has completely worn me out; you know the man, be so kind as to get on my horse, and go and persuade him to come here.' 'Aha!' thought the peasant, 'here is another who has no wick in his lamp!' 'Why should I not do you this favour?' said he, and mounted the horse and rode off in a quick trot. The youth remained sitting there till night fell, but the peasant never came back. 'The man from Heaven must certainly have been in a great hurry, and would not turn back,' thought he, 'and the peasant has no doubt given him the horse to take to my father.' He went home and told his mother what had happened, and that he had sent his father the horse so that he might not have to be always running about. 'Thou hast done well,' answered she, 'thy legs are younger than his, and thou canst go on foot.'

When the peasant got home, he put the horse in the stable beside the cow which he had as a pledge, and then went to his wife and said, 'Trina, as your luck would have it, I have found two who are still sillier fools than you; this time you escape without a beating, I will store it up for another occasion.' Then he lighted his pipe, sat down in his grandfather's chair, and said, 'It was a good stroke of business to get a sleek horse and a great purse full of money into the bargain, for two lean cows. If stupidity always brought in as much as that I would be quite willing to hold it in honour.' So thought the peasant, but you no doubt prefer the simple folks.

# *The Girl Without Hands*

A certain miller had little by little fallen into poverty, and had nothing left but his mill and a large apple-tree behind it. Once when he had gone into the forest to fetch wood, an old man stepped up to him whom he had never seen before, and said, 'Why dost thou plague thyself with cutting wood, I will make thee rich, if thou wilt promise me what is standing behind the mill?' 'What can that be but my apple-tree?' thought the miller, and said, 'Yes,' and gave a written promise to the stranger. He, however, laughed mockingly and said, 'When three years have passed, I will come and carry away what belongs to me,' and then he went. When the miller got home, his wife came to meet him and said, 'Tell me, miller, from whence comes this sudden wealth into our house? All at once every box and chest was filled; no one brought it in, and I know not how it happened.' He answered, 'It comes from a stranger who met me in the forest, and promised me great treasure. I, in return, have promised him what stands behind the mill; we can very well give him the big apple-tree for it.' 'Ah, husband,' said the terrified wife, 'that must have been the devil! He did not mean the apple-tree, but our daughter, who was standing behind the mill sweeping the yard.'

The miller's daughter was a beautiful, pious girl, and lived through the three years in the fear of God and without sin. When therefore the time was over, and the day came when the Evil-one was to fetch her, she washed herself clean, and made a circle round herself with chalk. The devil appeared quite early, but he could not come near to her. Angrily, he said to the miller, 'Take all water away from her, that she may no longer be able to wash herself, for otherwise I have no power over her.' The miller was afraid, and did so. The next morning the devil came again, but she had wept on her hands, and they were quite clean. Again he could not get near her, and furiously said to the miller, 'Cut her hands off, or else I cannot get the better of her.' The miller was shocked and answered, 'How could I cut off my own child's hands?' Then the Evil-one threatened him and said, 'If thou dost not do it thou art mine, and I will take thee thyself.' The father became alarmed, and promised to obey him. So he went to the girl and said, 'My child, if I do not cut off both thine hands, the devil will carry me away, and in my terror I have promised to do it. Help me in my need, and forgive me the harm I do thee.' She replied, 'Dear father, do with me what you will, I am your child.' Thereupon she laid down both her hands, and let them be cut off. The devil came for the third time, but she had wept so long and so much on the stumps, that after all they were quite clean. Then he had to give in, and had lost all right over her.

The miller said to her, 'I have by means of thee received such great wealth that I will keep thee most delicately as long as thou livest.' But she replied, 'Here I cannot stay, I will go forth, compassionate people will give me as much as I require.' Thereupon she caused her maimed arms to be bound to her back, and by sunrise she set out on her way, and walked the whole day until night fell. Then she came to a royal garden, and by the shimmering of the moon she saw that trees covered with beautiful fruits grew in it, but she could not enter, for there was much water round about it. And as she had walked the whole day and not eaten one mouthful, and hunger tormented her, she thought, 'Ah, if I were but inside, that I might eat of the fruit, else must I die of hunger!' Then she knelt down, called on God the Lord, and prayed. And suddenly an angel came towards her, who made a dam in the water, so that the moat became dry and she could walk through it. And now she went into the garden and the angel went with her. She saw a tree covered with beautiful pears, but they were all counted. Then she went to them, and to still her hunger, ate one with her mouth from the tree, but no more. The gardener was watching; but as the angel was standing by, he was afraid and thought the maiden was a spirit and was silent, neither did he dare to cry out, or to speak to the spirit. When she had eaten the pear, she was satisfied, and went and concealed herself among the bushes. The King to whom the garden belonged, came down to it the next morning, and counted, and saw that one of the pears was missing, and asked the gardener what had become of it, as it was not lying beneath the tree, but was gone. Then answered the gardener, 'Last night, a spirit came in, who had no hands, and ate off one of the pears with its mouth.' The King said, 'How did the spirit get over the water, and where did it go after it had eaten the pear?' The gardener answered, 'Some one came in a snow-white garment from heaven who made a dam, and kept back the water, that the spirit might walk through the moat. And as it must have been an angel, I was afraid, and asked no questions, and did not cry out. When the spirit had eaten the pear, it went back again.' The King said, 'If it be as thou sayest, I will watch with thee to-night.'

When it grew dark the King came into the garden and brought a priest with him, who was to speak to the spirit. All three seated themselves beneath the tree and watched. At midnight the maiden came creeping out of the thicket, went to the tree, and again ate one pear off it with her mouth, and beside her stood the angel in white garments. Then the priest went out to them and said, 'Comest thou from heaven or from earth? Art thou a spirit, or a human being?' She replied, 'I am no spirit, but an unhappy mortal deserted by all but God.' The King said, 'If thou art forsaken by all the world, yet will I not forsake thee.' He took her with him into his royal palace, and as she was so beautiful and good, he loved her with all his heart, had silver hands made for her, and took her to wife.

After a year the King had to take the field, so he commended his young Queen to the care of his mother and said, 'If she is brought to bed take care of her, nurse her well, and tell me of it at once in a letter.' Then she gave birth to a fine boy. So the old mother made haste to write and announce the joyful news to him. But the messenger rested by a brook on the way, and as he was fatigued by the great distance, he fell asleep. Then came the Devil, who was always seeking to injure the good Queen, and exchanged the letter for another, in which was written that the Queen had brought a monster into the world. When the King read the letter he was shocked and much troubled, but he wrote in answer that they were to take great care of the Queen and nurse her well until his arrival. The messenger went back with the letter, but rested at the same place and again fell asleep. Then came the Devil once more, and put a different letter in his pocket, in which it was written that they were to put the Queen and her child to death. The old mother was terribly shocked when she received the letter, and could not believe it. She wrote back again to the King, but received no other answer, because each time the Devil substituted a false letter, and in the last letter it was also written that she was to preserve the Queen's tongue and eyes as a token that she had obeyed.

But the old mother wept to think such innocent blood was to be shed, and had a hind brought by night and cut out her tongue and eyes, and kept them. Then said she to the Queen, 'I cannot have thee killed as the King commands, but here thou mayst stay no longer. Go forth into the wide world with thy child, and never come here again.' The poor woman tied her child on her back, and went away with eyes full of tears. She came into a great wild forest, and then she fell on her knees and prayed to God, and the angel of the Lord appeared to her and led her to a little house on which was a sign with the words, 'Here all dwell free.' A snow-white maiden came out of the little house and said, 'Welcome, Lady Queen,' and conducted her inside. Then they unbound the little boy from her back, and held him to her breast that he might feed, and then laid him in a beautifully-made little bed. Then said the poor woman, 'From whence knowest thou that I was a queen?' The white maiden answered, 'I am an angel sent by God, to watch over thee, and thy child.' The Queen stayed seven years in the little house, and was well cared for, and by God's grace, because of her piety, her hands which had been cut off, grew once more.

At last the King came home again from the war, and his first wish was to see his wife and the child. Then his aged mother began to weep, and said, 'Thou wicked man, why didst thou write to me that I was to take those two innocent lives?' and she showed him the two letters which the Evil-one had forged, and then continued, 'I did as thou badest me,' and she showed the tokens, the tongue and eyes. Then the King began to weep for his poor wife and his little son so much more bitterly than she was doing, that the aged mother had compassion on him and said, 'Be at peace, she still lives; I secretly caused a hind to be killed, and took these tokens from it; but I bound the child to thy wife's back and bade her go forth into the wide world, and made her promise never to come back here again, because thou wert so angry with her.' Then spake the King, 'I will go as far as the sky is blue, and will neither eat nor drink until I have found again my dear wife and my child, if in the meantime they have not been killed, nor died of hunger.'

Thereupon the King travelled about for seven long years, and sought her in every cleft of the rocks and in every cave but he found her not, and thought she had died of want. During the whole of this time he neither ate nor drank, but God supported him. At length he came to a great forest, and found therein the little house whose sign was, 'Here all dwell free.' Then forth came the white maiden, took him by the hand, led him in, and said, 'Welcome, Lord King,' and asked him from whence he came. He answered, 'Soon shall I have travelled about for the space of seven years, and I seek my wife and her child, but cannot find them.' The angel offered him meat and drink, but he did not take anything, and only wished to rest a little. Then he lay down to sleep, and put a handkerchief over his face.

Thereupon the angel went into the chamber where the Queen sat with her son, whom she usually called 'Sorrowful,' and said to her. 'Go out with thy child, thy husband hath come.' So she went to the place where he lay, and the handkerchief fell from his face. Then said she, 'Sorrowful, pick up thy father's handkerchief, and cover his face again.' The child picked it up, and put it over his face again. The King in his sleep heard what passed, and had pleasure in letting the handkerchief fall once more. But the child grew impatient, and said, 'Dear mother, how can I cover my father's face when I have no father in this world? I have learnt to say the prayer, 'Our Father, which art in Heaven,' thou hast told me that my Father was in Heaven, and was the good God, and how can I know a wild man like this? He is not my father.' When the King heard that, he got up, and asked who they were. Then said she, 'I am thy wife, and that is thy son, Sorrowful.' And he saw her living hands, and said, 'My wife had silver hands.' She answered, 'The good God has caused my natural hands to grow again;' and the angel went into the inner room, and brought the silver hands, and showed them to him. Hereupon he knew for a certainty that it was his dear wife and his dear child, and he kissed them, and was glad, and said, 'A heavy stone has fallen from off my heart.' Then the angel of God gave them one meal with her, and after that they went home to the King's aged mother. There were great rejoicings everywhere, and the King and Queen were married again, and lived contentedly to their happy end.

# *The Six Swans*

Once upon a time, a certain King was hunting in a great forest, and he chased a wild beast so eagerly that none of his attendants could follow him. When evening drew near he stopped and looked around him, and then he saw that he had lost his way. He sought a way out, but could find none. Then he perceived an aged woman with a head which nodded perpetually, who came towards him, but she was a witch. 'Good woman,' said he to her, 'can you not show me the way through the forest?' 'Oh, yes Lord King,' she answered, 'that I certainly can, but on one condition, and if you do not fulfil that, you will never get out of the forest and will die of hunger in it.'

'What kind of condition is it?' asked the King.

'I have a daughter,' said the old woman, 'who is as beautiful as anyone in the world, and well deserves to be your consort, and if you will make her your Queen, I will show you the way out of the forest.' In the anguish of his heart the King consented, and the old woman led him to her little hut, where her daughter was sitting by the fire. She received the King as if she had been expecting him, and he saw that she was very beautiful, but still she did not please him, and he could not look at her without secret horror. After he had taken the maiden up on his horse, the old woman showed him the way, and the King reached his royal palace again, where the wedding was celebrated.

The King had already been married once, and had by his first wife seven children, six boys and a girl, whom he loved better than anything else in the world. As he now feared that the step-mother might not treat them well, and even do them some injury, he took them to a lonely castle which stood in the midst of a forest. It lay so concealed, and the way was so difficult to find, that he himself would not have found it, if a wise woman had not given him a ball of yarn with wonderful properties. When he threw it down before him, it unrolled itself and showed him his path. The King, however, went so frequently away to his dear children that the Queen observed his absence; she was curious and wanted to know what he did when he was quite alone in the forest. She gave a great deal of money to his servants, and they betrayed the secret to her, and told her likewise of the ball which alone could point out the way. And now she knew no rest until she had learnt where the King kept the ball of yarn, and then she made little shirts of white silk, and as she had learnt the art of witchcraft from her mother, she sewed a charm inside them. And once when the King had ridden forth to hunt, she took the little shirts and went into the forest, and the ball showed her the way. The children, who saw from a distance that some one was approaching, thought that their dear father was coming to them, and full of joy, ran to meet him. Then she threw one of the little shirts over each of them, and no sooner had the shirts touched their bodies than they were changed into swans, and flew away over the forest. The Queen went home quite delighted, and thought she had got rid of her step – children, but the girl had not run out with her brothers, and the Queen knew nothing about her. Next day the King went to visit his children, but he found no one but the little girl. 'Where are thy brothers?' asked the King. 'Alas, dear father,' she answered, 'they have gone away and left me alone!' and she told him that she had seen from her little window how her brothers had flown away over the forest in the shape of swans, and she showed him the feathers, which they had let fall in the courtyard, and which she had picked up. The King mourned, but he did not think that the Queen had done this wicked deed, and as he feared that the girl would also be stolen away from him, he wanted to take her away with him. But she was afraid of her stepmother, and entreated the King to let her stay just this one night more in the forest castle.

The poor girl thought, 'I can no longer stay here. I will go and seek my brothers.' And when night came, she ran away, and went straight into the forest. She walked the whole night long, and next day also without stopping, until she could go no farther for weariness. Then she saw a forest-hut, and went into it, and found a room with six little beds, but she did not venture to get into one of them, but crept under one, and lay down on the hard ground, intending to pass the night there. Just before sunset, however, she heard a rustling, and saw six swans come flying in at the window. They alighted on the ground and blew at each other, and blew all the feathers off, and their swan's skins stripped off like a shirt. Then the maiden looked at them and recognized her brothers, was glad and crept forth from beneath the bed. The brothers were not less delighted to see their little sister, but their joy was of short duration. 'Here canst thou not abide,' they said to her. 'This is a shelter for robbers, if they come home and find thee, they will kill thee.' 'But can you not protect me?' asked the little sister. 'No,' they replied, 'only for one quarter of an hour each evening can we lay aside our swan's skin and have during that time our human form, after that, we are once more turned into swans.' The little sister wept and said, 'Can you not be set free?' 'Alas, no,' they answered, 'the conditions are too hard! For six years thou mayest neither speak nor laugh, and in that time thou must sew together six little shirts of starwort for us. And if one single word falls from thy lips all thy work will be lost.' And when the brothers had said this, the quarter of an hour was over, and they flew out of the window again as swans.

The maiden, however, firmly resolved to deliver her brothers, even if it should cost her life. She left the hut, went into the midst of the forest, seated herself on a tree, and there passed the night. Next morning she went out and gathered starwort and began to sew. She could not speak to anyone, and she had no inclination to laugh; she sat there and looked at nothing but her work. When she had already spent a long time there it came to pass that the King of the country was hunting in the forest, and his huntsmen come to the tree on which the maiden was sitting. They called to her and said, 'Who art thou?' But she made no answer. 'Come down to us,' said they. 'We will not do thee any harm.' She only shook her head. As they pressed her further with questions she threw her golden necklace down to them, and thought to content them thus. They, however, did not cease, and then she threw her girdle down to them, and as this also was to no purpose, her garters and by degrees everything that she had on that she could do without until she had nothing left but her shift. The huntsmen, however, did not let themselves be turned aside by that, but climbed the tree and fetched the maiden down and led her before the King. The King asked, 'Who art thou? What art thou doing on the tree?' But she did not answer. He put the question in every language that he knew, but she remained as mute as a fish. As she was so beautiful, the King's heart was touched, and he was smitten with a great love for her. He put his mantle on her, took her before him on his horse, and carried her to his castle. Then he caused her to be dressed in rich garments, and she shone in her beauty like bright daylight, but no word could be drawn from her. He placed her by his side at table, and her modest bearing and courtesy pleased him so much that he said, 'She is the one whom I wish to marry, and no other woman in the world.' And after some days he united himself to her.

The King, however, had a wicked mother who was

dissatisfied with this marriage and spoke ill of the young Queen. 'Who knows,' said she, 'from whence the creature who can't speak, comes? She is not worthy of a king!' After a year had passed, when the Queen brought her first child into the world, the old woman took it away from her, and smeared her mouth with blood as she slept. Then she went to the King and accused the Queen of being a man-eater. The King would not believe it, and would not suffer anyone to do her any injury. She, however, sat continually sewing at the shirts, and cared for nothing else. The next time, when she again bore a beautiful boy, the false stepmother used the same treachery, but the King could not bring himself to give credit to her words. He said, 'She is too pious and good to do anything of that kind; if she were not dumb, and could defend herself, her innocence would come to light.' But when the old woman stole away the newly-born child for the third time, and accused the Queen, who did not utter one word of defence, the King could do no otherwise than deliver her over to justice, and she was sentenced to suffer death by fire.

When the day came for the sentence to be executed, it was the last day of the six years during which she was not to speak or laugh, and she had delivered her dear brothers from the power of the enchantment. The six shirts were ready, only the left sleeve of the sixth was wanting. When, therefore, she was led to the stake, she laid the shirts on her arm, and when she stood on high and the fire was just going to be lighted, she looked around and six swans came flying through the air towards her. Then she saw that her deliverance was near, and her heart leapt with joy. The swans swept towards her and sank down so that she could throw the shirts over them, and as they were touched by them, their swan's skins fell off, and her brothers stood in their own bodily form before her, and were vigorous and handsome. The youngest only lacked his left arm, and had in the place of it a swan's wing on his shoulder. They embraced and kissed each other, and the Queen went to the King, who was greatly moved, and she began to speak and said, 'Dearest husband, now I may speak and declare to thee that I am innocent, and falsely accused.' And she told him of the treachery of the old woman who had taken away her three children and hidden them. Then to the great joy of the King they were brought thither, and as a punishment, the wicked step-mother was bound to the stake, and burnt to ashes. But the King and the Queen with their six brothers lived many years in happiness and peace.

# *Fundevogel*

There was once a forester who went into the forest to hunt, and as he entered it he heard a sound of screaming as if a little child were there. He followed the sound, and at last came to a high tree, and at the top of this a little child was sitting, for the mother had fallen asleep under the tree with the child, and a bird of prey had seen it in her arms, had flown down, snatched it away, and set it on the high tree.

The forester climbed up, brought the child down, and thought to himself: 'You will take him home with you, and bring him up with your Lina.' He took it home, therefore, and the two children grew up together. And the one, which he had found on a tree was called Fundevogel, because a bird had carried it away. Fundevogel and Lina loved each other so dearly that when they did not see each other they were sad.

Now the forester had an old cook, who one evening took two pails and began to fetch water, and did not go once only, but many times, out to the spring. Lina saw this and said, 'Listen, old Sanna, why are you fetching so much water?' 'If you will never repeat it to anyone, I will tell you why.' So Lina said, no, she would never repeat it to anyone, and then the cook said: 'Early tomorrow morning, when the forester is out hunting, I will heat the water, and when it is boiling in the kettle, I will throw in Fundevogel, and will boil him in it.'

Early next morning the forester got up and went out hunting, and when he was gone the children were still in bed. Then Lina said to Fundevogel: 'If you will never leave me, I too will never leave you.' Fundevogel said: 'Neither now, nor ever will I leave you.' Then said Lina: 'Then will I tell you. Last night, old Sanna carried so many buckets of water into the house that I asked her why she was doing that, and she said that if I would promise not to tell anyone, she would tell me, and she said that early tomorrow morning when father was out hunting, she would set the kettle full of water, throw you into it and boil you; but we will get up quickly, dress ourselves, and go away together.'

The two children therefore got up, dressed themselves quickly, and went away. When the water in the kettle was boiling, the cook went into the bedroom to fetch Fundevogel and throw him into it. But when she came in, and went to the beds, both the children were gone. Then she was terribly alarmed, and she said to herself: 'What shall I say now when the forester comes home and sees that the children are gone? They must be followed instantly to get them back again.'

Then the cook sent three servants after them, who were to run and overtake the children. The children, however, were sitting outside the forest, and when they saw from afar the three servants running, Lina said to

Fundevogel: 'Never leave me, and I will never leave you.' Fundevogel said: 'Neither now, nor ever.' Then said Lina: 'Do you become a rose-tree, and I the rose upon it.' When the three servants came to the forest, nothing was there but a rose-tree and one rose on it, but the children were nowhere. Then said they: 'There is nothing to be done here,' and they went home and told the cook that they had seen nothing in the forest but a little rose-bush with one rose on it. Then the old cook scolded and said: 'You simpletons, you should have cut the rose-bush in two, and have broken off the rose and brought it home with you; go, and do it at once.' They had therefore to go out and look for the second time. The children, however, saw them coming from a distance. Then Lina said: 'Fundevogel, never leave me, and I will never leave you.' Fundevogel said: 'Neither now; nor ever.' Said Lina: 'Then do you become a church, and I'll be the chandelier in it.' So when the three servants came, nothing was there but a church, with a chandelier in it. They said therefore to each other: 'What can we do here, let us go home.' When they got home, the cook asked if they had not found them; so they said no, they had found nothing but a church, and there was a chandelier in it. And the cook scolded them and said: 'You fools! why did you not pull the church to pieces, and bring the chandelier home with you?' And now the old cook herself got on her legs, and went with the three servants in pursuit of the children. The children, however, saw from afar that the three servants were coming, and the cook waddling after them. Then said Lina: 'Fundevogel, never leave me, and I will never leave you.' Then said Fundevogel: 'Neither now, nor ever.' Said Lina: 'Be a fishpond, and I will be the duck upon it.' The cook, however, came up to them, and when she saw the pond she lay down by it, and was about to drink it up. But the duck swam quickly to her, seized her head in its beak and drew her into the water, and there the old witch had to drown. Then the children went home together, and were heartily delighted, and if they have not died, they are living still.

# *The Valiant Little Taylor*

One summer's morning a little tailor was sitting on his table by the window; he was in good spirits, and sewed with all his might. Then came a peasant woman down the street crying: 'Good jams, cheap! Good jams, cheap!' This rang pleasantly in the tailor's ears; he stretched his delicate head out of the window, and called: 'Come up here, dear woman; here you will get rid of your goods.' The woman came up the three steps to the tailor with her heavy basket, and he made her unpack all the pots for him. He inspected each one, lifted it up, put his nose to it, and at length said: 'The jam seems to me to be good, so weigh me out four ounces, dear woman, and if it is a quarter of a pound that is of no consequence.' The woman who had hoped to find a good sale, gave him what he desired, but went away quite angry and grumbling. 'Now, this jam shall be blessed by God,' cried the little tailor, 'and give me health and strength'; so he brought the bread out of the cupboard, cut himself a piece right across the loaf and spread the jam over it. 'This won't taste bitter,' said he, 'but I will just finish the jacket before I take a bite.' He laid the bread near him, sewed on, and in his joy, made bigger and bigger stitches. In the meantime the smell of the sweet jam rose to where the flies were sitting in great numbers, and they were attracted and descended on it in hosts. 'Hi! who invited you?' said the little tailor, and drove the unbidden guests away. The flies, however, who understood no German, would not be turned away, but came back again in ever-increasing companies. The little tailor at last lost all patience, and drew a piece of cloth from the hole under his work-table, and saying: 'Wait, and I will give it to you,' struck it mercilessly on them. When he drew it away and counted, there lay before him no fewer than seven, dead and with legs stretched out. 'Are you a fellow of that sort?' said he, and could not help admiring his own bravery. 'The whole town shall know of this!' And the little tailor hastened to cut himself a girdle, stitched it, and embroidered on it in large letters: 'Seven at one stroke!' 'What, the town!' he continued, 'the whole world shall hear of it!' and his heart wagged with joy like a lamb's tail. The tailor put on the girdle, and resolved to go forth into the world, because he thought his workshop was too small for his valour. Before he went away, he sought about in the house to see if there was anything which he could take with him; however, he found nothing but an old cheese, and that he put in his pocket. In front of the door he observed a bird which had caught itself in the thicket. It had to go into his pocket with the cheese. Now he took to the road boldly, and as he was light and nimble, he felt no fatigue. The road led him up a mountain, and when he had reached the highest point of it, there sat a powerful giant looking peacefully about him. The little tailor went bravely up, spoke to him, and said: 'Good day, comrade, so you are sitting there overlooking the wide-spread world! I am just on my way thither, and want to try my luck. Have you any inclination to go with me?' The giant looked contemptuously at the tailor, and said: 'You ragamuffin! You miserable creature!'

'Oh, indeed?' answered the little tailor, and unbuttoned his coat, and showed the giant the girdle, 'there may you read what kind of a man I am!' The giant read: 'Seven at one stroke,' and thought that they had been men whom the tailor had killed, and began to feel a little respect for the tiny fellow. Nevertheless, he wished to try him first, and took a stone in his hand and squeezed it together so that water dropped out of it. 'Do that likewise,' said the giant, 'if you have strength.' 'Is that all?' said the tailor, 'that is child's play with us!' and put his hand into his pocket, brought out the soft cheese, and pressed it until the liquid ran out of it. 'Faith,' said he, 'that was a little better, wasn't it?' The giant did not know what to say, and could not believe it of the little man. Then the giant picked up a stone and threw it so high that the eye could scarcely follow it. 'Now, little mite of a man, do that likewise,' 'Well thrown,' said the tailor, 'but after all the stone came down to earth again; I will throw you one which shall never come back at all,' and he put his hand into his pocket, took out the bird, and threw it into the air. The bird, delighted with its liberty, rose, flew away and did not come back. 'How does that shot please you, comrade?' asked the tailor. 'You can certainly throw,' said the giant, 'but now we will see if you are able to carry anything properly.' He took the little tailor to a mighty oak tree which lay there felled on the ground, and said: 'If you are strong enough, help me to carry the tree out of the forest.' 'Readily,' answered the little man; 'take you the trunk on your shoulders, and I will raise up the branches and twigs; after all, they are the heaviest.' The giant took the trunk on his shoulder, but the tailor seated himself on a branch, and the giant, who could not look round, had to carry away the whole tree, and the little tailor into the bargain: he behind, was quite merry and happy, and whistled the song: 'Three tailors rode forth from the gate,' as if carrying the tree were child's play. The giant, after he had dragged the heavy burden part of the way, could go no further, and cried: 'Hark you, I shall have to let the tree fall!' The tailor sprang nimbly down, seized the tree with both arms as if he had been carrying it, and said to the giant: 'You are such a great fellow, and yet cannot even carry the tree!'

They went on together, and as they passed a cherry-tree, the giant laid hold of the top of the tree where the ripest fruit was hanging, bent it down, gave it into the tailor's hand, and bade him eat. But the little tailor was much too weak to hold the tree, and when the giant let it go, it sprang back again, and the tailor was tossed into the air with it. When he had fallen down again without injury, the giant said: 'What is this? Have you not strength enough to hold the weak twig?' 'There is no lack of strength,' answered the little tailor. 'Do you think that could be anything to a man who has struck down seven at one blow? I leapt over the tree because the huntsmen are shooting down there in the thicket. Jump as I did, if you can do it.' The giant made the attempt but he could not get over the tree, and remained hanging in the branches, so that in this also the tailor kept the upper hand.

The giant said: 'If you are such a valiant fellow, come with me into our cavern and spend the night with us.' The little tailor was willing, and followed him. When they went into the cave, other giants were sitting there by the fire, and each of them had a roasted sheep in his hand and was eating it. The little tailor looked round and thought: 'It is much more spacious here than in my workshop.' The giant showed him a bed, and said he was to lie down in it and sleep. The bed, however, was too big for the little tailor; he did not lie down in it, but crept into a corner. When it was midnight, and the giant thought that the little tailor was lying in a sound sleep, he got up, took a great iron bar, cut through the bed with one blow, and thought he had finished off the grasshopper for good. With the earliest dawn the giants went into the forest, and had quite forgotten the little tailor, when all at once he walked up to them quite merrily and boldly. The giants were terrified, they were afraid that he would strike them all dead, and ran away in a great hurry.

The little tailor went onwards, always following his own pointed nose. After he had walked for a long time, he came to the courtyard of a royal palace, and as he felt weary, he lay down on the grass and fell asleep.

Whilst he lay there, the people came and inspected him on all sides, and read on his girdle: 'Seven at one stroke.' 'Ah!' said they, 'what does the great warrior want here in the midst of peace? He must be a mighty lord.' They went and announced him to the king, and gave it as their opinion that if war should break out, this would be a weighty and useful man who ought on no account to be allowed to depart. The counsel pleased the king, and he sent one of his courtiers to the little tailor to offer him military service when he awoke. The ambassador remained standing by the sleeper, waited until he stretched his limbs and opened his eyes, and then conveyed to him this proposal. 'For this very reason have I come here,' the tailor replied, 'I am ready to enter the king's service.' He was therefore honourably received, and a special dwelling was assigned him.

The soldiers, however, were set against the little tailor, and wished him a thousand miles away. 'What is to be the end of this?' they said among themselves. 'If we quarrel with him, and he strikes about him, seven of us will fall at every blow; not one of us can stand against him.' They came therefore to a decision, betook themselves in a body to the king, and begged for their dismissal. 'We are not prepared,' said they, 'to stay with a man who kills seven at one stroke.' The king was sorry that for the sake of one he should lose all his faithful servants, wished that he had never set eyes on the tailor, and would willingly have been rid of him again. But he did not venture to give him his dismissal, for he dreaded lest he should strike him and all his people dead, and place himself on the royal throne. He thought about it for a long time, and at last found good counsel. He sent to the little tailor and caused him to be informed that as he was a great warrior, he had one request to make to him. In a forest of his country lived two giants, who caused great mischief with their robbing, murdering, ravaging, and burning, and no one could approach them without putting himself in danger of death. If the tailor conquered and killed these two giants, he would give him his only daughter to wife, and half of his kingdom as a dowry, likewise one hundred horsemen should go with him to assist him. 'That would indeed be a fine thing for a man like me!' thought the little tailor. 'One is not offered a beautiful princess and half a kingdom every day of one's life!' 'Oh, yes,' he replied, 'I will soon subdue the giants, and do not require the help of the hundred horsemen to do it; he who can hit seven with one blow has no need to be afraid of two.'

The little tailor went forth, and the hundred horsemen followed him. When he came to the outskirts of the forest, he said to his followers: 'Just stay waiting here, I alone will soon finish off the giants.' Then he bounded into the forest and looked about right and left. After a while he perceived both giants. They lay sleeping under a tree, and snored so that the branches waved up and down. The little tailor, not idle, gathered two pocketsful of stones, and with these climbed up the tree. When he was halfway up, he slipped down by a branch, until he sat just above the sleepers, and then let one stone after another fall on the breast of one of the giants. For a long time the giant felt nothing, but at last he awoke, pushed his comrade, and said: 'Why are you knocking me?' 'You must be dreaming,' said the other, 'I am not knocking you.' They laid themselves down to sleep again, and then the tailor threw a stone down on the second. 'What is the meaning of this?' cried the other 'Why are you pelting me?' 'I am not pelting you,' answered the first, growling. They disputed about it for a time, but as they were weary they let the matter rest, and their eyes closed once more. The little tailor began his game again, picked out the biggest stone, and threw it with all his might on the breast of the first giant. 'That is too bad!' cried he, and sprang up like a madman, and pushed his companion against the tree until it shook. The other paid him back in the same coin, and they got into such a rage that they tore up trees and belaboured each other so long, that at last they both fell down dead on the ground at the same time. Then the little tailor leapt down. 'It is a lucky thing,' said he, 'that they did not tear up the tree on which I was sitting, or I should have had to sprint on to another like a squirrel; but we tailors are nimble.' He drew out his sword and gave each of them a couple of thrusts in the breast, and then went out to the horsemen and said: 'The work is done; I have finished both of them off, but it was hard work! They tore up trees in their sore need, and defended themselves with them, but all that is to no purpose when a man like myself comes, who can kill seven at one blow.' 'But are you not wounded?' asked the horsemen. 'You need not concern yourself about that,' answered the tailor, 'they have not bent one hair of mine.' The horsemen would not believe him, and rode into the forest; there they found the giants swimming in their blood, and all round about lay the torn-up trees.

The little tailor demanded of the king the promised reward; he, however, repented of his promise, and again bethought himself how he could get rid of the hero. 'Before you receive my daughter, and the half of my kingdom,' said he to him, 'you must perform one more heroic deed. In the forest roams a unicorn which does great harm, and you must catch it first.' 'I fear one unicorn still less than two giants. Seven at one blow, is my kind of affair.' He took a rope and an axe with him, went forth into the forest, and again bade those who were sent with him to wait outside. He had not long to seek. The unicorn soon came towards him, and rushed directly on the tailor, as if it would gore him with its horn without more ado. 'Softly, softly; it can't be done as quickly as that,' said he, and stood still and waited until the animal was quite close, and then sprang nimbly behind the tree. The unicorn ran against the tree with all its strength, and stuck its horn so fast in the trunk that it had not the strength enough to draw it out again, and thus it was caught. 'Now, I have got the bird,' said the tailor, and came out from behind the tree and put the rope round its neck, and then with his axe he hewed the horn out of the tree, and when all was ready he led the beast away and took it to the king.

The king still would not give him the promised reward, and made a third demand. Before the wedding the tailor was to catch him a wild boar that made great havoc in the forest, and the huntsmen should give him their help. 'Willingly,' said the tailor, 'that is child's play!' He did not take the huntsmen with him into the forest, and they were well pleased that he did not, for the wild boar had several times received them in such a manner that they had no inclination to lie in wait for him. When the boar perceived the tailor, it ran on him with foaming mouth and whetted tusks, and was about to throw him to the ground, but the hero fled and sprang into a chapel which was near and up to the window at once, and in one bound out again. The boar ran after him, but the tailor ran round outside and shut the door behind it, and then the raging beast, which was much too heavy and awkward to leap out of the window, was caught. The little tailor called the huntsmen thither that they might see the prisoner with their own eyes. The hero, however, went to the king, who was now, whether he liked it or not, obliged to keep his promise, and gave his daughter and the half of his kingdom. Had he known that it was no warlike hero, but a little tailor who was standing before him, it would have gone to his heart still more than it did. The wedding was held with great magnificence and small joy, and out of a tailor a king was made.

After some time the young queen heard her husband say in his dreams at night: 'Boy, make me the doublet, and patch the pantaloons, or else I will rap the yard-measure over your ears.' Then she discovered in what state of life the young lord had been born, and next morning complained of her wrongs to her father, and begged him to help her to get rid of her husband, who was nothing else but a tailor. The king comforted her and said: 'Leave your bedroom door open this night, and my servants shall stand outside, and when he has fallen asleep shall go in, bind him, and take him on board a ship which shall carry him into the wide world.' The woman was satisfied with this; but the king's armour-bearer, who had heard all, was friendly with the young lord, and informed him of the whole plot. 'I'll put a screw into that business,' said the little tailor. At night he went to bed with his wife at the usual time, and when she thought that he had fallen asleep, she got up, opened the door, and then lay down again. The little tailor, who was only pretending to be asleep, began to cry out in a clear voice: 'Boy, make me the doublet and patch me the pantaloons, or I will rap the yard-measure over your ears. I smote seven at one blow. I killed two giants, I brought away one unicorn, and caught a wild boar, and am I to fear those who are standing outside the room.' When these men heard the tailor speaking thus, they were overcome by a great dread, and ran as if the wild huntsman were behind them, and none of them would venture anything further against him. So the little tailor was and remained a king to the end of his life.

# *Lily And The Lion*

A merchant, who had three daughters, was once setting out upon a journey; but before he went he asked each daughter what gift he should bring back for her. The eldest wished for pearls; the second for jewels; but the third, who was called Lily, said, 'Dear father, bring me a rose.' Now it was no easy task to find a rose, for it was the middle of winter; yet as she was his prettiest daughter, and was very fond of flowers, her father said he would try what he could do. So he kissed all three, and bid them goodbye.

And when the time came for him to go home, he had bought pearls and jewels for the two eldest, but he had sought everywhere in vain for the rose; and when he went into any garden and asked for such a thing, the people laughed at him, and asked him whether he thought roses grew in snow. This grieved him very much, for Lily was his dearest child; and as he was journeying home, thinking what he should bring her, he came to a fine castle; and around the castle was a garden, in one half of which it seemed to be summer-time and in the other half winter. On one side the finest flowers were in full bloom, and on the other everything looked dreary and buried in the snow. 'A lucky hit!' said he, as he called to his servant, and told him to go to a beautiful bed of roses that was there, and bring him away one of the finest flowers.

This done, they were riding away well pleased, when up sprang a fierce lion, and roared out, 'Whoever has stolen my roses shall be eaten up alive!' Then the man said, 'I knew not that the garden belonged to you; can nothing save my life?' 'No!' said the lion, 'nothing, unless you undertake to give me whatever meets you on your return home; if you agree to this, I will give you your life, and the rose too for your daughter.' But the man was unwilling to do so and said, 'It may be my youngest daughter, who loves me most, and always runs to meet me when I go home.' Then the servant was greatly frightened, and said, 'It may perhaps be only a cat or a dog.' And at last the man yielded with a heavy heart, and took the rose; and said he would give the lion whatever should meet him first on his return.

And as he came near home, it was Lily, his youngest and dearest daughter, that met him; she came running, and kissed him, and welcomed him home; and when she saw that he had brought her the rose, she was still more glad. But her father began to be very sorrowful, and to weep, saying, 'Alas, my dearest child! I have bought this flower at a high price, for I have said I would give you to a wild lion; and when he has you, he will tear you in pieces, and eat you.' Then he told her all that had happened, and said she should not go, let what would happen.

But she comforted him, and said, 'Dear father, the word you have given must be kept; I will go to the lion, and soothe him: perhaps he will let me come safe home again.'

The next morning she asked the way she was to go, and took leave of her father, and went forth with a bold heart into the wood. But the lion was an enchanted prince. By day he and all his court were lions, but in the evening they took their right forms again. And when Lily came to the castle, he welcomed her so courteously that she agreed to marry him. The wedding-feast was held, and they lived happily together a long time. The prince was only to be seen as soon as evening came, and then he held his court; but every morning he left his bride, and went away by himself, she knew not whither, till the night came again.

After some time he said to her, 'Tomorrow there will be a great feast in your father's house, for your eldest sister is to be married; and if you wish to go and visit her my lions shall lead you thither.' Then she rejoiced much at the thoughts of seeing her father once more, and set out with the lions; and everyone was overjoyed to see her, for they had thought her dead long since. But she told them how happy she was, and stayed till the feast was over, and then went back to the wood.

Her second sister was soon after married, and when Lily was asked to go to the wedding, she said to the prince, 'I will not go alone this time — you must go with me.' But he would not, and said that it would be a very hazardous thing; for if the least ray of the torch-light should fall upon him his enchantment would become still worse, for he should be changed into a dove, and be forced to wander about the world for seven long years. However, she gave him no rest, and said she would take care no light should fall upon him. So at last they set out together, and took with them their little child; and she chose a large hall with thick walls for him to sit in while the wedding-torches were lighted; but, unluckily, no one saw that there was a crack in the door. Then the wedding was held with great pomp, but as the train came from the church, and passed with the torches before the hall, a very small ray of light fell upon the prince. In a moment he disappeared, and when his wife came in and looked for him, she found only a white dove; and it said to her, 'Seven years must I fly up and down over the face of the earth, but every now and then I will let fall a white feather, that will show you the way I am going; follow it, and at last you may overtake and set me free.'

This said, he flew out at the door, and poor Lily followed; and every now and then a white feather fell, and showed her the way she was to journey. Thus she went roving on through the wide world, and looked neither to the right hand nor to the left, nor took any rest, for seven years. Then she began to be glad, and thought to herself that the time was fast coming when all her troubles should end; yet repose was still far off, for one day as she was travelling on she missed the white feather, and when she lifted up her eyes she could nowhere see the dove. 'Now,' thought she to herself, 'no aid of man can be of use to me.' So she went to the sun and said, 'Thou shinest everywhere, on the hill's top and the valley's depth — hast thou anywhere seen my white dove?' 'No,' said the sun, 'I have not seen it; but I will give thee a casket — open it when thy hour of need comes.'

So she thanked the sun, and went on her way till eventide; and when the moon arose, she cried unto it, and said, 'Thou shinest through the night, over field and grove — hast thou nowhere seen my white dove?' 'No,' said the moon, 'I cannot help thee but I will give thee an egg — break it when need comes.'

Then she thanked the moon, and went on till the night-wind blew; and she raised up her voice to it, and said, 'Thou blowest through every tree and under every leaf — hast thou not seen my white dove?' 'No,' said the night-wind, 'but I will ask three other winds; perhaps they have seen it.' Then the east wind and the west wind came, and said they too had not seen it, but the south wind said, 'I have seen the white dove — he has fled to the Red Sea, and is changed once more into a lion, for the seven years are passed away, and there he is fighting with a dragon; and the dragon is an enchanted princess, who seeks to separate him from you.' Then the night-wind said, 'I will give thee counsel. Go to the Red Sea; on the right shore stand many rods — count them, and when thou comest to the eleventh, break it off, and smite the dragon with it; and so the lion will have the victory, and both of them will appear to you in their own forms. Then look round and thou wilt see a griffin, winged like bird, sitting by the Red Sea; jump on to his back with thy beloved one as quickly as possible, and he will carry you over the waters to your home. I will also give thee this nut,' continued the night-wind. 'When you are half-way over, throw it down, and out of the waters will immediately spring up a high nut-tree on which the griffin will be able to rest, otherwise he would not have the strength to bear you the whole way; if, therefore, thou dost forget to throw down the nut, he will let you both fall into the sea.'

So our poor wanderer went forth, and found all as the night-wind had said; and she plucked the eleventh rod, and smote the dragon, and the lion forthwith became a prince, and the dragon a princess again. But no sooner was the princess released from the spell, than she seized the prince by the arm and sprang on to the griffin's back, and went off carrying the prince away with her.

Thus the unhappy traveller was again forsaken and forlorn; but she took heart and said, 'As far as the wind blows, and so long as the cock crows, I will journey on, till I find him once again.' She went on for a long, long way, till at length she came to the castle whither the princess had carried the prince; and there was a feast got ready, and she heard that the wedding was about to be held. 'Heaven aid me now!' said she; and she took the casket that the sun had given her, and found that within it lay a dress as dazzling as the sun itself. So she put it on, and went into the palace, and all the people gazed upon her; and the dress pleased the bride so much that she asked whether it was to be sold. 'Not for gold and silver.' said she, 'but for flesh and blood.' The princess asked what she meant, and she said, 'Let me speak with the bridegroom this night in his chamber, and I will give thee the dress.' At last the princess agreed, but she told her chamberlain to give the prince a sleeping draught, that he might not hear or see her. When evening came, and the prince had fallen asleep, she was led into his chamber, and she sat herself down at his feet, and said: 'I have followed thee seven years. I have been to the sun, the moon, and the night-wind, to seek thee, and at last I have helped thee to overcome the dragon. Wilt thou then forget me quite?' But the prince all the time slept so soundly, that her voice only passed over him, and seemed like the whistling of the wind among the fir-trees.

Then poor Lily was led away, and forced to give up the golden dress; and when she saw that there was no help for her, she went out into a meadow, and sat herself down and wept. But as she sat she bethought herself of the egg that the moon had given her; and when she broke it, there ran out a hen and twelve chickens of pure gold, that played about, and then nestled under the old one's wings, so as to form the most beautiful sight in the world. And she rose up and drove them before her, till the bride saw them from her window, and was so pleased that she came forth and asked her if she would sell the brood. 'Not for gold or silver, but for flesh and blood: let me again this evening speak with the bridegroom in his chamber, and I will give thee the whole brood.'

Then the princess thought to betray her as before, and agreed to what she asked: but when the prince went to his chamber he asked the chamberlain why the wind had whistled so in the night. And the chamberlain told him all — how he had given him a sleeping draught, and how a poor maiden had come and spoken to him in his chamber, and was to come again that night. Then the prince took care to throw away the sleeping draught; and when Lily came and began again to tell him what woes had befallen her, and how faithful and true to him she had been, he knew his beloved wife's voice, and sprang up, and said, 'You have awakened me as from a dream, for the strange princess had thrown a spell around me, so that I had altogether forgotten you; but Heaven hath sent you to me in a lucky hour.'

And they stole away out of the palace by night unawares, and seated themselves on the griffin, who flew back with them over the Red Sea. When they were half-way across Lily let the nut fall into the water, and immediately a large nut-tree arose from the sea, whereon the griffin rested for a while, and then carried them safely home. There they found their child, now grown up to be comely and fair; and after all their troubles they lived happily together to the end of their days.

# *The Pink*

There was once upon a time a queen to whom God had given no children. Every morning she went into the garden and prayed to God in heaven to bestow on her a son or a daughter. Then an angel from heaven came to her and said: 'Be at rest, you shall have a son with the power of wishing, so that whatsoever in the world he wishes for, that shall he have.' Then she went to the king, and told him the joyful tidings, and when the time was come she gave birth to a son, and the king was filled with gladness.

Every morning she went with the child to the garden where the wild beasts were kept, and washed herself there in a clear stream. It happened once when the child was a little older, that it was lying in her arms and she fell asleep. Then came the old cook, who knew that the child had the power of wishing, and stole it away, and he took a hen, and cut it in pieces, and dropped some of its blood on the queen's apron and on her dress. Then he carried the child away to a secret place, where a nurse was obliged to suckle it, and he ran to the king and accused the queen of having allowed her child to be taken from her by the wild beasts. When the king saw the blood on her apron, he believed this, fell into such a passion that he ordered a high tower to be built, in which neither sun nor moon could be seen and had his wife put into it, and walled up. Here she was to stay for seven years without meat or drink, and die of hunger. But God sent two angels from heaven in the shape of white doves, which flew to her twice a day, and carried her food until the seven years were over.

The cook, however, thought to himself: 'If the child has the power of wishing, and I am here, he might very easily get me into trouble.' So he left the palace and went to the boy, who was already big enough to speak, and said to him: 'Wish for a beautiful palace for yourself with a garden, and all else that pertains to it.' Scarcely were the words out of the boy's mouth, when everything was there that he had wished for. After a while the cook said to him: 'It is not well for you to be so alone, wish for a pretty girl as a companion.' Then the king's son wished for one, and she immediately stood before him, and was more beautiful than any painter could have painted her. The two played together, and loved each other with all their hearts, and the old cook went out hunting like a nobleman. The thought occurred to him, however, that the king's son might some day wish to be with his father, and thus bring him into great peril. So he went out and took the maiden aside, and said: 'Tonight when the boy is asleep, go to his bed and plunge this knife into his heart, and bring me his heart and tongue, and if you do not do it, you shall lose your life.' Thereupon he went away, and when he returned next day she had not done it, and said: 'Why should I shed the blood of an innocent boy who has never harmed anyone?' The cook once more said: 'If you do not do it, it shall cost you your own life.' When he had gone away, she had a little hind brought to her, and ordered her to be killed, and took her heart and tongue, and laid them on a plate, and when she saw the old man coming, she said to the boy: 'Lie down in your bed, and draw the clothes over you.' Then the wicked wretch came in and said: 'Where are the boy's heart and tongue?' The girl reached the plate to him, but the king's son threw off the quilt, and said: 'You old sinner, why did you want to kill me? Now will I pronounce thy sentence. You shall become a black poodle and have a gold collar round your neck, and shall eat burning coals, till the flames burst forth from your throat.' And when he had spoken these words, the old man was changed into a poodle dog, and had a gold collar round his neck, and the cooks were ordered to bring up some live coals, and these he ate, until the flames broke forth from his throat. The king's son remained there a short while longer, and he thought of his mother, and wondered if she were still alive. At length he said to the maiden: 'I will go home to my own country; if you will go with me, I will provide for you.' 'Ah,' she replied, 'the way is so long, and what shall I do in a strange land where I am unknown?' As she did not seem quite willing, and as they could not be parted from each other, he wished that she might be changed into a beautiful pink, and took her with him. Then he went away to his own country, and the poodle had to run after him. He went to the tower in which his mother was confined, and as it was so high, he wished for a ladder which would reach up to the very top. Then he mounted up and looked inside, and cried: 'Beloved mother, Lady Queen, are you still alive, or are you dead?' She answered: 'I have just eaten, and am still satisfied,' for she thought the angels were there. Said he: 'I am your dear son, whom the wild beasts were said to have torn from your arms; but I am alive still, and will soon set you free.' Then he descended again, and went to his father, and caused himself to be announced as a strange huntsman, and asked if he could offer him service. The king said yes, if he was skilful and could get game for him, he should come to him, but that deer had never taken up their quarters in any part of the district or country. Then the huntsman promised to procure as much game for him as he could possibly use at the royal table. So he summoned all the huntsmen together, and bade them go out into the forest with him. And he went with them and made them form a great circle, open at one end where he stationed himself, and began to wish. Two hundred deer and more came running inside the circle at once, and the huntsmen shot them. Then they were all placed on sixty country carts, and driven home to the king, and for once he was able to deck his table with game, after having had none at all for years.

Now the king felt great joy at this, and commanded that his entire household should eat with him next day, and made a great feast. When they were all assembled together, he said to the huntsman: 'As you are so clever, you shall sit by me.' He replied: 'Lord King, your majesty must excuse me, I am a poor huntsman.' But the king insisted on it, and said: 'You shall sit by me,' until he did it. Whilst he was sitting there, he thought of his dearest mother, and wished that one of the king's principal servants would begin to speak of her, and would ask how it was faring with the queen in the tower, and if she were alive still, or had perished. Hardly had he formed the wish than the marshal began, and said: 'Your majesty, we live joyously here, but how is the queen living in the tower? Is she still alive, or has she died?' But the king replied: 'She let my dear son be torn to pieces by wild beasts; I will not have her named.' Then the huntsman arose and said: 'Gracious lord father she is alive still, and I am her son, and I was not carried away by wild beasts, but by that wretch the old cook, who tore me from her arms when she was asleep, and sprinkled her apron with the blood of a chicken.' Thereupon he took the dog with the golden collar, and said: 'That is the wretch!' and caused live coals to be brought, and these the dog was compelled to devour before the sight of all, until flames burst forth from its throat. On this the huntsman asked the king if he would like to see the dog in his true shape, and wished him back into the form of the cook, in the which he stood immediately, with his white apron, and his knife by his side. When the king saw him he fell into a passion, and ordered him to be cast into the deepest dungeon. Then the huntsman spoke further and said: 'Father, will you see the maiden who brought me up so tenderly and who was afterwards to murder me, but did not do it, though her own life depended on it?' The king replied: 'Yes, I would like to see her.' The son said: 'Most gracious father, I will show her to you in the form of a beautiful flower,' and he thrust his hand into his pocket and brought forth the pink, and placed it on the royal table, and it was so beautiful that the king had never seen one to equal it. Then the son said: 'Now will I show her to you in her own form,' and wished that she might become a maiden, and she stood there looking so beautiful that no painter could have made her look more so.

And the king sent two waiting-maids and two attendants into the tower, to fetch the queen and bring her to the royal table. But when she was led in she ate nothing, and said: 'The gracious and merciful God who has supported me in the tower, will soon set me free.' She lived three days more, and then died happily, and when she was buried, the two white doves which had brought her food to the tower, and were angels of heaven, followed her body and seated themselves on her grave. The aged king ordered the cook to be torn in four pieces, but grief consumed the king's own heart, and he soon died. His son married the beautiful maiden whom he had brought with him as a flower in his pocket, and whether they are still alive or not, is known to God.

## *Sweetheart Roland*

There was once upon a time a woman who was a real witch and had two daughters, one ugly and wicked, and this one she loved because she was her own daughter, and one beautiful and good, and this one she hated, because she was her stepdaughter. The stepdaughter once had a pretty apron, which the other fancied so much that she became envious, and told her mother that she must and would have that apron. 'Be quiet, my child,' said the old woman, 'and you shall have it. Your stepsister has long deserved death; tonight when she is asleep I will come and cut her head off. Only be careful that you are at the far side of the bed, and push her well to the front.' It would have been all over with the poor girl if she had not just then been standing in a corner, and heard everything. All day long she dared not go out of doors, and when bedtime had come, the witch's daughter got into bed first, so as to lie at the far side, but when she was asleep, the other pushed her gently to the front, and took for herself the place at the back, close by the wall. In the night, the old woman came creeping in, she held an axe in her right hand, and felt with her left to see if anyone were lying at the outside, and then she grasped the axe with both hands, and cut her own child's head off.

When she had gone away, the girl got up and went to her sweetheart, who was called Roland, and knocked at his door. When he came out, she said to him: 'Listen, dearest Roland, we must fly in all haste; my stepmother wanted to kill me, but has struck her own child. When daylight comes, and she sees what she has done, we shall be lost.' 'But,' said Roland, 'I counsel you first to take away her magic wand, or we cannot escape if she pursues us.' The maiden fetched the magic wand, and she took the dead girl's head and dropped three drops of blood on the ground, one in front of the bed, one in the kitchen, and one on the stairs. Then she hurried away with her lover.

When the old witch got up next morning, she called her daughter, and wanted to give her the apron, but she did not come. Then the witch cried: 'Where are you?' 'Here, on the stairs, I am sweeping,' answered the first drop of blood. The old woman went out, but saw no one on the stairs, and cried again: 'Where are you?' 'Here in the kitchen, I am warming myself,' cried the second drop of blood. She went into the kitchen, but found no one. Then she cried again: 'Where are you?' 'Ah, here in the bed, I am sleeping,' cried the third drop of blood. She went into the room to the bed. What did she see there? Her own child, whose head she had cut off, bathed in her blood. The witch fell into a passion, sprang to the window, and as she could look forth quite far into the world, she perceived her stepdaughter hurrying away with her sweetheart Roland. 'That shall not help you,' cried she, 'even if you have got a long way off, you shall still not escape me.' She put on her many-league boots, in which she covered an hour's walk at every step, and it was not long before she overtook them. The girl, however, when she saw the old woman striding towards her, changed, with her magic wand, her sweetheart Roland into a lake, and herself into a duck swimming in the middle of it. The witch placed herself on the shore, threw breadcrumbs in, and went to endless trouble to entice the duck; but the duck did not let herself be enticed, and the old woman had to go home at night as she had come. At this the girl and her sweetheart Roland resumed their natural shapes again, and they walked on the whole night until daybreak. Then the maiden changed herself into a beautiful flower which stood in the midst of a briar hedge, and her sweetheart Roland into a fiddler. It was not long before the witch came striding up towards them, and said to the musician: 'Dear musician, may I pluck that beautiful flower for myself?' 'Oh, yes,' he replied, 'I will play to you while you do it.' As she was hastily creeping into the hedge and was just going to pluck the flower, knowing perfectly well who the flower was, he began to play, and whether she would or not, she was forced to dance, for it was a magical dance. The faster he played, the more violent springs was she forced to make, and the thorns tore her clothes from her body, and pricked her and wounded her till she bled, and as he did not stop, she had to dance till she lay dead on the ground.

As they were now set free, Roland said: 'Now I will

go to my father and arrange for the wedding.' 'Then in the meantime I will stay here and wait for you,' said the girl, 'and that no one may recognize me, I will change myself into a red stone landmark.' Then Roland went away, and the girl stood like a red landmark in the field and waited for her beloved. But when Roland got home, he fell into the snares of another, who so fascinated him that he forgot the maiden. The poor girl remained there a long time, but at length, as he did not return at all, she was sad, and changed herself into a flower, and thought: 'Someone will surely come this way, and trample me down.'

It befell, however, that a shepherd kept his sheep in the field and saw the flower, and as it was so pretty, plucked it, took it with him, and laid it away in his chest. From that time forth, strange things happened in the shepherd's house. When he arose in the morning, all the work was already done, the room was swept, the table and benches cleaned, the fire in the hearth was lighted, and the water was fetched, and at noon, when he came home, the table was laid, and a good dinner served. He could not conceive how this came to pass, for he never saw a human being in his house, and no one could have concealed himself in it. He was certainly pleased with this good attendance, but still at last he was so afraid that he went to a wise woman and asked for her advice. The wise woman said: 'There is some enchantment behind it, listen very early some morning if anything is moving in the room, and if you see anything, no matter what it is, throw a white cloth over it, and then the magic will be stopped.'

The shepherd did as she bade him, and next morning just as day dawned, he saw the chest open, and the flower come out. Swiftly he sprang towards it, and threw a white cloth over it. Instantly the transformation came to an end, and a beautiful girl stood before him, who admitted to him that she had been the flower, and that up to this time she had attended to his house-keeping. She told him her story, and as she pleased him he asked her if she would marry him, but she answered: 'No,' for she wanted to remain faithful to her sweetheart Roland, although he had deserted her. Nevertheless, she promised not to go away, but to continue keeping house for the shepherd.

And now the time drew near when Roland's wedding was to be celebrated, and then, according to an old custom in the country, it was announced that all the girls were to be present at it, and sing in honour of the bridal pair. When the faithful maiden heard of this, she grew so sad that she thought her heart would break, and she would not go thither, but the other girls came and took her. When it came to her turn to sing, she stepped back, until at last she was the only one left, and then she could not refuse. But when she began her song, and it reached Roland's ears, he sprang up and cried: 'I know the voice, that is the true bride, I will have no other!' Everything he had forgotten, and which had vanished from his mind, had suddenly come home again to his heart. Then the faithful maiden held her wedding with her sweetheart Roland, and grief came to an end and joy began.

# *King Grisly-Beard*

A great king of a land far away in the East had a daughter who was very beautiful, but so proud, and haughty, and conceited, that none of the princes who came to ask her in marriage was good enough for her, and she only made sport of them.

Once upon a time the king held a great feast, and asked thither all her suitors; and they all sat in a row, ranged according to their rank — kings, and princes, and dukes, and earls, and counts, and barons, and knights. Then the princess came in, and as she passed by them she had something spiteful to say to every one. The first was too fat: 'He's as round as a tub,' said she. The next was too tall: 'What a maypole!' said she. The next was too short: 'What a dumpling!' said she. The fourth was too pale, and she called him 'Wallface.' The fifth was too red, so she called him 'Coxcomb.' The sixth was not straight enough; so she said he was like a green stick, that had been laid to dry over a baker's oven. And thus she had some joke to crack upon every one: but she laughed more than all at a good king who was there. 'Look at him,' said she; 'his beard is like an old mop; he shall be called Grisly-beard.' So the king got the nickname of Grisly-beard.

But the old king was very angry when he saw how his daughter behaved, and how she ill-treated all his guests; and he vowed that, willing or unwilling, she should marry the first man, be he prince or beggar, that came to the door.

Two days after there came by a travelling fiddler, who began to play under the window and beg alms; and when the king heard him, he said, 'Let him come in.' So they brought in a dirty-looking fellow; and when he had sung before the king and the princess, he begged a boon. Then the king said, 'You have sung so well, that I will give you my daughter for your wife.' The princess begged and prayed; but the king said, 'I have sworn to give you to the first comer, and I will keep my word.' So words and tears were of no avail; the parson was sent for, and she was married to the fiddler. When this was over the king said, 'Now get ready to go — you must not stay here — you must travel on with your husband.'

Then the fiddler went his way, and took her with him, and they soon came to a great wood. 'Pray,' said she, 'whose is this wood?' 'It belongs to King Grisly-beard,' answered he; 'hadst thou taken him, all had been thine.' 'Ah! unlucky wretch that I am!' sighed she; 'would that I had married King Grisly-beard!' Next they came to some fine meadows. 'Whose are these beautiful green meadows?' said she. 'They belong to King Grisly-beard, hadst thou taken him, they had all been thine.' 'Ah! unlucky wretch that I am!' said she; 'would that I had married King Grisly-beard!'

Then they came to a great city. 'Whose is this noble city?' said she. 'It belongs to King Grisly-beard; hadst thou taken him, it had all been thine.' 'Ah! wretch that I am!' sighed she; 'why did I not marry King Grisly-beard?' 'That is no business of mine,' said the fiddler: 'why should you wish for another husband? Am not I good enough for you?'

At last they came to a small cottage. 'What a paltry place!' said she; 'to whom does that little dirty hole belong?' Then the fiddler said, 'That is your and my house, where we are to live.' 'Where are your servants?' cried she. 'What do we want with servants?' said he; 'you must do for yourself whatever is to be done. Now make the fire, and put on water and cook my supper, for I am very tired.' But the princess knew nothing of making fires and cooking, and the fiddler was forced to help her. When they had eaten a very scanty meal they went to bed; but the fiddler called her up very early in the morning to clean the house. Thus they lived for two days: and when they had eaten up all there was in the cottage, the man said, 'Wife, we can't go on thus, spending money and earning nothing. You must learn to weave baskets.' Then he went out and cut willows, and brought them home, and she began to weave; but it made her fingers very sore. 'I see this work won't do,' said he: 'try and spin; perhaps you will do that better.' So she sat down and tried to spin; but the threads cut her tender fingers till the blood ran. 'See now,' said the fiddler, 'you are good for nothing; you can do no work: what a bargain I have got! However, I'll try and set up a trade in pots and pans, and you shall stand in the market and sell them.' 'Alas!' sighed she, 'if any of my father's court should pass by and see me standing in the market, how they will laugh at me!'

But her husband did not care for that, and said she must work, if she did not wish to die of hunger. At first the trade went well; for many people, seeing such a beautiful woman, went to buy her wares, and paid their money without thinking of taking away the goods. They lived on this as long as it lasted; and then her husband bought a fresh lot of ware, and she sat herself down with it in the corner of the market; but a drunken soldier soon came by, and rode his horse against her stall, and broke all her goods into a thousand pieces. Then she began to cry, and knew not what to do. 'Ah! what will become of me?' said she; 'what will my husband say?' So she ran home and told him all. 'Who would have thought you would have been so silly,' said he, 'as to put an earthenware stall in the corner of the market, where everybody passes? But let us have no more crying; I see you are not fit for this sort of work, so I have been to the king's palace, and asked if they did not want a kitchen-maid; and they say they will take you, and there you will have plenty to eat.'

Thus the princess became a kitchen-maid, and helped the cook to do all the dirtiest work; but she was allowed to carry home some of the meat that was left, and on this they lived.

She had not been there long before she heard that the king's eldest son was passing by, going to be married; and she went to one of the windows and looked out. Everything was ready, and all the pomp and brightness of the court was there. Then she bitterly grieved for the pride and folly which had brought her so low. And the servants gave her some of the rich meats, which she put into her basket to take home.

All on a sudden, as she was going out, in came the king's son in golden clothes; and when he saw a beautiful woman at the door, he took her by the hand, and said she should be his partner in the dance; but she trembled for fear, for she saw that it was King Grisly-beard, who was making sport of her. However, he kept fast hold, and led her in; and the cover of the basket came off, so that the meats in it fell about. Then everybody laughed and jeered at her; and she was so abashed, that she wished herself a thousand feet deep in the earth. She sprang to the door to run away; but on the steps King Grisly-beard overtook her, and brought her back and said, 'Fear me not! I am the fiddler who has lived with you in the hut. I brought you there because I really loved you. I am also the soldier that overset your stall. I have done all this only to cure you of your silly pride, and to show you the folly of your ill-treatment of me. Now all is over: you have learnt wisdom, and it is time to hold our marriage feast.'

Then the chamberlains came and brought her the most beautiful robes; and her father and his whole court were there already, and welcomed her home on her marriage. Joy was in every face and every heart. The feast was grand; they danced and sang; all were merry; and I only wish that you and I had been of the party.

*Contents*